"You know, I'll only be here for a short time," Allie sai[...] instincts kickin[...] to lead her som[...] not prepared to [...] more than a week or so, and then I'll be back off to my old life again, solving crimes and dodging bad guys."

"So what if we agreed now," Jones asked, "to keep anything that might happen in that time span casual? Because tonight's dinner might've been fantastic—but suddenly I'm craving just a taste of something sweet."

Reaching up, his fingertips skimmed her jawline, his gaze searching, testing, probing for permission.

The answering flutter of excitement she felt had her flirting right back. She said, "I don't know, Jones. Could be you'd find me spicy—or salty if you're especially annoying."

"Let's find out if I'm annoying you, then, shall we?" he asked before he leaned in even closer, their lips tentatively testing the territory of a kiss.

* * *

Colton 911: Chicago—Love and danger come alive in the Windy City...

* * *

If you're on Twitter, tell us what you think of Harlequin Romantic Suspense! #harlequinromsuspense

Dear Reader,

As a writer, I'm something of a connoisseur of characters, not only the kind we find in fiction, but those fascinating people we run across in real life. Some of them tend to be outgoing, warm and friendly, at ease around groups large or small. They're the easiest to get to know, since they enjoy seeking out and discovering new people.

But I've often found it worth the time and trouble to draw out those who prefer to remain out of sight, quietly absorbed in some pursuit of their choosing, whether it's a hobby or a profession I know nothing about. Some, like Allie Chandler, the hacker–private investigator heroine of my latest, *Colton 911: Hidden Target*, are true introverts, choosing to hide their real selves in order to pursue their passions—and to save themselves the hurt of the rejection they've experienced too often in the past.

Jones Colton, however, isn't about to be easily brushed off. For one thing, he quickly realizes that, despite the inconvenience of the close quarters they're forced to share, the woman he's hired to unravel the murders that have been tormenting his family offers his best chance at finding justice. Even more than that, in Allie he recognizes a kindred soul, someone who's following her own drummer—and fighting to overcome a tragedy that shaped her. It's that common bond that he somehow senses might be the key to bringing both of them redemption.

In writing this story, it's my hope that each of us will learn to look beyond the barriers that so many hide behind and see through to the potential—or find someone like Jones who will see past our own defenses to all we have to offer.

Colleen Thompson

COLTON 911: HIDDEN TARGET

Colleen Thompson

Special thanks and acknowledgment are given to Colleen Thompson for her contribution to the Colton 911: Chicago miniseries.

Recycling programs for this product may not exist in your area.

ISBN-13: 978-1-335-62893-0

Colton 911: Hidden Target

Copyright © 2021 by Harlequin Books S.A.

This edition published by arrangement with Harlequin Books S.A.

For questions and comments about the quality of this book, please contact us at CustomerService@Harlequin.com.

Harlequin Enterprises ULC
22 Adelaide St. West, 40th Floor
Toronto, Ontario M5H 4E3, Canada
www.Harlequin.com

Printed in U.S.A.

The Texas-based author of more than thirty novels and novellas, **Colleen Thompson** is a former teacher with a passion for reading, hiking, kayaking and the last-chance rescue dogs she and her husband have welcomed into their home. With a National Readers' Choice Award and multiple nominations for the RITA® Award, she has also appeared on the Amazon, BookScan and Barnes & Noble bestseller lists. Visit her online at www.colleen-thompson.com.

Books by Colleen Thompson

Harlequin Romantic Suspense

Colton 911: Chicago

Colton 911: Hidden Target

Passion to Protect
The Colton Heir
Lone Star Redemption
Lone Star Survivor
Deadly Texas Summer

The Coltons of Mustang Valley

Hunting the Colton Fugitive

Cowboy Christmas Rescue
"Rescuing the Bride"

Silhouette Romantic Suspense

Deadlier Than the Male
"Lethal Lessons"

Visit the Author Profile page at Harlequin.com for more titles.

To Kim and Joy, for their unwavering friendship, wisdom and support, along with the shared understanding that a large TBR pile, a hot cup of tea and a good canine companion are all essential ingredients of the writing process.

Chapter 1

According to the information Allie Chandler read on the glass door as she rushed up, panting in her dripping wet clothes, the Lone Wolf Brewery wouldn't open for another hour. With a groan of pure frustration, she smacked the heel of her hand beneath the grinning wolf's head logo—and sucked in a startled breath when the unlocked door pushed open.

At least she could add this to the very short list of things that had gone her way this morning, since the ceiling of her hotel room had sagged down and given way to a waterfall moments after she'd returned from her run. Shrieking with horror, she'd scrambled about frantically, first rescuing her expensive computer equipment and peripherals, followed by all the shoes and clothing she could salvage.

Someday you'll look back on this and laugh, she tried to tell herself. At the moment, however, that was almost impossible to imagine as she struggled to haul her bulky suitcase, large backpack and an equally out-size tote bag inside the small bar area to confront the man who'd put her up at the four-star hotel, where he'd assured her all of his family's business associates had been happily staying for decades.

Wrestling her temper, she reminded herself the flood—the result of a guest on the floor above hers falling asleep while running a bath—wasn't his fault. Nor had he arranged for the heavy early May sky to open up on her way over here from the train station, as if to make up for the fact that the hotel deluge had missed her. Still, as her dripping running clothes and bags slowly formed a puddle around her feet and thunder rumbled with a sound like giants bowling overhead, she couldn't help thinking she'd look more like a private investigator and less like a half-drowned rodent fished out of floodwaters if the man could have simply answered his phone this morning like a reasonable person.

A bronze-skinned woman with silvering hair in tiny, beaded braids climbed down from the stepladder she had been using to reach the industrial-style stainless-steel light fixture she'd been polishing, one of a number hanging above a bar dominated by rustic woods and wood-and-metal stools. Wearing a leather black vest over her Lone Wolf T-shirt and a row of silver piercings along one ear, she appraised Allie coolly.

"Hate to send you back out in that weather," she said, nodding toward Allie's bags, "but the bus station's a couple of blocks down."

"Oh, no," Allie said, understanding her mistake. As raindrops pelted the high-set exterior windows, she explained, "I'm not looking to catch a bus. I was just hoping to—"

"Sorry, but our restrooms are for paying customers only, and besides, we aren't even open yet. I'm not sure which of those two geniuses unlocked the door so early."

The bartender cast an aggrieved look toward the floor-to-ceiling glass wall at the rear of the room, which gave a clear view of the craft microbrewery's production floor. There, Allie spotted two young men in protective coveralls and boots working, one spraying down enormous steel hoppers while another scrubbed a large kettle in an oversize sink. Neither appeared to notice the older woman's irritation.

"I need to see the owner," Allie told her before nodding in the direction of a tall, dark-haired man, who appeared oblivious as he sat with his back to them at far end of the bar. The sleeves of his linen shirt were rolled up, and he had a tablet computer lying in front of him. But what truly caught her eye was his focus on a wooden paddle holding four small glasses containing liquids in varying shades of amber, which he'd bent forward to examine at eye level, as if he were sizing up the head of foam on each. She doubted that any man she'd ever dated had ever regarded her with the same degree of appreciation.

Brushing aside the odd thought, and the light shiver that went with it, she said, "I'm pretty sure that's him."

"That's Jones Colton, yeah," said the bartender, whose dark brown eyes hadn't softened, "but I'm not about to interrupt the man while he's in the zone and testing product. Besides, if you're here selling something or looking to apply for work, you need to drop a note online, same as everybody else."

"I'm not selling anything, and the fact is," Allie said, so frustrated by this point that she let slip, "I already work for him, the same as you do."

Colton straightened to type rapidly on his tablet without ever looking their way. Which was less surprising now that Allie noticed the earbuds he was wearing.

"Then how come you aren't sure what he looks like?" the bartender challenged.

"Because we haven't met in person. *Yet*," Allie fired back, chilled to her soaked skin and tired enough of this game that she put her head down and strode directly toward the man who'd offered her this out-of-town job by phone only three days earlier—which had proven to be perfect timing, as far as she was concerned.

Tossing aside the cleaning rag she'd been using, her self-appointed gatekeeper lunged and made a grab for her, shouting, "Hey you, hold up right there! *Jones!*"

Allie, whose agility more than made up for what she lacked in height, let go of the suitcase and ducked around the taller, more solidly built woman. But she hadn't allowed for the wider tote that she was carrying, which clipped the top of a stool as she passed by and sent it crashing down onto the polished concrete floor.

In the high-ceilinged space, the sound rang loud as a gunshot beneath the weathered wooden crossbeams. Startled by the noise, Jones leaped to his feet, whipping around to stare down at the two women with startled, deep blue eyes.

Gorgeous eyes, Allie couldn't help but notice, set in a face even more handsome than his photo from the microbrewery's website, with a polished, yet effortlessly casual appearance that made her all too aware of how shabby she must look with her lack of makeup, long, sodden ponytail, black leggings and running shoes, and a long-sleeved T-shirt now clinging to her sports bra like a second skin.

"What on earth's going on here?" he demanded, removing the earbuds as he looked from Allie to the bartender. "Yolanda?"

"You tell me." Shrugging, the older woman gestured angrily toward Allie. "She just came sloshing in through the front door, claiming that she works for you."

"It's Allie, Allie Chandler." Squelching forward, she thrust out her hand. "We've spoken on the phone and via email. I just got into town last night."

"Ms. *Chandler*?" Ignoring her outstretched hand, his eyes flared as he stepped back to give her a head-to-toe once-over. "What on earth? You're soaked through and shivering—just look at her, Yolanda. The poor woman's lips are practically blue."

Giving her a once-over, Yolanda grimaced. "Let me go grab a couple of dry towels out of the storeroom—and a mop, too, before somebody breaks their neck on this wet floor."

"I've got a mop right here. You just worry about the towels," Jones said before she hurried off.

"Th-thanks," Allie called, her face heating, "and sorry about the dramatic entrance."

She'd hoped to make a better impression on this client, who had lured her here with the offer of a bonus big enough to convince her to turn down the law enforcement agencies for which she normally consulted. And unlike the last department she had worked with, this guy was desperate enough for answers that she doubted he would get too particular about her methods—or try to stiff her if she colored outside the lines.

"I can't imagine it was your choice to show up drenched," Jones said, gesturing for her to take a seat. "But I'm glad for the chance to meet you in person. I don't understand, though. I thought you said you'd be bringing yourself up to speed for the next few days, mostly working from the hotel."

"I'm afraid that place is no longer an option," she said before telling him about the impromptu appearance of Niagara Falls in her room.

"That's terrible about you losing half of your clothes and shoes," he said, sounding properly appalled as he grabbed a mop from behind the bar and quickly swabbed at the floor where she'd been dripping. "Buy whatever you need to replace them, or send anything salvageable to a dry cleaner. Send me the receipts, and I'll be sure to reimburse you."

She nodded her appreciation. "Thanks for that, but the important thing is, I saved all my equipment, along with the research I've done so far into your father's and your uncle's...deaths."

She chose the word carefully, barely stopping herself from using the more emotionally charged *assassination*. The more she'd learned about the simultaneous long-range shooting of the twin brothers outside of their sixty-million-dollar intellectual property corporation, Colton Connections, the more she'd come to suspect the brothers' unsolved murders qualified as such. Not that she'd gotten a lot to go on from her brief conversation with Joe Parker, the Chicago PD detective who'd run the investigation until the FBI had stepped in more recently after two more men—with no known connections to the original victims—were killed under similar mysterious circumstances with an equally frustrating lack of leads or progress. But then, she was never brought in to unravel easy cases, which was exactly the reason that she loved her work.

"About that." Holding the mop handle like a staff, Jones Colton raised one palm and looked around as if to reassure himself that none of his employees was in earshot. "If it's all the same to you, let's just keep what you're doing for me quiet for the moment. As far as anybody here's concerned, you're an old college friend visiting from out of town."

As a cover story, it would have played well, since she'd learned in her background research that the two of them were the same age: twenty-seven. Even so, she shook her head. "I'm afraid that I've already blown that. When I couldn't get past your bartender, I let it slip that I work for you, too. I hope that's not an issue."

"Yolanda's my bar manager," Jones corrected, replacing the mop where he had grabbed it, "and you didn't tell her what you were doing for me, did you?"

"No. I wouldn't do that," Allie assured him, still upset with herself about her earlier slip, no matter how cold and wet and stressed out she'd been feeling.

"Good." He sounded relieved. "But getting back to your hotel issue, I don't understand. Why couldn't they just move you to another room?"

"Several rooms were damaged, and they're completely full," she added. "Besides that, they're saying that because of that big music festival being at the same time as a couple of conventions, they're unable to assist with alternate arrangements. Although, in my opinion, *unwilling* is more like it."

Jones shook his head. "That's damned disappointing. I'm sorry I ever put you up there, but don't worry. We'll find you somewhere else to stay. I'm afraid it may not have quite as many amenities or be as upscale, but—"

"I need privacy and security, not fancy bars and turn-down service, and definitely somewhere," she said as an errant lock of hair sent a drip down her nose, surprising her with a sneeze she barely covered in time, "a whole lot drier. Excuse me."

After blessing the sneeze, he said, "I promise you I'll see to it. I only wish you'd called the moment you ran into trouble instead of getting yourself soaked coming here."

Crossing her arms, she made a face. "Before you get too invested in that lecture, you might want to check your cell phone."

"My *phone*?" But he dutifully pulled it out of his back pocket, and then winced, undoubtedly seeing evidence of the missed calls and texts from her numerous attempts to reach him.

Sheepishly, he looked up at her. "I owe you an apology, I see. I've been getting so many junk calls lately that I turned off the ringer while I was testing this last flight before tonight's big tasting dinner. Wish you'd thought to phone the brewery."

"The number rang and rang when I tried, so I took a shot and grabbed a train here when I couldn't find a car."

"You took the L here?" he asked. "The nearest stop's four blocks away."

"Funny," she said, her flatly, "it seemed much farther in a downpour."

"So, the hotel was a bust, your new boss's let you down and even the sky here's opened up and drenched you," he said in summary. "Other than that, Ms. Chandler, how're you finding Chicago so far?"

As uncomfortable and out of sorts as she felt, she found herself laughing in response to his wry smile. "Let's just say if you were trying to motivate me to quickly sort out your case and get back to the Southern California sunshine, you're off to a great start."

Despite the jest, Allie meant to avoid returning home for at least a few weeks, even if she had to book a room under an alias once this job was finished. And she'd be keeping a close watch over her shoulder, possibly for a good long time to come.

Sobering abruptly, Jones's gaze latched on to hers. "*Quickly* would be ideal."

In his voice, she heard not only hope, but the strain of a brand of desperation that she remembered all too well herself. Swallowing back the ache of old grief, she felt the weight of the challenge she was facing, the responsibility of bringing to justice the killers— Chicago PD's forensics had determined there had definitely been a pair of them, each simultaneously firing a long-range rifle from a different vantage—to allow a shattered family to heal.

Whatever it takes to break this case wide open, I promise you, I won't let you down.

Her mood lifted when she spotted Yolanda bustling toward them, a pair of folded towels in her arms.

Handing one to Allie, she said, "I just pulled these out of the dryer, so they're nice and warm for you."

With a sigh of pure relief, Allie wrapped it around her upper body. "You're a lifesaver," she said gratefully as she snuggled into the blessed heat.

The dark brown eyes softened. "How about I start some coffee, too, to warm you up?"

"A cup would be most welcome. Thanks," said Allie. "Was it Yolanda?"

"Yolanda Miller," she responded with a curt nod.

"And I'm—"

"This is Allie Chandler," Jones broke in, cutting her a look that warned her to go along with his explanation. "I've flown her here all the way from Los Angeles to lend the business her eagle eye. She may look a little soggy at the moment—" his smile was sympathetic "—but she's actually a very successful brand and marketing consultant."

"A *brand* consultant?" Yolanda blinked in confusion before abruptly going on the defensive. "What do we need one of those for? We're doing just fine, aren't we? *Better* than fine, since we were featured on that segment of *Chicago Weekender* and all the ladies gotta load of that handsome mug of yours on their TV screens."

Allie smirked at Jones's look of exasperation—and the swift flush that rose from his collar.

"Come on, Yolanda," he said, clearly attempting to recover his dignity. "Every business owner wants to rise to the next level—especially now that we're going all respectable, being served at True." Glancing at Allie, he explained, "My cousin's restaurant's been quite the hit, especially since word's gotten out that she was nominated for a James Beard award in just her second year of operation."

Allie, who traveled so much and worked such odd hours that her knowledge of the restaurant landscape was largely limited to takeout and delivery, still knew enough to say, "That's *quite* impressive."

"We're all very proud of Tatum," he said. "I just want to be sure my product and my brand are both up to the challenge."

Yolanda assured Jones, "Course you're good enough," before turning a fierce look on Allie. "Now this fancy California branding stuff's all well and good, but don't mess with our smiling wolf's head logo, Miz LA. That boy's got some *sass* to him, just like *this* one."

When she nodded toward Jones, he flashed a grin

framed by a perfect set of dimples. "You heard my right-hand woman, Allie. The logo stays."

After studying if for several moments to give her so-called *expert* opinion credence, Allie agreed, "I wouldn't change a thing about it."

With a satisfied nod, Yolanda said, "I think we're gonna get along just fine, then. But as soon as I start that coffee, I'd best get back and run through our bar bites menu with the new short order cook and make sure she's ready for her first shift."

"I've got the coffee. Thanks, Yolanda," Jones said, moving behind the bar and grabbing a pot to fill it.

As the bar manager hurried toward a doorway leading to what must be a kitchen, he measured out grounds from a canister and started the pot brewing before turning back to lean on his forearms on the bar. "It was her younger son who designed my logo," he explained, his tone hushed. "That'd be Harrison, the nineteen-year-old she and her husband lost in an accident last year. He was quite the artist, and their pride and joy."

"I'm sorry to hear that." Allie might not be much of a people person, but she felt a surge of genuine compassion. Pulling the towel a little tighter around her, she claimed the barstool across from Jones and shrugged. "And if it makes you feel any better, I really *do* think your wolf's pretty cute."

"He's supposed to be edgy, not *cute*." Straightening, he folded well-muscled arms across a broad chest that tapered toward narrow hips and an admirably flat stomach. "And maybe a little bit badass, but a lot discerning."

Allie couldn't suppress a smile. "Let me guess—because that's how you see yourself, right?" In her experience, men as good-looking and successful as Jones Colton had no shortage of ego. Though she'd learned he'd walked away from the family business—and the guaranteed path to success that went with it—at a young age to find his own path, she could imagine he would instinctively look down on someone like her, who remembered all too well what it had felt like going to bed hungry and still clipped coupons out of habit. Not that it was any skin off her teeth what he thought.

"It's nothing to do with me," he scoffed, gesturing toward the gleaming silver tanks on the floor of the brewery beyond the glass wall. "It's about what my *customers* aspire to, how they see their best selves, whether they're twenty-five-year-old Cubs fans stopping on the way home from Wrigley Field for a cold one or well-heeled, serious beer tourists."

"Beer tourists come to Chicago? I thought that was just a thing in Germany."

"Good draft beers are brewed all over, with different styles for different tastes and regions, even seasons of the year—but I know you didn't come here to talk drafts, especially while you're standing around courting mildew in those wet things."

"No, I definitely didn't," she admitted. "Fortunately, I do have some dry clothes inside my suitcase."

"I'll tell you what, then," he suggested. "How about I take you back to my office—I have a little bathroom with a shower in there, too, if you'd care to avail yourself? That'll give you a chance to get all cleaned up while I help out my people through the opening rush. Then we can talk at length, in comfort."

"Right now, that sounds about perfect. And if I finish up before you're ready, I can always pull out my laptop and get some work done."

"Great, then. Let me bring your coffee. How do you take it?" he asked.

"Black, with one sugar," she said decisively.

"Coming right up," he told her, "though eventually I plan to prove to you that I'm a better brewmeister than a barista."

She nodded, forcing what she hoped passed for a smile before saying, "Not before I show you that I'm a better PI than I am a more-than-slightly-soggy marketing consultant."

His expression sobering, he cut a look around them, once more checking as if to make certain that no one else was in earshot. "Right now, I'm just praying you'll turn out to be the miracle worker your references were claiming—because I'm afraid that's what it's going to take to find the cowardly sons of bitches who've torn my family apart."

Two hours later, Jones shifted the flat, white box he was carrying to one hand and knocked at the door of his office so as not to startle the woman he had left inside. A woman he'd been warned had a one-track mind when it came to her work, without a lot left over in the way of social graces.

"Oh, if anybody can get the job done, I reckon she's the one to do it," one of her references had told him. The sheriff of a rural West Texas county, the man had given her full credit for cracking a money-laundering ring the prior summer.

"Whatever tricks she picked up hackin' as a teenager had her runnin' circles around everybody on our task force, even that computer forensics expert the Feds sent out to help us," the lawman had told him. "But she's an odd duck, that little lady. She'd rather stay in all night grindin' over that computer than bend an elbow with the fellas once the shift was over. And if you try and crack a joke around her, she'll as likely as not ask you to shut the door behind you on your way out of whatever broom closet you've got her workin' in as give you the time of day."

"I'm not hiring her for a hostess at my bar—or looking for a girlfriend, either," Jones had told him. Even if he weren't running himself ragged lately trying to keep up with the demands of the microbrewery while dealing with the fallout of the murders, he had a strict personal policy against getting involved with women he employed, knowing it would end up far too awkward when he inevitably grew restless after a short time and moved on. "So her being focused on her work sounds ideal to me."

"Yeah, well," the sheriff had confided, "it never hurts a gal to put on a pretty smile now and again instead of scowlin' every time somebody kids her about brewin' up another pot of coffee for the boys."

Figuring the man was lucky she hadn't dumped that scalding coffee on him for his so-called sense of humor, Jones entered the office at Allie's invitation.

"Sorry, I kept you waiting so long," he told her, the mouthwatering aroma from the white box wafting around him. "We had a delivery of hops come in that I had to personally check out, and then one of the hoses broke loose on the number three tank. It made quite the mess before we got it…"

He forgot what he was saying as his gaze found Allie, who was sitting behind his desk, looking completely in her element as she worked at a slim, modern-looking laptop. But it wasn't her equipment, or even the flattering pair of tortoiseshell-rimmed glasses she now wore that surprised him, but how thoroughly she'd transformed her appearance since he'd last seen her.

"You look a lot more comfortable," he said once he found his tongue.

"I feel like a new woman, now that I'm all cleaned up and out of those wet running clothes. Thanks for the use of your shower and your office." With a pleasant smile, she pushed back the glasses on her head, where they sat like a tiara atop her light brown hair, which hung long, loose and sleekly straight, now that she had dried it.

She'd dressed simply, donning a lightweight white sweater over a pair of jeans. But with her fresh-scrubbed face and slim, ringless hands, with their neatly trimmed and buffed nails, he found that he didn't miss the higher-maintenance frills so many of the women he'd dated seemed obsessed with.

"I've brought some lunch to make up for the wait—and my lousy hotel recommendation," he told her, setting the box on an empty corner of the desk.

She sniffed appreciatively at the scents of Italian herbs and cheesy goodness, her eyes smiling as she stood. "So *this* is what you call an apology?"

"You like Chicago thin-crust pizza? I ordered one, tavern-cut with all the good stuff on it, from a place just down the block."

"I'm not sure about that particular style, but my rumbling stomach has decided that it *smells* a whole lot like forgiveness."

After he produced a roll of paper towels from a storage cabinet, he offered her a cold beer to wash it down.

"I'd love the chance to sample your brews another time," she said, "but I'll stick with water during work hours."

"Even if your new boss gives you a pass?"

"Especially then," she said solemnly, her gaze connecting with his own, "since any employer who shows up on my first full day with fresh, hot pizza and an offer of fine craft brew is an employer who deserves the very best work I can give him—just the way your father and your uncle deserve justice."

He nodded, sensing that she absolutely meant what she was saying. And feeling more optimistic than he had in months. It was enough to convince him that he'd done the right thing after all, going behind his family members' backs in hiring a woman with a reputation for getting answers that the police—and more recently even the FBI—couldn't.

After grabbing them both bottled waters from the mini fridge, Jones claimed one of the two chairs on the opposite side of the desk, only to glance over and see her still standing behind the desk, her light brown gaze locked in on the screen of her laptop.

"Allie?" he asked, her intensity reminding him of a lioness from a nature documentary, who might at any moment burst from cover to take down the zebra she'd been stalking.

"Sorry," she said with a shake of her head. "I was just checking out some of the chatter from area bulletin boards for gun enthusiasts in the weeks before the murders, looking for offers or inquiries regarding private gun sales, or maybe somebody asking about a gunsmith who hand loads the particular ammo that was used—"

"Hand loads?" he asked, shaking his head.

"That's when the gunpowder and other components are reloaded and pressed into an existing casing. Shooting enthusiasts often prefer it because they can customize the load to the weapon they're using. When you're planning to shoot from long range, little details like that can make all the difference."

"The police never said anything about that."

"Ballistics weren't clear on the casing, but it was a place for me to start, especially since the members of this bulletin board imagine they're safe from enterprising snoopers like myself, with their paltry little password. *Amateurs.*"

"Have you found anything yet?" he asked, excitement building to hear what sounded to him like a great idea.

"Not yet, and it might prove to be a total bust. But I'm afraid I can be like a dog with a bone, once I zero in on an idea."

"Don't apologize for that," he assured her, as he struggled to drag his hopes back to a more realistic level. "After all, it's the reason that I hired you."

What looked like relief eased her expression, the relief of someone he suspected was used to being an outsider, a young woman judged for not happily pouring coffee and deferring to the older cops she often worked with.

The insight prompted him to offer a smile. "Better hurry, before your lunch gets cold."

Closing the laptop, she came and joined him. "Thanks."

As Allie bit into her first slice of supreme pizza— after discreetly picking off the mushrooms and hiding them inside her paper towel—she murmured happily and closed her eyes, chewing slowly. "Mmmm. This... This is..."

"Good, huh?" he asked, surprisingly turned on watching this petite hacker-turned-PI lost in a world of her own pleasure. It got him to wondering what other Chicago delights he might introduce her to, a thought that had his imagination running in an altogether new direction before he clamped down ruthlessly on his libido.

The sheriff had been right. She was pretty enough—beautiful, even, when she flashed one of those fleeting smiles his way, but he warned himself to forget it. *Put everything about her out of your mind but the job she's here to do. A job you can't risk distracting her—or yourself—from for a single second if you ever want another good night's sleep.*

Heaven only knew, he hadn't had one lately, not without the nightmares about learning of the murders. And the guilt that plagued him still, remembering how he'd gotten wasted—falling down drunk—the night before the funeral and then shown up disgustingly hung over... as if it wasn't bad enough knowing that he'd never have the chance to truly make his father proud.

I'll make it up to you, Dad and Uncle Alfie. I'll spend whatever I have to, take any risk that's needed, to find whoever took you from us.

"This is amazing. *Thank* you," Allie said, sighing over her a second slice with an air of blissed-out reverence before wiping off her hands.

"Then how about another?" he asked as he finished up his own.

Lowering her water bottle, she shook her head. "Thanks, but I'd better quit while I'm ahead. Otherwise, you'll just find me snoring in your office later—unless you've already somehow managed to find me someplace to stay?"

"I took a look at the vacation rental site online, and Yolanda checked a different app as well, but I'm afraid there're no vacancies available anywhere I'd be comfortable recommending. I do have an idea, though, if you'll hear me out instead of walking out."

"Why would I—"

"I'm talking about you staying at *my* place. I have a

house, you see? A restored bungalow with a nice guest room—"

She frowned, her forehead creasing. "I don't know about *that*, Jones. I need my own space to work, and plenty of privacy to focus."

"Well, that makes two of us," he admitted, knowing that his territoriality about his living quarters, his need to decompress alone after his noisy, social shifts, was a large part of why his previous relationships hadn't lasted longer, as well as the reason his siblings and cousins had started referring to him as the family's lone wolf long before he'd ever thought of starting up the brewery. "But I'm sure we can make this work. The truth is, I'm not spending all that much time at home lately, between the business and checking in on family."

She still looked uncertain. "Your family..."

"Mostly my aunt and mother. They're twins, you know, just like my father and his brother were, and it's great that they have each other to lean on, and their business to distract them, too. Still, this has been a terrible time for them—for them and all the family, since we got the news."

"I'm sorry to hear that, but...would it be possible that you could stay with one of them?"

"Stay with my family?" he asked, not understanding.

She flushed slightly. "Instead of at the house, with me, I mean, so I can work uninterrupted?"

Frowning, he shook his head, taken aback by her request. "Listen, Allie, I'm already putting myself out offering to share my space, but I'm not willing to let you root me out of my own home. If you're worried I'm thinking of trying something inappropriate with you, I give you my solemn word right now that I'm *absolutely* not interested in anything like—"

"Oh, no, it isn't that." She shook her head and raised her palms, color flaming in her cheeks. "I'm sure you understand completely…the professional boundaries of our arrangement."

"Good," he said, the word coming out more harshly than he meant it to, mostly because he was irritated over his earlier attraction to her, "because the *only* thing only I want from you is directions to the sons of bitches I mean to see pay for my dad's and uncle's murders."

I've done it again, Allie realized, watching Jones duck his head against another light shower to load her things into the trunk of a sleek blue BMW.

"Don't forget to buckle up," he advised as they climbed inside, his admonition so stiff that she knew her instinct was on target.

I've definitely alienated one more person I'm going to have to work with within hours of meeting him by saying the wrong thing. Or maybe it was the right thing, said in the wrong way. She'd never known exactly. She only understood there was something missing in her makeup. Some factor that made smooth social interactions simpler for others than they seemed to be for her.

By this time, it should come as no surprise, nor should it bother her as long as she was left in peace to unravel the perplexing—and deeply fascinating—cases that stymied investigators whose hands were tied by a frustrating array of laws and regulations. Laws and regulations that she considered on a case-by-case basis, some of which she deemed…debatable. Trivialities to be dispensed with to stop the kinds of men and women who brought families to grief.

Including happy families such as her own had once been, so she understood the impotent rage Jones must be feeling, his burning need for justice, even if she couldn't put those feelings into words.

But even in the name of setting the greatest wrongs right, there were lines she knew better than crossing. And judging from what he'd said, she realized it was time to set him straight on the issue before she invested any more of herself into this venture.

"When I took on your case," she said as the car glided along wet streets hemmed in by modern mid-rise buildings, "I agreed to help you find the killers."

He slowed to a stop, leading a small pack of traffic, as ahead of them, a light cycled from amber to red.

Flipping on his wipers long enough to clear a few leaves and strands of pollen from the glass, he challenged, "Don't tell me you're already trying to manage my expectations."

"No." She shook her head. "I'm trying to manage your behavior *afterward*, once I've tracked down these killers."

"*If* you track them down, don't you mean? Or do you already know something I don't?" He darted a glance her way, hope flaring in his blue eyes. "Is there something you need to tell me?"

She shook her head. "Not yet, or I already would have. I just want to make it clear, if I find evidence I believe may be strong enough to convince a prosecutor, I'll need your word that you aren't planning to do anything crazy."

He kept his gaze trained straight ahead and asked her in a low voice, "So tell me, Ms. Chandler, how does a former criminal like yourself define *crazy*, exactly?"

As the light changed, he sped forward, just as her heart leaped at the mention of her past missteps. Yet he wasn't the first client who'd tried to rattle her by blindsiding her with some unsavory detail discovered from her background, so she controlled her breaths and delivered her answer, cool and smooth as glass.

"*Suspected* criminal." None of the hacking charges against her, all of which had occurred while she was still a juvenile, had ever gone to trial, thanks to the FBI special agent in charge and a merciful judge who had given her the chance to get her act together and serve the greater good—along with law enforcement—instead of using her skills to independently dole out punishment to those she decided had it coming. "One who'd rather remain free to hunt *true* criminals than being locked up for, say, abetting murder."

"Who said anything about murder?" Jones asked as the small sedan zipped over into the left lane ahead of traffic and quickly caught a green arrow at the next intersection. "Is that what you think I'm plotting, some sort of eye for an eye vengeance for my dad's and uncle's deaths?"

"Can you honestly tell me it hasn't crossed your mind?" she asked, turning her head to take note of the low-slung black sports car that had zipped behind them through the left turn.

Scowling, he drove on, silent for so long that it surprised her when he finally erupted a few blocks later. "Could you really blame me if it has? They were shot down by a pair of snipers and left dying, as if they were garbage, nothing to anybody—not the backbone of a family, a support I never fully appreciated until—until the day it was lost forever."

"I'm sorry," she said simply, but he continued speaking as though he hadn't heard.

"So, yeah," he admitted, "I *have* fantasized about tracking down these cowards and making them pay for what they've done. After comforting my grandmother, who's lost *two* sons, when she was crying, and holding my poor mother when she broke down after the funeral, I even had dreams where I had my father's killer on his knees, begging me not to blow his worthless head off."

Moved by the anguish in Jones's voice, she admitted, "As a girl, I had those same dreams. Sometimes, I still do."

He jerked a look in her direction, surprise splashing over his face. *"What?"*

Her stomach flipped, making her wish she could take back what she said. But there was no reversing it, so she forced herself to struggle forward, the words like thorns in her throat. "When I was a kid, my—my dad went missing. The police didn't find his remains for another seventeen months."

"I—I had no idea," he said.

"It's not something I share often," she told him, though *ever* would have been far closer to the truth. "But you were honest with me, so I'm being straight with you now, too."

"So he—your father was—murdered, like my dad and Uncle Alfred?"

"There was never officially a ruling, but yes," she said, as memories of searing grief and helpless rage bubbled to the surface. "I have zero doubt that it was murder, nor about who killed him—not that an eleven-year-old was in a position to do anything about it." And by the time she had been, she had lacked the maturity and judgment to handle things the way that she now wished she would have.

"That must've been horrible, especially as a child. I'm sorry you had to go through that."

As they passed a public library, she waved off his

sympathy. "It was a long time ago, and I didn't bring it up because I'm dying to rehash it. I just wanted you to know I get it, what it's like to want to kill someone who's destroyed the core of your family, along with your sense of safety and of who you—who you are in this world."

He glanced her way, their gazes connecting for the barest fraction of a second. Yet it was enough that she felt a ripple of awareness of their shared experience running through her, as clear as the rainwater sluicing off the windows outside.

"You hit the nail on the head," he said, his eyes back on the road. "That's exactly what it's destroyed. Before all this went down, I knew who I was—the youngest of the Chicago Colton cousins, the one who was always so slow to get his act together."

"What do you mean, slow to get your act together?" she asked as they were delayed by traffic that had slowed to move around a fender bender. "Correct me if I'm wrong, but aren't you here right now, driving a nice car on your way to your own home after leaving the thriving microbrewery that's generating all sorts of excitement, all well before the age of thirty?"

"All true, and I don't mean to sound a bit ungrateful, except…" He blew out a long breath. "When you're born into a family of high achievers, where everybody seemed to come out of the gate so certain of what they were meant to do and what steps were needed to achieve it— and they had such damned *noble* goals, too—continuing the work of Colton Connections, with its focus on inventions that would better society, or helping kids, or teaching at a university or creating cutting-edge cuisine—"

"All worthy ambitions, but none of them for you, I take it?"

"Exactly, but let me tell you, my father was none too impressed by my decision to drop out of the college business program he'd talked me into enrolling in when I couldn't figure out a major for myself." Jones gave a rueful chuckle. "It's a wonder he didn't track me down and throttle me after he found out I'd withdrawn and used the money for my semester to go backpacking around Europe to investigate a few different opportunities. That was when he cut me off financially."

So, Jones *hadn't* voluntarily turned his back on his family's wealth after all… Her interest piqued, she said, "I imagine that didn't help the relationship between you."

"Let's just put it this way," he said as he continued driving, crossing an overpass above a freeway into what appeared to be an older residential area. "The two of us didn't really speak for years, until I finally came to realize that being forced to go it on my own was the best thing that ever happened to me, and the only reason on this earth I've gotten to the point that I have now."

"In other words, you grew up." Having tired of dating the kind of men who never would, she nodded her approval.

"Grew up, but I'm afraid it didn't make me any less stubborn because I could never bring myself to come out and admit to my father that I knew he'd done me a favor in the long run. Just like he never got around to telling me that I'd actually done well with my *'beer slinging'* after all, not in so many words, at any rate."

"So that explains why you hired me…because the two of you had unfinished business."

"We did. But understand this. It damned well didn't mean I didn't love the man. It didn't mean that at all."

"Of course not," she said, glancing toward him and

then craning her neck to look behind them at the same black sports car she'd taken note of earlier, following them through the intersection.

"Jones," she warned, her stomach clenching. "That car—"

Before she could say more, a gold SUV merged into their lane just behind them, coming between them and the black car and blocking it from sight.

"What's up?" he asked. "Is there some problem?"

"I—I'm not sure," she said, her heart pounding out a warning. *They're here. They've found you! How? And does this mean you're putting your new client—and anyone you come into contact with—in danger?*

"Is something going on? You're dead pale. Tell me," Jones demanded.

Once more, the SUV, whose driver seemed to be in a huge hurry, pulled out of his lane, this time roaring past them. Only now, the black sports car had dropped off out of sight.

Where could he have gone? Or had she only been imagining they were being followed?

"I'm sorry," she told Jones, improvising on the spot. "I saw that guy in the gold SUV coming up behind us, driving so aggressively—people like that make me really nervous."

He cast a sharp-eyed look in her direction. "Is that right? A woman who goes after hardened criminals is terrified of bad Chicago drivers?"

Knowing a challenge when she heard him, she hit back bluntly, "You know how many people die every year from road rage incidents and reckless driving?"

"Too many, I'm certain, and I'm not trying to make light of it. But you were shaking, Allie. I saw it. You can't tell me that's all about anything as impersonal as accident statistics."

"I guess I'm still on edge after my stressful morning, that's all," she said. "It's nothing, really. Or nothing you need to worry about, anyway."

"If you say so." He didn't sound at all convinced. "But if you ever decide that you do want to talk about it…"

"Thanks, but I'll be fine," she said, wanting desperately to change the subject, to bring the conversation back around to his relationship with his father. But she grew tongue-tied at the thought, and so the next few minutes were spent in awkward silence until finally, Jones turned onto a shaded street mainly consisting of restored older homes.

"It's just up ahead," he told her, casually waving toward the right. "My humble abode."

"This is what you call *humble*?" she asked, her self-consciousness falling away as he pulled into the drive of a handsome, tan brick bungalow, whose bow-front enclosed porch and numerous window frames were painted an eye-catching dark green.

"Hard to believe the place was a partially gutted drug den when I bid on it. When my sister, Carly, saw it for the first time, I believe 'apocalyptic horror' was the term she used to describe it." Snorting at the memory, he grinned and shook his head. "She and Heath, my older brother, both thought I'd lost my mind, and my cousins were about ready to stage an intervention."

"So you've had all this done since?" Though she'd watched shows about such projects on her favorite cable TV networks—had even secretly fantasized about renovating a fixer-upper of her own—the combination of sky-high real estate prices in the LA region and her own lack of skills and knowledge had her conceding it was nothing but a pipe dream.

"A lot of it I did myself, or worked on with a couple of buddies in the contracting business—but for the plumbing and electrical, I hired professionals."

"Well, I'm impressed that you did any of it. The place is absolutely gorgeous, right down to the landscaping." She gestured toward the glossy-leafed shrubbery bordering the walkway.

"It's taken me *years*, between this and getting the brewery on its feet," he told her as he shut off the engine, "and I should warn you, some parts of the interior are still a work in progress."

"I can't wait to see it," she said, fascinated to discover this unexpected facet of the one-time black sheep of the Colton family.

After grabbing her things, he led her inside. There, her jaw nearly dropped at the sight of beautifully restored wooden floors, gray walls with simple white molding that led the eye into a living area furnished with a blue sectional and several splashes of brighter color. The clean, modern lines of the furnishings perfectly complemented a tiled fireplace and built-in bookcase that formed the first floor's focal point.

"You have an amazing eye," she said, which drew an immediate, self-deprecating snort.

"Actually, I have a mom and an aunt in the home decorating business, so I was smart enough to listen when they told me I needed to do better than the old collector electric guitar and vintage beer ad posters I'd originally put up—at least if I ever hoped that any woman might want to set foot in the space, much less stick around to share it for more than a couple of sleepovers."

She laughed at that. "So what happened to the cool

stuff? Don't tell me you let them shame you into dumping it."

"It's currently living in my basement man cave with my pool table, workout gear and all the unfinished projects that I'm hiding."

"Sounds like the perfect place for it."

After putting down her stuff, he gave her a quick tour of the remainder of the floor, which included a modernized gray-and-white kitchen, a dining room, and a beautifully renovated master bed and bathroom.

"Your room'll be upstairs," he said, grabbing her suitcase on his way to the steps. Their footsteps echoed as they both ascended, and soon, he was showing her a welcoming room with a comfortable-looking bed situated between two, tall lace-curtained windows.

"These upstairs bedrooms were so tiny, I knocked the wall out between two of them to make a guest room that wouldn't feel so much like an old-school phone booth," he said.

"It's lovely," she told him, admiring the woodwork and the little antique dresser as he set down the suitcase and she lowered her backpack to the bed.

"I'm sorry there's no room for a desk in here," he said, "but you're welcome to spread out and work wherever you'd like in the house. For as long as you're here, please make yourself at home."

"Sounds great. Thanks. So, are you heading back over to the brewery to work?"

Shaking his head, he told her, "I thought I'd take a few hours before I need to get ready for this evening's tasting dinner—which reminds me. Yolanda was asking if you'd be there tonight, and it got me to thinking, why wouldn't you? You know, as my new marketing consultant?"

"At True? This evening?" She stiffened, feeling the blood drain from her face as she imagined herself among all those well-dressed, undoubtedly well-heeled people, the kind of people who seemed to come equipped with a sixth sense that informed them the likes of her did not belong. Shaking her head, she took a step back. "No, I don't think so, Jones. I can't— I couldn't possibly, on such short notice."

"Why not?" he asked her. "After all, most of the family's going to be there. It'll give you a chance to meet them, add your first impressions to whatever other background research you've been doing."

"I don't— That isn't really necessary," she said, forcing out the words with difficulty as her throat began to tighten.

Looking nearly as uncomfortable as she felt, Jones confessed, "By the way, I haven't told any of them about you except my sister, Carly, and to be honest, I'd rather not let the others know what you're really here for, either. I don't want to get their hopes up, after so many months of disappointment, just in case nothing turns up."

"That's a good idea," she agreed. "The last thing I need is your family calling me for updates or to run their individual theories by me. It would only slow me down."

"But I still think you should come tonight. You'll need dinner later anyway, and you did say you wanted to try out my beers, didn't you?"

She shook her head. "Don't you remember? Half my clothes were damaged in this morning's flood. I don't even really know what it was I salvaged and stuffed inside my suitcase, but I'm sure it's not suitable for a—"

"It's not the opera, Allie. It's a dinner with a beer

tasting. I do have to show up on the early side to shake some hands and say hello as guests arrive, but I promise you, no one's going to be all that dressed up. I'll be wearing jeans myself."

"You're a guy," she pointed out, her heart fluttering like the wings of a trapped moth. "And basically, the star of the show tonight besides, so the rules are different for you."

"I've got an idea, then," he said, snapping his fingers as it came to him. "Let me text Tatum. She's just about your size, and I'll bet she'd be able to help you out with something."

"I said *no*, Jones, so don't bother your cousin while she's getting ready for this dinner," Allie blurted, seeing in his eyes that she was coming across as shrill and difficult, but the idea of being backed into a corner, put on display and forced to act out some farce he'd chosen for her was pushing all her buttons. "I told you I need peace and quiet and space, so I'll be happier—*far* happier—working here. *Alone.*"

Chapter 2

Peering at her through narrowed eyes, Jones wondered what on earth was with this woman, who once more looked and sounded on the edge of panic. "This doesn't have anything to do with that gold SUV that made you so nervous on the way here, does it?"

"It wasn't the— *No*," she insisted. "It absolutely doesn't. I'd just like some peace and quiet so I can focus on finding your father's and uncle's killers. Is that too much to ask?"

As bright and engaging as he'd found her earlier, he couldn't help thinking back to the sheriff's calling her an odd duck, and wondering if the man might have had a point. Certainly, the warmth she'd shown him earlier had iced over, as suddenly as if an out-of-season cold front had blown in off Lake Michigan.

"Have it your way," he told her, sensing that any further attempts would only prompt her to dig her heels in deeper. "But if you change your mind, my offer to come as my guest still stands. Meanwhile, I'll leave you to your work. The bathroom next door's all yours. You'll find fresh towels under the sink and just about anything you might need during your stay."

She nodded curtly but said nothing.

"If you think of anything else, you'll find me down in the man cave—" after dealing with the perplexing woman, he could use some time to decompress "—or in the master bedroom getting ready. I need to be over there around six thirty."

"Thank you, and I really do appreciate your hospitality." She barely met his gaze. "You've been very kind."

"You're more than welcome—especially if you're half as good as your references promise."

She looked up quickly. "If you don't agree I am, I'll tell you what. We'll split my expenses getting out here, but I won't charge you a penny for my time."

"You're that confident you'll get the killers?"

"Not necessarily," she admitted before the barest smile lifted one corner of her mouth. "But I'm a hundred percent certain that I'd rather you not spend the whole time I'm here worrying that this has all been a colossal waste of money. So do we have a deal?"

"Sounds like I'd be a fool to say no," he said, though he couldn't imagine stiffing her, or a woman as serious as she seemed doing less than her best, "so sure thing, Allie."

"Great." Though her smile widened, it was fleeting, and he saw the relief flash through her eyes when he nodded goodbye before heading down to the partially finished basement.

Something more than this case has her worried, he realized as he put on some music and racked up some balls on his pool table. He was reminded of a female bartender he'd once worked with before he'd owned his own place, who'd grown jumpy after an ex-boyfriend had started following her. She'd been nervous, too, in public spaces, and had reacted badly if anyone tried to press her into going out after her shifts, at least until her ex was arrested for violating his restraining order—and the terms of his parole—by showing up at their workplace waving around a weapon.

Could Allie possibly have something like that going on back in California? If so, might she have seen a face in traffic she'd momentarily mistaken for her stalker?

At the idea of some brute harassing or even hurting her, Jones felt a rush of anger, followed by an even stronger desire to keep her safe.

Scowling, he grabbed his favorite cue stick and told himself he was leaping to conclusions—and allowing his family's recent tragedy to make him overprotective of everyone around him. Including a woman he suspected would be quite perturbed if she had any inkling that he had lapsed into a fantasy of rescuing her from some imaginary ex who might be out to harm her.

As he lined up one shot after another, he once more felt the darkness calling: the black hole that had threatened to engulf him following his dad's and uncle's deaths. As hard as the grief and anger had hit him, it had grown even tougher not having any answers—and when he'd learned that his troubled relationship with his father was making the authorities take an extra-hard look at his alibi and motivation, he'd been absolutely crushed to imagine that for even a second any of his family members might have entertained the same suspicions. Even after they'd all been cleared, Jones still had to wonder. Did his siblings, his cousins and the others ever still look at him and wonder if he was only pretending to be grieving? Did they wonder every time he smiled or laughed if he might be feeling relief that he no longer had to worry about his father's judgment?

He hid his turmoil as best he could, being as supportive as he knew how for his loved ones and pasting on his most convincing approximation of a charming smile for his customers at the brewery. But with the weight of grief and shame gnawing at him, Yolanda had begun calling him out for his distraction—or for his increasing surliness over the minor snafus and complaints that were a part of every business owner's day.

"After this tasting dinner, you need a vacation, something to take your mind off all this stress you've been under before you drive off any more of our employees," she'd suggested last week, after he'd sent back so many plates to the short order cook to be remade that Javier had finally pronounced him impossible and stormed off in a huff, never to return. "Maybe a few days chilling in Las Vegas would sort you out. Or how about Cozumel or somewhere? I'm pretty sure some time poolside ogling bikinis would be good for your soul."

"The last thing I need is time alone to brood over everything that's happened," he'd said, "and the fact that the killers are still out there, probably sitting back and laughing while we—"

"Then don't go alone," Yolanda had suggested. "Why not invite one of those little groupies you always have running around after you, pretending like they really give a damn about where various hops varieties are grown and their relative merits and weaknesses?"

"Who *wouldn't* care about a fascinating topic like that?" he'd teased.

Yolanda rolled her eyes. "The kind of pretty things

who check to make sure you're not listening before they whisper over the bar to ask me if I could maybe hook them up with a wine cooler… But that doesn't mean they couldn't serve as company—or stress relief, if you catch my drift."

He certainly had, but in his gut, Jones had known that he needed answers way more than the sort of fleeting horizontal distraction that might have served him in the past. And if this last-ditch effort, hiring Allie, couldn't get his family the justice that they all craved, maybe it was time to pull up stakes, sell off the bar, the brewery, everything he owned here and start his life anew someplace where no one knew him…

And in a city far less haunted by the ghosts of his regrets.

After showering and shaving for the long-anticipated beer dinner later that afternoon, he changed into his best jeans with a fresh shirt that he left unbuttoned at the collar. He shrugged on a slim-cut tan sports jacket, the suspicion creeping up on him, not for the first time, that Tatum had only suggested his involvement in tonight's event, whose proceeds would be benefiting one of the children's charities that her sister January worked with, out of a sense of familial obligation. Would others be whispering behind his back, saying that he hadn't earned a place at the table or all the attention he'd been getting in local media?

Knowing it was only a late-breaking case of nerves talking, he glared at his reflection in the bathroom mirror. "Since when do you give a damn what anybody else thinks? You've worked your tail off for this, and the proof is in the product."

Yet for a fleeting moment, he imagined he glimpsed his father, standing behind his reflection with his strong arms crossed, his skeptical expression saying he was reserving judgment.

"You just wait and see then," Jones said, his old resentment twisted up inside a knot of grief and longing. *Who knew I'd still miss you so much that I'd keep inventing ways to keep even our old arguments going?*

Only in Jones's imaginary conversations with his father, he was never compared unfavorably to his older brother, Heath, his sister, Carly, or any of his cousins. And he always somehow managed to get in the last word.

As if to counter the idea, a knock interrupted his thoughts, making Jones jump before he belatedly remembered that he had a guest. Shaking his head at how keyed up he was, he crossed the room and opened his bedroom door to Allie.

"You've changed again," he noted, taking in yet another transformation. This time, she'd pulled up her long hair in a simple, yet elegant twist that showed off the shoulder-baring turquoise top she was wearing over a calf-skimming black skirt with sandals. A pair of silver earrings dangled, sparkling like tiny chandeliers. It was on the tip of his tongue to ask her, *How is it you manage to look more beautiful every time I see you?*

Instead, he said, "I thought you were staying in to work."

When she shrugged, he had to make an effort to keep his gaze from lingering on her well-formed shoulders, along with the sweet curve of her neck… But he noticed she was blushing.

"I—I'm sorry about before, upstairs," she stammered. "I'm such a— I'm not always great when I'm put on the spot like that and pressed, especially when it comes to being thrust into a new group of people."

"So you're a little introverted," he said. "Some of the smartest people I've ever known are."

As her light brown eyes searched his, he sensed her attempting to assess whether he was being honest or mocking her for her admitted weakness. In that moment, he understood that she had spent a lifetime apologizing for who she was.

"I get it," he said, knowing what it was like not to feel accepted and relieved to think it was something as straightforward as a little shyness problem, rather than anything more ominous, that had caused her to behave as she had earlier. "In the future, I'll try not to come on quite so strong."

"You were right, though," she admitted, "about the tasting dinner being the perfect opportunity for me to meet and observe each of your family members. I'd like to come along, if you'll still have me. I thought this outfit might do."

"You look *very* nice," he assured her, noticing that she'd played up her beautiful eyes and full lips, applying her makeup with a light touch. He picked up, too, on some fresh and faintly citrusy fragrance, so subtle that it made him want to lean closer to try to breathe it in more deeply. To breathe *her* in, but he held firm, reminding himself that he knew better.

"I thought that maybe, on the way over, you could fill me in a little about your business's marketing efforts and plans for the future so I don't come off like a complete idiot if someone asks me for my take on the Lone Wolf Brewery."

Smiling, he nodded, and for the next twenty minutes gave her a rundown on the microbrewery's history, his work over the past few years and what he had in mind to grow his brand. As they headed out to his car, she seemed genuinely interested, asking astute questions about his idols and his inspirations and even where he hoped to be in five years.

"In *five years*?" he echoed as he opened the car door for her. By then he would be the same age as his older brother, now the president of the multimillion-dollar Colton Connections, with all the responsibilities—and the pressures—that entailed. Though Heath seemed happy enough now, especially since he and his right-hand woman, Kylie Givens, had gotten together, Jones had a hard time imagining himself as settled, content knowing that his future lay with one career and one company, or even still living in the home he'd so pains-takingly remodeled.

"Try thinking ahead," she said once he had climbed into his own side of the vehicle. "Can you see yourself expanding to get your products in other bars or maybe grocery stores? Or maybe opening additional locations in other cities?"

"To be honest, I'm a lot less interested in making and selling a whole lot *more* beer than I am in figuring out how to make it *better*. That means keeping every-thing directly under my own supervision and maybe partnering with more foodie and beer tourism venues. I'd much rather do that than focus on just one or two products with the kind of mass appeal for suburban su-permarket chains."

"In other words, you're more of an artisan brewer, not really in this for the money."

"Don't get me wrong. I'm no rich kid dilettante, doing this for love alone. I've gotta keep the lights on and my people taken care of," he conceded. "But if big profit were really what made me tick, my father would've understood me a whole lot better."

"So what *does* excite you, Jones?" she asked as he checked for traffic and backed out the car into the street.

Hitting the brakes a little harder than he'd meant to, he clumsily shifted into drive.

"A-about your work, I mean," she stammered.

He glanced over to catch her blushing, or maybe it was only the sunset staining her face a deep rose color.

Smiling her way, he said, "Traveling around to pick the brains of old craftsmen all over the world. Meeting new brewers on the cutting edge, people who are so passionate about what they're doing that they live and breathe their product. Introducing casual, occasional beer drinkers—"

"Like me," she pointed out.

Nodding, he continued, "—to our signature craft brews and seeing their eyes light up as their palates come alive."

"The way you look, when you talk about it, I can see why people have been flocking to your brewery. That kind of passion's a rare thing. People restless with the humdrum day-to-day grind want a taste of that in their lives."

"Yeah, well, I'd like to think my product's really good, too," he said, impressed with how intently she had listened—and seemed to get the essence of what he was saying, where so many others assumed he was just talking and his true end game was to sell out to some big company that would slap his label over an inferior, watered down version of his beer.

"I'm looking forward to finding out, and to getting a chance to connect some of your family members' names with faces, too."

"I know we talked about this earlier, but you aren't looking at any of them as suspects, are you?"

"From the information Detective Parker was kind enough to share with me, he's pretty much exhausted that avenue of inquiry, along with most of your father's and uncle's major business rivals and associates—anyone the two of them were known to have bad blood with. And if that wasn't enough," she added, "there are no connections anyone can find between any of them and the more recent set of murder victims that appear to have the same MO."

"So who *are* you looking at, then?"

When a dark-colored sports car passed them, she went quiet, her eyes following it as her body stiffened.

"Allie?" he asked, foreboding zinging through him. *I wasn't imagining it earlier. She's definitely looking out for trouble.*

"Sorry." She shook her head before returning to what she'd been saying. "Instead of investigating individuals linked with your father and uncle at this point, the only approach that makes sense is to cast the widest possible digital net for evidence and see where that leads me."

Letting her watchfulness go for the time being, he asked, "Evidence like that gun forum you were reading?"

She nodded. "All sorts of social media."

As he stopped for a traffic signal, he asked, "What exactly are you looking for?"

"I'm not sure I can explain my methods, other than to say that they're more art than science. Online rants and ravings, even calls for violence have gotten so commonplace, they're more like white noise, so even specific threats aren't the best of indicators. More often, I've found, it's what *isn't* said that's most telling."

"Like the negative space between the object of a picture and the frame's edge?" he asked before shrugging.

"A graphic designer who was putting some ads together for the brewery was telling me about it."

"That's a great way of thinking of it. There's something about that creepy unspoken part in a conversation—a chill runs through me when I imagine the words between the lines. Like this afternoon, when I came across—" She cut herself short.

"When you came across *what*?"

She only shook her head. "What I think might have been some coded chatter between friends, that's all. Half a conversation, and so far, it's mostly a gut feeling. I don't want to jinx anything by speaking up too soon."

He wanted to prod further, but the light was already turning green, and they had nearly reached the restaurant. Still, Jones hung his hopes on Allie's instincts, feeling those same chills that she claimed to sometimes feel...

Along with a premonition that whatever this smart, capable and gorgeous woman had come across would finally bring an end to the questions that had been tormenting his family for the past five months. But, he wondered, would they find the answers they discovered any easier to live with?

Though Allie continued to keep an eye on traffic, she'd more or less convinced herself during the course of the afternoon that she'd only imagined she'd been tracked here, in spite all her precautions. After double-checking the encryption securing the online booking of her trip and reminding herself that she'd told no one where she was traveling, she could imagine no other way the men she feared could have any idea where she'd disappeared to.

After all, her enemies, for all their ruthlessness,

didn't possess supernatural powers. And she reminded herself that the threat had been mailed to her home address three weeks before, and for all of her lost sleep, fancy new alarm system for her condo and one-on-one refresher sessions from her old self-defense instructor, she hadn't had a whisper of real trouble so far.

Tonight, she told herself, she wasn't about to let anxiety throw her off her game, not when she needed to focus on sorting out the various Coltons to aid in her investigation. Besides, when was the last time she'd enjoyed a nice dinner in the company of a handsome and intriguing man? As long as she only tasted from each the alcoholic offerings instead of going wild, there was no reason she couldn't at least try to have a little fun while she was at it.

She wasn't certain what she'd been expecting from Tatum Colton's North Center area restaurant. Marble columns, perhaps, and a maître d' in a fancy black tuxedo, looking down his nose at anyone—beginning with her—he felt didn't measure up.

Instead, she found True to be as warm and welcoming a space as she could wish for. A renovated warehouse, its spacious interior was marked by tall front windows and high ceilings painted a soothing shade of green. The glossy leaves of healthy potted plants, the rich, polished grain of the wooden tables and the long, marble bar—where dozens of patrons were dining—had her smiling as she took them in, along with the friendly background chatter of numerous conversations.

"This place has the air of its own little peaceful kingdom," she told Jones as they approached the hostess stand, "one where I'd like a linger awhile and sample whatever it is I'm smelling." She sniffed appreciatively, her mouthwatering with the tantalizing aromas wafting their way.

"You'll have to tell Tatum that was your first impression," he said. "I'm sure she'd love to hear it."

"I can't wait to meet her." Allie nodded toward a sign explaining that the downstairs dining room was closed this evening for a sold-out private event. "Sounds like your beer's been quite the draw."

"It's more than likely Tatum's special menu," he said, waving off the compliment, "or charitable donors looking to support children in need. You can get my cousin January to tell you all about the organization that's benefiting from tonight's event. Here she comes now, with her fiancé, Sean Stafford."

They turned toward a couple just arriving, and Jones formally introduced his tall, blond cousin, who looked to be about their own age, and a strong-looking man with wavy, light brown hair.

As the two men shook hands, Jones said, "Hey, Detective, don't be such a stranger over at the brewery. I've missed seeing you lately."

Allie perked up at the title, wondering if he might be with Chicago PD or even work with Detective Parker. But since she couldn't imagine any way to broach the subject at a crowded social function, or ask him if he'd heard anything about the FBI's investigation into the recent murders, she could only hope that the topic came up during the course of casual conversation.

"Everyone in Homicide's been pulling a lot of overtime of late," explained Sean, whose muscular build was offset by an affable expression, "but I'll try to get by sometime this week."

"This is Allie Chambers," Jones said, introducing

her. "She's a marketing consultant I've flown in from LA to put fresh eyes on my branding."

"Welcome to Chicago," January told her. "So nice to meet you. Shall we head downstairs instead of crowding up here near the entrance?"

"Definitely," Jones said.

A smiling hostess arrived, greeting Jones and January each by name and welcoming them all before ushering them toward the staircase and wishing them a pleasant evening.

On the way down, Allie happened to overhear Jones quietly telling his cousin, "I know I'm likely to get mobbed as we're being seated, and Allie's jet-lagged from her trip out and, to be honest, a little on the shy side. Do you think you could maybe take her under your wing a little? Introduce her to some of the family and help get her settled at our table?"

"Absolutely. I'd be glad to," January assured him as they entered a dining room where a large group of people stood talking, greeting each other and shaking hands while they stood in line waiting to be seated.

"I didn't mean for Jones to pawn me off on you like an unwanted kitten," Allie told her as he was dragged off by his brother Heath—who, though somewhat older and fairer-haired than Jones, was every bit as easy on the eyes—to shake the hands of a couple of the dinner's sponsors who were apparently clamoring to meet him. "I'm perfectly capable of fending for myself."

"Now why would you want to do that when you could hang with the fun people?" January's infectious grin had Allie instantly warming to her.

As she expected, January proved to be as helpful as she was kind, advising her while Sean chatted with another of the men in line, "It's bound to get a little crazy for the next few minutes, but stick with me and I'll steer you toward where we'll be sitting, with Jones and his bar manager."

"I appreciate that, and Yolanda's great," Allie said. "By the way, I've been thinking since Jones introduced us what a great dress that is you're wearing. That color's perfect on you." She normally paid little heed to styles, but that shade of violet really brought out the taller woman's green eyes.

"Thanks! I'll have to tell my big sister, Simone. She's wasn't able to make it tonight, but she helped me pick it out, when I managed to lure her away from work for once."

Since she would choose work over clothes shopping any day of the week, Allie could relate. "Well, she definitely has good taste."

"Speaking of which," January added, "I may have to steal those earrings from you."

Uncomfortable with the attention, Allie nodded her thanks before quickly changing the subject. "I hear you're involved with the children's charity this event's benefiting,"

"I am." January went on to explain how, during her time as a social worker, she'd seen the group do wonders keeping children living in battered women's and homeless shelters from falling through the cracks of the educational system. "If these kids get the chance to graduate and get job training or higher education, we have hard data showing we can break the cycle of suffering."

As she finished, Sean turned to tease, "You'd better watch yourself, Allie, or my fiancée will be twisting your arm for a donation while she's holding you captive."

"I was already thinking of offering," Allie said honestly. "It's the least I can do, since Jones invited me to this dinner as his guest."

"That's so kind of you, and you're in for a real treat," January promised. "My sister gave me a sneak peek at the menu."

"And Jones is debuting a new beer that I can't wait to try," Sean said before introducing the strikingly good-looking Latino man he'd been chatting with. "This is my coworker, Cruz Medina—"

"Who happens to be Tatum's fiancé," January interjected. "So, Cruz, are we going to get a peek tonight at those mad knife skills my sister's been telling me you've been putting to work for her in the kitchen?"

"Only in the service of a good cause," Cruz deflected, looking thoughtful as he ran a thumb along the line of jet-black beard that defined his strong jaw.

"Please, don't get her started on good causes or we'll be here awhile," Sean warned, grinning. "They're trying to get everybody seated, so let's go grab our table."

Jones arrived to claim the seat to Allie's right, bringing with him Yolanda, who drew raves in her feminine-cut tuxedo-style suit, while her husband, Roderick, a thick-waisted retired Chicago firefighter, beamed with pride. But his deep brown eyes truly lit up with the arrival of the first course, a pair of plump seared scallops on a crisp, thin biscuit smeared with some unidentifiable but unimaginably delicious paste, topped with delicate ginger-scented wildflower petals.

"It's almost too beautiful to eat," Allie said, basking in the sight beside the pale ale they'd started out with.

"If you really think that, you can pass that dainty nibble my way," Roderick ventured, before Yolanda elbowed him and warned him, "You mind your manners, Roddy, and keep those big fingers outta my plate if you don't want my fork to find your knee."

Their good-natured teasing set the tone for a pleasant conversation, which mostly centered around the various courses and especially Jones's newest offering, a special, darker brew that perfectly complemented the juniper-flavored honeyed duck breast with watercress.

"I never knew that food like this existed," Allie gushed as she washed down another bite. "And I was totally prepared to simply *pretend* to like your beer just to be polite, you know, as your marketing adviser. But this has been—oh, my goodness. You've ruined me forever for whatever six-pack's on sale at the local discount store."

Grinning, he laid a hand over his heart, miming a solemn look in her direction. "Then I feel my life's work hasn't been in vain. But I hope you've saved room for dessert."

"Maybe a bite or two," she said, patting her full stomach before whispering to January, "Hey, do you have any idea why that redhead over there keeps giving me the evil eye? Or am I just imagining things?"

Just then, the young woman in question, who wore a black dress with a plunging neckline, sent another annoyed looked in her direction.

January whispered, "She's probably just another of Jones's flock of admirers, mad to see that you're the woman on this arm."

"But we're not—"

"Maybe not, but he's been *awfully* attentive, I can't help but noticing…and I understand you're staying at his house."

Allie felt her cheeks heat. "Where on earth did you hear that?"

"Mmm…maybe when I stepped into the ladies' room earlier, and Yolanda happened to breeze through."

"I hope she told you about my hotel disaster," Allie whispered urgently. "And I certainly hope no one's thinking I'm out to worm my way into Jones's bed or something."

"Of course not. Relax. We both understand it's only a temporary professional arrangement, even if the two of you *would* make a cute couple."

Allie made a scoffing sound, but decided not to encourage more speculation by protesting too much.

"It may not be so comfortable for you," January said, speaking in hushed tones, "but I'm actually thrilled to see Yolanda joking again and taking an interest in Jones's love life. After what happened with their son last year, she and Roderick went through some really tough times. It gives me hope that someday, things will get a little better for my family."

Allie touched her arm, seeing the sadness in her green eyes. "Jones told me about your losses, and I'm so sorry."

January gave a pained smile. "I'm sorry for bringing up such sadness on a night we're all supposed to be celebrating."

Shaking her head, Allie said, "You're learning to live with something very, very big. Never apologize for however long that takes you. It's a process."

"Thank you." January patted the top of her hand and then looked away when Sean asked if she was doing okay.

Giving the two of them privacy, Allie turned, her interest piqued as she overheard Jones quietly ask Cruz if he'd heard any more updates from Special Agent Howard. But Cruz only shook his head and grinned as a blonde wearing an updo and apron over her dress headed their way. "Oh, there's the woman of the hour now." Coming to his feet, he kissed Tatum in greeting.

"I thought I'd join you for dessert at least," True's owner told them, turning a happy smile onto Jones, "*after* I've led a toast the permanent inclusion of the Lone Wolf Brewery's beers on our menu."

"I—I don't know what to say," Jones said, clearly overcome as he rose to embrace her.

"That'd be a danged first," Yolanda hooted, and Allie found herself laughing as well, happy she'd decided to be part of this gathering after all.

Later, as they walked back toward the parking lot where they had left Jones's car, she told him, "Congratulations on the dinner. From what I could see, it was an enormous success." She found herself wishing that his father had been there to see it, that Jones could've gotten seen his dad's nod of approval or even hear him acknowledge out loud that the one-time black sheep of the family had turned out well.

"It was a fun night," he agreed. "And January tells me the directors of the foundation are thrilled with the amount in pledged donations it's brought in."

"That's excellent," Allie said. "It sounds as if they're using it to change a lot of lives."

"What about you, though?" he asked. "Did you manage to muddle through dealing with my family and friends all evening unscathed? I know big events like this aren't really your thing."

"You and January eased me into the onslaught nicely. And all that delicious food and beer didn't hurt a bit," she said, as they passed a bicycle shop that had closed up for the evening. "But *you* hardly drank a thing, I noticed."

"I knew I'd be driving, for one thing."

"And?" she prompted, sensing there was more.

"And…I might've been a little nervous," he confessed with a shrug that made him look almost boyish. "I heard through the grapevine there were a couple of pretty high-powered critics in attendance."

"I wonder if January could've been nervous, too," Allie speculated. "She was only having water, even when Tatum led her toast, though January did make a point earlier of telling me how much she loves your brews."

"Normally, she does," he said. "And she'd never miss the unveiling of a new beer."

"Well," Allie said, smiling as another explanation occurred to her. "There *are* other reasons a happily engaged young woman might decide to forego alcohol altogether."

"You aren't suggesting that she might be *pregnant*? She didn't say anything, did she?"

Allie shook her head. "No, but I did notice a couple of looks between her and Sean—and he seemed especially solicitous, asking if he could go and grab a sweater from the car at one point when she mentioned being a little chilled from the ventilation. But you know what? I hardly know them. So please forget I said anything. I'm probably dead wrong."

At the entrance to the parking lot, Jones stopped walking, keys jingling in his hand.

"What?" she asked, turning to stare at him.

A slow grin spread over his face—a smile that set off an answering flutter beneath her stomach. She reminded herself that any attraction she felt was purely physical—and as ill-timed as it was unwise.

"Come on," she prodded, pulling herself back on track. *"Spill."*

"I just think your PI instincts are right on target, that's all, and I couldn't be more delighted for them," he said, chuckling as they continued walking toward the waiting car, parked among a couple of dozen others. "I'm happy, too, that you and January were getting on so well. Did she happen to introduce you to Heath or Carly? I'm sorry I didn't get a chance to."

"She pointed out your sister, but she and her—is it her fiancé?—were across the room, so—"

"Yes, she and Micha are taking things slower this time around."

"This time?" Allie asked.

"Yes, they were together once before, but— It's quite a long story. Clearly, they're doing great now though, since they've recently told us they're engaged, too."

"There seems to be a lot of that going around in your family."

He nodded, looking somber. "Maybe because when you see how suddenly life can be taken from you, it makes you step back and take a second look at how you're living yours."

"I can see that. I know, sometimes I wonder if I've been wasting—" Pulling up short as a tall shadow emerged from between two parked SUVs they were approaching, she cried, "Jones, *look out*!"

"Hey, watch it, buddy*,"* Jones barked, but the man was too close to avoid when he seemingly stumbled, thrusting one angular elbow into Jones and knocking him off balance.

Caught midstride, Jones went down, shouting, *"Allie!"*

But her instincts and self-defense training had already taken over. Pivoting away from the stranger—a thin, pale man in a watch cap and a grimy raincoat—she fought off panic, her right hand plunging into her bag, an action she'd mentally rehearsed a hundred times these past two months. Whether she had paranoia, preparation or blind luck to thank for it, her fingers closed immediately on the item she'd moved from her checked-through luggage to her purse earlier today.

Her gaze met the stranger's, his dark and determined, as he bared crooked teeth in a snarl. She thumbed off the safety and engaged the switch as she let the purse fall to the ground.

A buzzing, crackling sound filled the air, with the blue-white flickering of the arcing spark flashing off the stranger's hollow-eyed face.

"Back off, right now!" she warned, raising the stun gun higher as she took a step closer. "Don't think for a second I won't shock you!"

Recoiling, the man whimpered, raising his arms to block the light. "No need to hurt me, lady," he said, his speech slurred. "I didn't mean to—to knock nobody over. All I wanted was a fiver, a dollar even, maybe. That's all, for my med'cine."

His pleading words cut off abruptly as his gaze fell to her fallen purse, and she saw the calculating gray eyes weigh their chances.

She imagined him wondering, would she dare come within reach, close enough to shock him? Or if he were bold and swift enough, could he make off with her bag, with her cell phone and her wallet?

As his gangly body dropped into a crouch, one long arm reaching downward, Jones came up behind him, warning, "I wouldn't chance that if I were you." Clamping his hand around the man's elbow, Jones hauled him upright, his tone firm but also reassuring. "After the scare you just gave both of us, my lady friend here looks nervous enough to light up the two of us—and probably most of the Great Lakes region—with that thing."

Jones hadn't been kidding about Allie looking nervous. Her face glowed, sickly pale beneath the lot's security light, and the stun gun she was holding was quivering rapidly. But her jaw was set, and her eyes burned with a look of fierce determination—one that told him that she neither knew nor cared that the weapon in her hand was technically illegal in this jurisdiction. She was clearly prepared to use it, if that was what it took to protect the two of them.

The man who'd knocked him off his feet, whose unkempt sandy-colored hair and tattered raincoat made him appear to be one of the homeless population occasionally encountered in the area, struggled to pull away from Jones.

"Let me go! Don't hurt me!" he pleaded, his voice crackling with a terror that competed with the snapping of the stun gun.

"No one's going to hurt you," Jones said, shooting a look toward Allie, who silenced the weapon, killing its blue-white spark. "I'm just offering you a helping hand up. That's all…"

And giving Allie the chance to pick up her bag before you think any harder of making off with it. Though Jones hated to assume the worst of those down on their luck and always tried to help where he could, he wasn't naive enough to miss the way this guy had been eyeing Allie's handbag.

As Allie scooped it up, the gaunt man's tone grew wheedling. "You got a few loose bills on you, don't you? Then I can go somewhere else to grab some dinner. Haven't had a solid meal in—hell, I don't remember when."

"You're saying now you're hungry?" Allie's skepticism reminded Jones of how earlier the man had mentioned "med'cine." Probably a reference to whatever illicit drugs he was using.

But to Jones, that didn't matter right now so much as did the dozen or so other diners he spotted heading toward their vehicles, most of them in pairs or small groups. Diners whose evenings he wouldn't want spoiled by a persistent—and unusually aggressive—panhandler.

Glaring pointedly at Allie, the thin man answered, "Hungry, sick go ahead and take your damned pick. So how about somethin' outta that fancy purse for me, unless you're the kind of sick little girl who'd rather get her jollies hurtin' a poor man?"

"I'm no little girl," Allie said, eyes flashing, "and I wouldn't've had to defend myself if you hadn't deliberately *assaulted* my companion, so quit playing like you're the victim here."

"I didn't assault nobody! You quit spoutin' lies about me, sister, or I swear I'll—"

"Hey, I'll tell you what," Jones said, concerned that this guy wasn't acting like any other panhandler he'd encountered, but still thinking he could handle this and get Allie and himself both safely on their way. "Before we end up having to trouble my cop friend over there across the street—" he nodded toward where he spotted Sean and January heading in the opposite direction, both seemingly oblivious to the encounter "—why don't we grab you some meal vouchers out of my car. I have a flyer in there, too, with information on where you can cash them in for food and find a warm, safe place to stay for the night."

There was a tense moment as the man in the raincoat shifted from foot to foot and licked his chapped lips nervously. "You sure you couldn't maybe throw me just a little cash money?"

"Are *you* sure you wouldn't rather spend the night in jail?" Allie asked, more firmly. "Because that can be arranged, too."

The suddenness of the man's lunge took Jones off guard, along with the crude obscenity exploding from his sneering mouth as he ripped free and vaulted toward Allie with shocking speed and strength. Jones's own shout, along with her shriek of alarm, added to the chaos as she raised the stun gun.

Jones saw it go flying from her grasp and heard her grunt as she spun halfway around from a blow to her left shoulder. Horrified that she'd been struck, Jones spotted a silvery flash, reflected off the streetlight from the hand that her assailant drew back.

"Knife!" Jones shouted, adrenaline pumping through him as the attacker slashed at her face.

Allie ducked, the blade whistling through the air only inches above her head. But in her mad scramble backward, her feet tangled and she sat hard, then rolled onto her back.

Jones's fist slammed into her attacker's face, snapping the man's head sideways before a second punch plowed into his solar plexus, hitting harder than he'd ever struck another person in his life.

"Ungh!" the thin man grunted, the air exploding from his mouth as he dropped to his knees and then fell sobbing. Landing on his side, he curled into a fetal

position, clearly desperate to protect his face and mid-section from further damage.

With the approach of footsteps, a new voice, deep and familiar, emerged from the darkness just behind them. "Grab his knife, Jones! At your three o'clock."

"Got it. Thanks, Micha," Jones said, grateful for the arrival of his sister Carly's new fiancé, since he knew of no one he'd rather have in his corner in a pinch than the former Special Forces soldier.

Sure enough, by the time Jones had secured the weapon—a wicked-looked four-inch switchblade, Micha had knelt beside the downed man and made quick work of securing his hands behind his back with some parachute cord that he'd produced from some-where.

Nodding his appreciation, Jones stared at where Allie sat only steps away, her eyes huge and her face even paler as one hand covered the top of her shoulder.

"How bad is it?" he asked. "Should I call an ambulance?"

"I'm not quite sure—" Turning her palm over, she looked down at the shiny wetness staining her hand—the same blood Jones saw spreading across her shoulder. "I thought—thought he'd only *hit* me. I didn't realize that he'd— The knife— It must've—"

"Allie!" He dropped to his knees on the hard concrete between two parked SUVs, catching her as her eyes rolled back and she slumped over. "Allie, wake up!"

His sister, Carly, rushed over, her blue eyes wide and her phone in hand as the silvery skirt of her dress flut-tered around her legs. "I've called 911 already. Now, lay her down, carefully, and let me in to assess the injury and check her vitals." A pediatric nurse by trade, she visibly fought back her emotions before pleading with him, "Help me help her, Jones."

"I thought he was just a panhandler, but he— I think he might've *stabbed* her." His heart constricted as he carefully pulled aside the sodden material of Allie's shirt slightly—how much blood had she lost? He couldn't tell in this light. The wound looked fairly small, perhaps no more than an inch or so in length. But how deep had the blade plunged? Could it have pierced major blood vessels?

"Move over," Carly ordered, more firmly this time. "Or better yet, switch on your phone's flashlight for me so I can see what we have here."

Scooting over, he fumbled for his cell, but the phone squirted from his blood-slick hands, clattering to the concrete before he managed to retrieve it and activate the light.

"I'm damned useless here. I'm sorry," he said, feeling both helpless and furious at himself for his clumsiness, his slowness—and for not having recognized and stopped the threat before Allie could be hurt in the first place.

After failing to protect her, would he now be forced to watch her bleed out, the way his father and Uncle Alfie had in another parking lot a few short months ago? He couldn't let it happen—couldn't watch the vibrant, beautiful woman he'd been talking to, even laughing with, only a few minutes before, die.

"There's not so much blood, not really," Carly told him. "And her pulse and respiration are both strong and steady. I'm just applying a bit of pressure here to slow the flow."

"Here, take this. It's sterile and absorbent," Micha

said, tearing open a small, sealed packet he'd pulled from his sport jacket to hand to her.

Curious about what other oddments he might have squirreled away on his very capable person in case of emergency, Jones caught the scarred veteran's eye but decided to save the inquisition for another occasion.

The man in the raincoat attempted to roll to his feet, which prompting Micha to turn and push him to the ground before advising in an eerily cool voice, "You can either stay down, or *I'll* put you down—and trust me, friend, you won't like my methods."

As Carly pressed the cloth to Allie's wound, Allie groaned and tried to push her hand away, rousing enough to complain, "Ah, don't...where is—? What's going—"

Eyes fluttering open, she looked around, clearly confused, from Carly to Jones.

"I'm Carly Colton," his sister said. "You've had an accident."

"Some accident," Allie said, frowning in the direction of her assailant, who now sat hunched and sulking under Micha's supervision. "And this is *so* not how I'd hoped to meet Jones's sister—after passing out at the sight of my own blood."

"I'm sure you're in pain," Carly said, "and there has been some blood loss."

Allie grimaced, looking from Carly to Jones before confessing, "It's happened before, I'm afraid. I'm fearless about heights, closed spaces—I can even bluff like crazy if called upon, but as for blood—don't surprise me with the red stuff, especially my own, or it's lights out."

"You mean you aren't *dying*?" Jones stammered. "He *stabbed* you, only inches from your heart!"

"It's nowhere near there. Come on," she chided. "This is embarrassing enough, a woman in my line of work, fainting over a silly thing like a little—"

"*You're* the PI, aren't you?" Carly said. "Jones told me he was hiring someone."

"Allie Chandler, in the flesh," she said with a nod of her head. At the sound of sirens, she made a face and looked at Jones. "Please tell me you didn't call an ambulance, not over a cut shoulder."

"No, but *I* did," Carly told her, "and it's a decision that I stand by. I don't care if you are a PI. You can't play off a stab wound like it's nothing."

Allie stiffened, paling further. "I just need a shower, some antiseptic ointment and an adhesive bandage or two, that's all."

"Carly's a registered nurse," Jones informed her. "You need to listen to her."

"That's right," Carly put in, "and I'm telling you, you'll need a tetanus shot and antibiotic, probably with several stitches, at the very minimum—and that's if there's no damage to underlying structures."

"You might as well give up and listen," Micha advised her. "I can already tell you, arguing with Carly when she plays the nurse card is a losing proposition—and anyway, she's right. You don't want to end up with some infection. Trust me."

"I'm *not* riding in an ambulance," Allie insisted, "not over some nick from a random nutcase."

"How's this, then?" Jones offered as the first emergency lights came into view. "As long as your bleeding's not too bad and you stay conscious, I'll take you to an urgent care center to get checked out as soon as we finish talking to the police and make sure this guy goes straight to jail where he belongs before he hurts someone else. Fair enough?"

She took a moment before conceding. "I guess that makes sense."

"And then you're going to tell me *exactly* why you've been on guard for trouble practically since the moment you arrived here."

She didn't look happy about it, but she nodded. "As long as there's no ambulance, you've got yourself a deal."

Chapter 3

It was after one in the morning when Jones finally drove her home from the urgent care center. By that time, Allie was sore, aching and mentally and physically exhausted after dealing with both the police and the doctor who'd stitched her wound.

As badly as she needed sleep, what she craved even more was time alone to sort through her thoughts and make a plan for what to do next. But judging by the way Jones was blocking her path to the staircase, he wasn't about to let her go without the private conversation she'd been dreading.

"You've put me off long enough. It's time for some real answers," he said, his blue eyes tired but his gaze determined. "That story you told the police earlier about being totally blindsided this evening—it wasn't the whole truth and we both know it."

She looked away for a moment, wavering under the strength of his direct stare.

"I thought so," he said, sounding as confident as if she'd admitted it aloud. "You *knew* someone was looking for you. You've damned well known it since you got here."

She shook her head to argue the point—a mistake since it pulled at her fresh stitches.

When she hissed through her teeth, Jones grimaced and then nodded toward the sectional. "Please, grab a seat. I'll get you a glass of water so you can take one of these pain pills from your prescription."

"I'm not sure I'll need it."

"Better to get ahead of it, don't you think? For one thing, you'll sleep better if you're not hurting."

"Right now, I'm pretty sure I could conk out if you propped me up in a dark corner." She yawned, pointedly.

"You might think that now," he said, "but you're probably pretty wound up. And remember what the doctor said. Pain control aids healing."

She tried for a smile. "Now you're sounding like your sister." Though they'd declined Carly's offer to accompany them to the urgent care center, she'd texted repeatedly to check in or remind Allie of things to ask the doctor about while she and Jones were still waiting to be seen.

"I'll take that as a compliment," Jones called from the kitchen, where she soon heard the clinking of ice cubes falling into a glass from the refrigerator-door dispenser.

Returning, he met her at the sectional, where she'd kicked off her shoes and tucked her feet up under her skirt. Shaking out a single pill from one of the prescrip-

tion bottles they'd picked up at a twenty-four-hour drug-
store on the way home, she thanked him before washing
down the tablet.

"You know," Jones said, his knee accidentally bump-
ing hers as he sat down at an angle to her, "you scared
the hell out of me tonight, when you looked down at
that blood and fainted."

She groaned at the reminder, but he held up a palm.

"Hear me out, Allie. I was afraid that you'd— That
the street thug might've killed you right in front of
me, while I just stood there, helpless to protect you."
His normally bright blue eyes looked haunted by the
thought.

"I feel terrible about scaring you like that," she said,
seeing that he looked nearly as wrung out as she felt.
"And even sorrier for ruining what should've been a
joyous evening for you."

"It wasn't *your* fault that guy went ballistic about my
not offering him the cash he wanted."

"I don't know about that. If I hadn't been so confron-
tational with him, threatening him with a night in jail
the way I did, then maybe he wouldn't have exploded
that way."

"You had no way of knowing he had a long history
of violent behavior with women," Jones said, referring
to what the police had told them about her assailant, a
homeless ex-con named Curtis Stubbs, who would now
be returned to the same jail he'd only recently been released from on prior assault charges. "There's no reason to blame yourself—is there?"

She frowned at the attempt to press her for more information. But as her attention settled on the smear of
dried blood staining his lapel—*her* blood—she decided
that she owed him something. "As I explained before,

both to the police *and* you, my work with various law enforcement agencies over the past few years has led to the breakup of a number of big-time criminal enterprises. They don't tend to have much of a sense of humor about it when their operations are disrupted, so threats come with the territory."

"*Deadly* territory," he said, his brow furrowing.

"Not if you're careful, which is why I always work behind the shroud of false identities online and virtual private networks, along with data traps I've set up to warn me if anyone might be sniffing too close to the real me on the web."

"So is that what's going on here? Was one of those traps triggered?"

"I'm sorry." She shook her head, putting the glass down on a coffee table coaster. "I'm not following."

"Clearly, something's had you on edge ever since you've gotten here. I saw it from the first time you were in the car with me. You nearly lost it—as if you'd seen something—someone you *knew* following—"

"I was— It was nothing like that." The words came tumbling out too quickly, forcing her to scramble to come up with some excuse. "It was only—for a split second I saw someone I was sure I recognized, someone I know from California— Haven't you ever had that happen? Your brain playing tricks on you when you're in a strange place?"

"Except you did it again on the way to the restaurant this evening. *And* you're lying to me now. You've definitely been expecting trouble."

It was a statement, rather than a question. And a measure of her fatigue—or perhaps, her guilt over what she'd put him through this evening—that she nodded rather than denying it once more.

"All right," she relented. "It wasn't a data trap that clued me in, or any kind of online threat, but a typed envelope and message mailed directly to my home recently, one bearing no return address and an illegible postmark. Whoever sent it made sure to use my full name—my real name—in the threat, along with a photo taken through what I assume to be high-powered zoom lens, of me on my morning run. The picture was marked with a set of crosshairs."

"Not exactly subtle."

"You were expecting, what? Shakespearean allusions out of hardcore cutthroats?"

"Point taken," he said grimly. "I certainly hope you changed your running route and habits afterward."

"Do I look to you like the kind of person who wants to end up as—how was it they put it? Oh yes, as 'compost in various, unmarked locations'?"

He winced. "So who, exactly, are these people?"

She shook her head. "For your own safety, Jones, it's better I don't tell you, because they have an ugly history of making good on such threats."

Taking her by surprise, he reached to cover her hand with his, giving it a squeeze. "The only thing that's putting me in danger is your keeping me in the dark. Now tell me. I can handle it."

"Can you?" she demanded. "Because if you go running to the cop engaged to your family member with any of this story, you could end up costing me my life."

"You have my word," he said, those blue eyes drilling into her. "Just explain this so I can watch my back and help you watch out for yours, too, as long as you're under my protection."

"That's where you've got this wrong," she told him. "You don't owe me your protection. I'm working for you, that's all—though I certainly appreciated the way you took down that Stubbs guy tonight."

"You think I'd look the other way, let somebody hurt you if I had the power to stop it?" He shook his head. "I'm sorry, Allie, that's not the way I'm built. But tonight, I'd at least like to *understand* why I need to go and ice my knuckles."

Maybe it was the late hour, the aftermath of stress, or the medication slowly spreading through her bloodstream. Or maybe it was the weight and warmth of his touch, and the fact that she'd had no one else to talk to, no one she could trust, since her mother's death two years before, but Allie found the pressure inside her building until there was nothing left to do but talk to the decent, honorable man who was offering to stand by a near-stranger.

"All right," she said. "I have no proof, of course, but my gut and the timing both tell me this goes back to my last big job, a major sex trafficking outfit. A network of manipulative monsters who trick poor families into believing they're sending their daughters, some of them as young as eleven or twelve, out of their war-torn and gang-violence ravaged countries for legitimate work and a shot at a better life."

"I've read about those scumbags, basically modern-day slavers."

She nodded in agreement. "Honestly, I'd spend my days wreaking havoc in their lives for free if I weren't getting paid to do it. It's taxing, wading through the human misery, but so rewarding, knowing there's a road to home and healing for many of those abused kids."

"Sounds emotionally brutal, seeing the reality up close. I'm not sure I could handle that," he admitted.

"Not everybody can," she said. "But I try to channel my feelings into action and harness the rage I feel at the monsters responsible to motivate myself to work harder. Then it's oh-so satisfying when I help smash their ugly empires all to pieces."

"Sounds like you find the work worth the risk," he said, rubbing at the back of his neck. "But how do you think it went wrong this time? Did the traffickers hire some superhacker to break through your electronic defenses?"

"I almost wish they had," she said. "It'd been easier to deal with than betrayal."

"Betrayal?" Straightening, he seemed to shrug off his fatigue. "You mean someone *gave* those guys your real name and tipped them off on where to find you? Who would—?"

"Detective Oz Sullivan," she said, spitting out a name that would always taste bitter on her tongue. "He was the lead detective in charge of the task force I was brought in to assist by the police chief after their investigation of two years had stalled. Sullivan was furious with the chief—apparently he'd been feuding with her since the day she was sworn in—and when he saw *I* was another female, and half his age to boot, he made such a stink about it that he ended up being forced into retirement."

"Sounds like he was lucky not to get outright fired and *lose* his retirement, while he was at it," Jones said.

"You'd think so, wouldn't you?" asked Allie, outraged all over again over the situation. "But even though he acted like a fool and completely jeopardized the entire investigation, a lot of his colleagues sympathized with his wounded pride. I can tell you, it didn't make my job any easier after I reported that he'd threatened to, excuse the language, 'beat the tits off' me if I came within a mile of his precious files."

"He actually *said* that?"

"Oh, yeah. And in front of witnesses. That was before his last day, when he got so paranoid that someone would share the material on his days off that he started shredding his case notes wholesale so they wouldn't fall into the 'wrong hands.'"

"Sounds like the guy really lost it."

"Yet you would've thought he was an innocent martyr, driven out the door by the evil chief, if you'd've listen to his colleagues."

"That must've made your time there damned unpleasant."

Her mouth pulled tight as she recalled being frozen out of social conversations, having doors closed in her face even when coming in with fresh pastries for the task force in the morning, and finding her rental car's tires flattened one evening when she was the last to leave at the end of a long shift. "I considered it motivational. I was hell-bent on proving to them that I could get their job done better than they could, in an insanely tight time frame. Which I did."

"Good for you," he said, smiling in what looked like admiration.

"I thought so, too, until they dragged their feet on my payment afterward and then this threat showed up in my mail," she said.

"So you think this Sullivan guy, the detective, doxed you to someone involved with these sex traffickers."

"I honestly can't think of anyone who'd enjoy the thought of my ending up as compost more…which is why I took steps to protect myself."

"Like that stun gun in your purse."

"Among other things," she said. "But honestly, considering all the precautions I've taken—and the fact the I told no one in California where I was going, I can't imagine any way they could've tracked me here to Chicago."

Jones crossed his arms over his chest. "I'm calling bull on that one, Allie. I think that you *can* imagine it—probably in horrific detail. Which is why you're so afraid that tonight's attack wasn't random."

"I'm not— Okay I *am* afraid, but that's just stress talking. Common sense tells me that this Stubbs guys is just who the police say, a habitual criminal with a low tolerance for frustration. The fact that we ran across him tonight was just lousy luck," she said, selling the idea with everything she had.

It occurred to her, however, that the person she was working hardest to convince was not Jones, but herself. Maybe because she hoped that when she finally fell into bed, she wouldn't feel the need to sleep with one eye open.

But the look Jones gave her was skeptical. "I don't know about that," he said, "but I am happy you're pressing charges. Still, don't you think you ought to mention the particulars of the threat against you to the local police just in case?"

"Absolutely not," she said firmly. "You need to understand this, Jones. I am not about to go to the cops accusing another officer, even a retired one from a suburban department outside of Phoenix, of anything. If I do that without hard proof in hand, no matter if it happens to turn out later that the guy is as guilty as sin, I'll never get work consulting for another law enforcement agency again."

"But that's not right at all, and he did threaten you."

"Right or wrong doesn't matter. I already have two strikes against me, being female and practically looking like I just got out of high school, if I'm not careful with how I dress and wear my makeup. If they get the idea that I'm some kind of plant who's really there to snitch on cops, the thin blue line will become a wall of resistance like you would not believe."

"But I personally know cops, *great* cops who'd never tolerate that sort of—"

She speared him with a look. "So do I, and plenty of them, but you'll have to trust me on this one, Jones. It's the world I live in."

"That's all very well as long as you *do* get to live in it, instead of dying," he insisted, "so as long as you're staying here, working on my issues, I'll be taking extra precautions, to keep both of us safe."

"What kind of precautions?" she asked.

"I'll be arming my home alarm system, which I admit I'm normally pretty lax about when I'm here," he told her. "There's also a pistol I usually keep locked in a gun safe. But I plan to take it out and make sure it's loaded and within reach, just in case."

"You know how to use it, I presume?"

He nodded. "I've had some training and gotten licensed to carry here, as well as in Colorado."

"Why Colorado?" she asked.

"I originally got licensed so I could transport the money from a bar out in Denver I used to manage to the bank at nights back before I bought my own place."

She gave him an appraising look. "You mean you didn't start out as top dog in this business?"

He laughed. "*Hardly.* But I've learned important lessons from every sort of work I've done. Lessons that I hope have made me a better boss and a better human being."

Abruptly aware that he hadn't moved the hand that rested on top of hers, she felt her fingers tingling with awareness. And appreciation of how much compassion he'd shown her over the past few hours.

"From what I've seen of you so far," she said, lifting her gaze to meet his, "you're already a fine person, caring and considerate to everyone around you—even the geeky former hacker you only met this morning."

He leaned in closer, studying her intently before his voice dropped to a sexy rumble. "Don't put yourself down, Allie. There's nothing at all strange about you... except maybe for the effect you're having on me."

As the pad of his thumb rhythmically bumped across her knuckles, the fine hairs on her forearms lifted, and the tingling she'd been feeling intensified, her lips parting slightly. How long had it been since she'd allowed herself to be so very attracted to a man? And how long since she had let her guard down, even this much?

Thinking back, she drew a blank, reminded painfully of the day she had decided to wall herself off from the world. But it was a lonely space, inside that barricade, she knew, feeling herself waver.

"You know, I'll only be here for a short time," she said, her self-preservation instincts kicking in to warn her body not to lead her somewhere her heart was not prepared to follow. "Most likely no more than a week or so, and then I'll be back off to my old life again, solving crimes and dodging bad guys."

"So what if we agreed now," he asked, "to keep anything that might happen in that timespan casual? Because tonight's dinner might've been fantastic—but suddenly I'm craving just a taste of something sweet."

Reaching up, his fingertips skimmed her jawline, his gaze searching, testing, probing for permission.

The answering flutter of excitement she felt had her flirting right back, saying, "I don't know, Jones. Could be you'd find me spicy—or salty if you're especially annoying."

"Let's find out if I'm annoying you, then, shall we?" he asked before he leaned in even closer, their lips tentatively testing the territory of a kiss.

Jones knew he was a fool to be playing this game with her, but it had been so long since he'd felt the slightest flicker of interest in any woman that he'd been unexpectedly bowled over by his reaction to the beautiful if slightly awkward PI working for him. Though part of it was physical, it wasn't lost on him that he'd been indifferent to the charms of far flashier beauties since the murders had occurred. Still, his interest had ramped up throughout the evening as Allie had joined in the conversation at their table—shyly at first, but with increasing warmth and occasional laughter as, drawn out by January's kindness, she warmed to those around her.

Though she'd listened more than she spoke and wasn't the type to command the entire conversation at the table, he'd overheard her as she spoke to each person in turn, asking an intriguing question and then listening closely for an answer. She might then briefly share a similar experience or make a low-key, but funny, sometimes self-deprecating observation. By evening's end, both January and Sean were flashing him thumbs-up signs, and even Yolanda had murmured into his ear when Allie slipped off to the restroom, "This marketing guru of yours hasn't said anything about any boyfriend back in California, has she? And I haven't seen a ring on that girl's finger, either."

"Would you quit trying to fix me up with anything

that moves?" he'd whispered to her. "I told you, I am *not* looking for a relationship."

"That doesn't mean that you can't take the edge off so you'll quit running off my help and drivin' me half-crazy," she'd countered.

Still, Jones had only scoffed at the idea of using Allie—or anyone—that way. But the hours he'd spent with her since then, seeing her at her most vulnerable, and coaxing her to open up to him, had only added fuel to the fire of his attraction.

And now, fitting his mouth to hers, he carefully sampled a sweetness far more layered than any of True's most decadent desserts. The flavors invited him to linger as she tipped back her head to deepen the kiss and her hands reached up behind him, a rumbling in her throat as she pulled him even closer, wriggling enticingly against his body.

A hunger roared up inside him in response, a need so fierce and urgent that it tempted him to push her back into the cushions and begin a thorough exploration. But as his hand found the soft mound of her breast, she caught her breath, a sharp sound of pain escaping.

Backing off, he shook his head. "You're hurting—of course you're hurting. You were just *stabbed*, for heaven's sake. I'm sorry. I shouldn't have— A gentleman would never—"

"Maybe I wasn't looking for a *gentleman* at the moment," she said, her light brown hair tousled and her lips glistening and swollen. "So don't apologize. But I *am* sore...and getting sleepy."

As if triggered by her words, a yawn broke free.

"No surprise there, especially after that pain pill you took, so why don't you let me help you up to your room."

She made a scoffing sound. "I'm perfectly capable of walking up to bed."

"Humor me. That old staircase is pretty steep, and— you can at least let me carry up a fresh glass of water for you."

She smiled at him and snorted. "Sure, Jones. You can escort me up those *treacherous* steps—as long as we both understand that you'll be heading straight back downstairs…to sleep."

After making certain the alarm system was set and returning to the master suite afterward, Jones unlocked his pistol from the gun safe in his bedroom closet and checked to make certain the .40-caliber semiautomatic had been left both properly cleaned and loaded. He moved it to the top drawer of his bedside table before heading to the bathroom for a quick shower, eager to wash away the lingering traces of what had turned out to be a very long night. But unsettling memories of this evening's encounter with the disturbed man clung to him, along with what Allie had told him about the thugs threatening her life—thugs put on her trail by a vindictive former police detective. As hard as she had tried to convince him that the two situations must be unrelated, Jones was no longer certain what to think.

All he knew was that throughout the evening, a bond had taken root between them. Despite his own suggestion—a wise one, considering their circumstances—that they keep anything that might happen between them low-key, there was nothing at all casual about his concerns for her safety…

Concerns that, along with the lingering taste of her on his lips, kept sleep at bay for several hours longer.

Chapter 4

Worn down by stress, trauma and the effects of the painkiller, Allie had dropped into a deep sleep practically the moment she'd crawled into the comfortable guest bed. Awakened at a little after seven when she accidentally rolled over onto her sore shoulder, she found herself unable to return to sleep, her brain crawling with worries…and not a little regret.

She wished now she'd followed her initial instincts, skipping the beer dinner to continue pecking around the edges of the potential lead she'd happened upon yesterday afternoon. Whether or not that panned out, if she'd remained here working, she never would have been hurt. But the injury frightened her far less than the fact that she had lowered her guard with a man she'd known for such a short time, telling him a secret with the power to rain real trouble down on both their heads.

Compared to that misstep, the foolishness of their

flirtation, and of the kiss whose memory sent a white heat spiraling through her, meant nothing. Yet it was that simple human contact and the dangerously swift connection she'd felt with a man she didn't really know at all—couldn't possibly, in such a short time—that had her rolling out of bed, her brain buzzing with the need to get to work, to get the job done and get clear of this place before she got in any deeper.

After cleaning up, she dressed, choosing a comfortably loose-fitting olive-colored top with jeans and a pair of casual slip-on sneakers. Deciding to skip the heavy-duty pain pill to keep her head clear, she instead took an over-the-counter headache tablet from her purse, along with the antibiotic she'd been prescribed.

Considering how late their night had run, she wasn't surprised to find the door to Jones's room still closed and the house dim and quiet. But since he'd invited her to make herself at home, she set about doing what she needed, making a second trip upstairs for the rest of her equipment before preparing toast and coffee in the kitchen.

With her hunger sated, she grabbed her mug and took it to the table, where she had set up her main laptop, a large secondary screen, her tablet computer and a portable multifunction printer/copier/scanner.

Once seated, she went back for a closer look at the social media account that had caught her eye the previous afternoon. From the screen, a photo of a sullen-eyed nineteen-year-old named Leo Styler glowered out at her from beneath a shaggy fringe of unkempt-looking dark hair. His page listed him as a student of a Chicago-area community college, whose interests ranged from combat-simulation-style paintball to ominous-looking tattoos to the kinds of bands whose lyr-

ics couldn't be played on commercial radio. Scrolling
past his recent shares of antigovernment conspiracy
theories, rants over so-called "infringements" of his
freedoms and complaints against other males the opin-
ionated Leo considered "soft" or "weaklings," she noticed that the camo-and-black-clad teen professed an
interest in relationships with women but appeared to
have few if any female friends.

"Surprise, surprise," she muttered, suspecting he
had no clue why females might be turned off—or flat-
out terrified—by the testosterone-steeped hostility he
projected.

Unfortunately, angry young men were depressingly
common online. Allie would have scrolled past this one,
just as she had so many others from the Chicago area,
were it not for the posting she'd found dating back to the
morning after the murders of Alfred and Ernest Colton.

Scored, it stated simply, followed by the notation,
1 of 2.

So you finally got to first base with a lady, one of
his paintball buddies had wised off in the comments.

Hickey pictures or it didn't happen! another one
had chimed in. *And not from the hose of your vacuum
cleaner this time!*

Leo, to his credit, had ignored their provocation. And
Allie might have dismissed the exchange herself except, in another of her wanderings, she'd come across
a social media page on the same platform. Though it
didn't appear to have been updated in some time, this
one belonged to a more wholesome-looking blond kid
with a nice smile who was listed as a graduate of a
high school in the same affluent Oak Brook neighborhood Leo hailed from. Unlike Leo, however, Jared Garner seemed to have plenty of attractive female friends

around his own age. He also had photos posted from his days on his school's golf team and appeared to be involved in a community recycling organization.

But he, too, had made a single post on the day after Ernest and Alfred Colton had been shot down.

Scored, it read. *2/2.*

Not long afterward, the account appeared to have gone dormant.

Still, she'd warned herself not to get overly excited. There were dozens of other possible explanations for the pair of postings.

This morning, though, she resumed her digging, checking out a newer social media platform, where she found that Mr. Clean-Cut, Jared Garner, was currently spending far more time. Goose bumps rose when she discovered that he was now attending Western Community College, the same school as his angry former classmate Leo Styler, but there was something different about Jared in the newer photos posted on this page. Though they still depicted the good-looking blond guy with the breezy smile of a popular young football jock, in every instance now, his gaze was slightly off, never connecting with that of the photographer. Observing all the shots together, the combined effect sent a chill clean through Allie, as if she were looking at someone who'd gone dead inside in the space of a few months' time.

Don't read so much into a few lousy pictures, she scolded herself, knowing that when a person spent long enough drifting through the white noise that comprised social media, her mind could start inventing patterns that didn't really exist.

But when she later discovered the two nineteen-year-olds' brief exchange regarding another pair of "scores" in the video comments section of a combat paintballer who went by the name of Kap'n K-Oz, wild exhilaration ricocheted through her...

Excitement that fizzled like a bottle rocket crashing down into ice water as she imagined Jones's and his family's heartbreak when they finally learned the real reason for their loved ones' deaths.

It was well past noon by the time Jones finally emerged from his room, only to find that much of his house's first floor had been taken over.

Not only had Allie left out the bread, her plate and utensils, and the peanut butter and cherry preserves from which she'd evidently made herself breakfast earlier, he frowned to see that she'd left only the dregs in the coffee she'd made but had never thought of brewing a second pot nor cleaning up her mess. As he finished tugging a sweatshirt over his jeans, he found her stretched out on the living room sectional, her eyes glued to her laptop, though he noticed she had other items, along with a pen and papers, scattered across his dining table, as well.

"Glad to see you've made yourself at home," he said dryly, barely able to fathom the scope and swiftness of what felt like a full-scale invasion.

With her long hair clipped in a messy updo and the tortoiseshell glasses she apparently used for computer work perched on the end of her nose, she somehow still managed to look effortlessly sexy as she held up an index finger, gesturing for him to wait a minute as she finished tapping with her right hand.

"Sorry," she said distractedly, her gaze never straying from the screen to meet his. "Just need to— I have to make sure I've copied, pasted and documented all of... Hmm..."

Lowering her finger, she went on clicking and tapping until he lost patience and retreated to the kitchen, deciding he wasn't ready to deal with the combination of annoyance and raw attraction—or sort one from the other—without a healthy jolt of caffeine. While waiting for the fresh pot to brew, he put away the food and was just finish cleaning up from Allie's breakfast when he finally noticed her frowning in his direction.

"Oh," she said, her mouth twisting in a look of chagrin. "I was just about to deal with that. You didn't need to—"

"Before or after the health department showed up?" he asked as he used a sponge to wipe a smattering of crumb from the counter. Realizing how grumpy he sounded, he shook his head and added, "Seriously, it's no big deal. It's just I've never been the greatest about sharing my space—especially before caffeine."

"I figured you might at least cut a *stabbing* victim a little slack," she fired back. "Especially since I've just fou—"

"You're absolutely right. I'm sorry." Racked with guilt, he used his fingers to flip back his sleep-mussed hair. "How are you feeling today? Did you sleep all right?"

"I'm feeling fine," she said. *"Better* than fine, considering."

"Then why do you look so worried?" he asked, trying to make sense of the tension lining her face. "That hunch that you had yesterday—do you think you have something?"

"Let's put it this way," she said with a grimace, "those chills I mentioned having have by now gone subzero. I think I may've found the guys—the pair who killed your dad and uncle."

He thumped down his mug so hard on the lamp table that some of the hot liquid sloshed over its edges. "Who, Allie? Who are they?" he demanded, his heart punching at his sternum and his mouth going dry. "And what could they have possibly had against my family to put us through this hell?"

She gently covered his hand with hers. "Why don't you sit down and let me walk you through the evidence I've uncovered so you'll understand where we are and what we need to do next?"

Jones dropped down to the seat beside her. A thousand questions clamored, but all he could do was stare, his stomach throbbing.

Compassion softening her beautiful face, she gave his hand a squeeze. "I want to briefly lay out the thumbnail profile I was working off and the progression of leads I—"

"I don't need all of that yet. Just tell me what *happened* to my family," he burst out, his voice breaking. "That's why I hired you, after all, for your professional opinion—and because I need to know *why*. Who would hate them so much, or us, the Colton family?"

Her eyes misting, she turned completely away from the computer to give him her full attention. "All right, but that's the thing. These guys *didn't* hate your family, or your father or your uncle either. I'm pretty sure they never even knew them."

"Then why on earth would they *kill* them?"

"You have to understand, Jones," she said quietly. "They're basically just a couple of dumb kids. Unspeakably cruel, but—"

His vision darkened. "I don't understand—you're saying a couple of *children* murdered my dad, my uncle?"

She shook her head. "I shouldn't have put it that way. Legally and morally, they're grown men, a couple of nineteen-year-old college freshmen. I'm afraid—I believe the two of them have dreamed up some kind of sick sniper game, a twisted extension of the legitimate league play they appear to be involved with. Apparently, even combat-style mag-fed paintball wasn't lethal enough for these two sociopaths' tastes."

He stared at her, dumbfounded. "A *game*? You're talking about something with *points* and *scores*?"

When she nodded, his heart thrashed in his chest. "That can't be right. How can you possibly believe that—"

"As I told you, I have good reason. If I didn't, I never would've brought it up."

Her gaze, intelligent as it was unwavering, reminded him of her experience presenting evidence to law enforcement. But it was the compassion he saw written there that convinced him she was telling him the absolute truth as she saw it—a truth that struck him like a mallet.

"So you're saying—you're telling me these—these losers took two people I love, people who can never be replaced for—for *what*?" he demanded. "Sick *kicks*? Because they were freaking *bored* one day and couldn't think of anything better to do?"

Standing, he turned away from her and wiped an arm across his face, beyond caring if she saw the tears of rage and pain streaming down his face. Because right now, his heart was breaking as he tried to imagine how the hell he could possibly tell his mother and his aunt what had happened to their husbands? And what about his grandmother, who had lost the twin sons so precious to her? And he couldn't even bear to think about his siblings and his cousins.

He thought he would be sick.

"I—I'm so sorry, Jones," she said, stepping up behind him and wrapping her arms around his waist. As she laid her head against his back, she added, "For you and all your family, I truly am. I *know* what this is, wanting more than anything to know the truth until—until you finally get some inkling how awful it might be—"

Too upset to accept her touch, he pulled away and started pacing. "Those bastards won't get away with this. I swear, I'll damned well show them—"

"Jones, I need you to listen to me, because it's not only *your* family's justice that's at stake here. I've come across another posting where each of them is boasting about 'scoring' after the second pair of men were murdered, too, where one of them—maybe you don't need to hear this."

"I *insist* you tell me. What did he write?"

Her sigh was filled with regret. "'Another rando bites the dust.'"

He stopped to stare at her. "Another *rando*?"

"You know, like a random person?" she clarified. "It's what makes me believe they didn't know any of the four men they've murdered so far. They probably figured—and correctly—that if they chose victims they had no connections with whatsoever, they'd be highly unlikely to get caught."

"But they were *bragging* about these killings online?" Rage hammered at his temples. "Why hasn't someone turned them in before now? I can't believe this!"

"Some of these postings were in strange spots where

most people wouldn't look, and they seemed generic enough that they could've referred to all sorts of things, so unless someone was specifically looking with the proper context, it's highly unlikely they'd put it all together," she explained. "But the dates line up—and considering these guys' interests and their profiles, it's a solid enough lead to go to the authorities for further investigation."

"A lead? Not *proof* enough to get them off the streets before they can strike again?"

"Oh, Jones," she said. "I'm sorry, but we're still a long way from putting anybody behind bars. Right now, my instincts are telling me these *are* our guys, but it's going to take a lot of solid investigative work—background, interviews, checking out of any physical evidence or alibis—before charges can be filed. I'll do everything I can to help, of course, for as long as you want me here."

He nodded to show he understood, though he was still struggling to wrap his brain around this new reality. "All right then. Now, can you run past me what you have, just the way you plan to for the authorities? I want all the details, Allie. No holding back to spare my feelings."

She studied him for a moment, clearly weighing her options before saying, "Why don't you have some coffee and grab something to eat first?"

"You think I could *eat* after hearing news like this?" He waved his hands in disbelief. "Are you kidding me?"

"Then go ahead and get dressed. I'll need a ride soon to the FBI field office. I've made an appointment to see Special Agent Brad Howard there, since Detective Parker told me he's now heading up the investigation. Then you can see everything, along with him."

"Why not tell me now?"

She shrugged. "Because I'm not taking a chance on you."

Shaking his head, he raised a palm. "A *chance*? What are you talking about?"

She grimaced. "I'm worried about you gleaning enough identifying information on our two suspects that you might decide to run off and do something dangerous— or downright crazy—on your own."

Allie's pulse picked up speed as she watched raw fury flash through Jones's eyes.

"We've been through this before." His brow furrowed. "I told you, I have no absolutely no intention of—"

"I know you did, but that was before I hit you with this kind of news." She forced herself to take steady, measured breaths and moderate her tone and volume. "Before you realized that a couple of likely sociopaths, who've never for a moment considered that their targets might have families or feelings, were behind—"

"They'll damned well know it by the time I get through with—" He cut himself off, eyes closing as if he'd realized he wasn't exactly bolstering his case.

She stepped nearer, instinctively extending her hand before remembering how he'd tensed before and pulled away from her touch.

"It's been a lot of years," she told him, reaching with her voice instead, "but please remember, I've been where you're standing. I know what it is to want nothing more than to utterly destroy whoever ruined things for you and your loved ones."

"Then at least they'd know," he said, his fists knotted and his face flushing. "They'd know for certain that I really did care about my father."

"From the little I've interacted with your family," she said, daring to move even closer, "I've already gotten the message that they love you unconditionally. Which means the only person you have something to prove your loyalty to is yourself, Jones."

"You've only just arrived here, and you've barely scratched the surface of my family," he argued. "You have no idea what any of them really think."

"All right," she conceded, "but I do know this much. You won't be doing anybody any favors, robbing them of a chance at a trial and a guilty verdict. And even if you do find some way to get some kind of street justice, it'll never give you the satisfaction you imagine."

His eyes narrowed. "And how are you so sure of this?"

Her flesh quivered, the skin crawling as if a fly had tracked across it as she remembered the sight of the sheet-draped body being wheeled out of the house. Shaking her head to dispel the awful memory—and the buzzing sound of the insects swarming the garage where he'd been found that hot, August day, she said, "You're just going to have to take my word for it that I am—and I wouldn't want you to make the same mistake for something that can't bring back your loved ones... or leave you with a burden you'll have to live with for the rest of your life."

It was a burden she would wish on no one, though some might call it justice. But only those who hadn't learned, as she had, that true justice—the restoration of the murdered loved one—was beyond the human grasp.

"You tracked down whoever killed your father, didn't you?" He pressed the issue. "What did you do to him, Allie?"

"If it makes you feel any safer, it was *his* choice to

take his own life after I sent him proof that *I* knew, nothing I'd planned for or seen coming." At only fourteen, she'd lacked the foresight, or any idea of how horrible she would feel, watching from her bicycle as his estranged wife and his mother had pulled up, both of them in hysterics. "So you don't have to worry about any bodies buried under my patio out in California."

"That's a relief, anyway."

"Maybe it shouldn't be," she warned, giving him a pointed look, "since that means there's still plenty of room for anybody who gets it in his stubborn head to muck up my investigation and jeopardize my good standing with law enforcement."

He chuckled at her mild threat, and she breathed a sigh of relief as some of the tension between them lifted. Still, she wondered if, considering the bad news she'd delivered, the two of them would ever again find their way back to what had last night felt so easy and natural between them.

Better for both of you to take a deep breath, dial things back to a strictly professional relationship, she told herself. *You both have too much going on to throw in a case of serious bad judgment.*

"All right," Jones agreed, looking better than he had any right to, even slightly rumpled and unshaven. "I promise you, I won't do anything to jeopardize a legal case against these losers."

"Great, but that's going to mean one other thing. I'll need your silence for the time being."

"My *silence*? Do you know how long my family's waited, and now you're telling me that I can't offer them a sliver of hope or let them know we have a lead on these two?"

"That's exactly what I'm saying. Because if any one

of you goes off half-cocked and does something—or spooks these guys into running, it could ruin everything."

Turning to pace the room, he scrubbed at his jaw, clearly wrestling with the necessity. "I hear what you're saying, but what if—if I swore my mother, say, to secrecy?"

"Would that be fair to her—or to whoever she told, because you know she'd confide in someone, at least her sister or maybe her mother, if this doesn't pan out? Do you really want to watch their hearts break all over again?"

Sighing, he shook his head. "I hate to admit it, but you're right. It wouldn't be fair to do that to any of them. I'll carry this alone."

"I promise, you won't be alone," she said, offering a smile. "Not as long as I'm here anyway, leaving crumbs and dishes all over your counters."

One corner of his mouth lifted. "Don't tell me that's a habit."

"You know, I *was* going to leave this establishment a good online review," she teased, "but the room service is lacking and the help's a little naggy."

Smile fading, he said, "Seriously, Allie, you're fine. I do have one request, though."

"What's that?"

"I need to see these guys, their faces—the snipers you suspect killed my father and my uncle. Just their photos, please. I don't want to be blindsided at the special agent's office without—without seeing exactly what kind of sick pieces of garbage could be capable of randomly destroying lives."

After considering the request, she nodded before going to her laptop. Keeping the screen turned away from Jones, she pulled up two photos of the pair and enlarged them, positioning them side by side before turning the computer so he could see them. On the left, Leo Styler's angry, dark eyes smoldered like a pair of burning cigarette butts from beneath his thick, dark bangs. To his right, the handsome, blond Jared Garner managed to look equally disturbing, with his empty gaze eerily askew.

But Jones had a different take.

"They look so…*normal*," he said, sounding baffled. "Just like any average white guys you might see walking down a city street or run across on any college campus."

"That's how the monsters move among us, by looking just like anybody else."

But in her heart, Allie knew the truth was more complex…knew that all of them had the capacity to commit monstrous actions if they fell prey to their worst impulses. It was why she clung so fiercely to her own code, even if it wasn't always strictly in accordance with the absolute letter of the law. At least she could live with her actions, and help bring families like Jones's some peace in the wake of tragedy.

Later that afternoon, Special Agent Brad Howard stood from his desk before coming around to shake their hands. A broad-shouldered man in his midthirties with a conservative dark brown haircut, he cut a neat figure in his dark suit and subtly patterned tie. Within a short time, Allie concluded that his mind was even sharper.

"Thanks for coming in today and turning over this information, both of you," he told them after she'd finished reviewing what she'd found, his hazel eyes astute and focused. "This is very impressive work, Ms. Chandler, and you can rest assured we'll immediately start looking into these two young men to see if there's anything to these suspicions."

"Suspicions?" Jones blurted, clearly no longer able to stifle the emotions he'd before forced to bottle up as Allie had laid out her case about the subjects fitting the profiles of potential team serial killers. "She showed you what those guys wrote—*and* the dates they wrote them. There's no way I'm buying that's all coincidental."

The special agent nodded, his expression sincere. "I understand your feelings, but for all we know, they're referring to some online game they're into, or an impromptu paintball practice round they were playing. These posts could even relate to some disgusting competition involving their sexual conquests—"

"I so did *not* need that picture in my head," said Allie, visibly shuddering as she flipped closed the screen of her laptop and tucked it back into the leather tote she'd combined with professionally pulled-back hair, a light blazer and freshly applied lipstick—all of which she'd found helpful in keeping law enforcement types from dismissing her as some glorified underaged hacker.

"You two don't really believe that, do you?" asked Jones, who had also neatened his look for their trip to the office, changing into an untucked button-down shirt and a pair of dark-gray slacks but passing on the jacket.

"No, of course not," Howard told him, "but I absolutely *do* believe that's the kind of story any defense attorney worth their salt will come up with, if we jump the gun and arrest these two on the thin evidence you've brought us now."

"He's right," Allie confirmed for Jones's sake before focusing on the special agent, "but I'd bet my retainer you'll find plenty more on those two once you get to digging."

Howard smiled. "I'd like nothing more than for your instincts to be proven right, but in the meantime—" his gaze turned toward Jones "—I'll need to ask for your discretion on this."

Jones nodded. "Allie's already explained why that's important, so I'll be sure to keep it to myself until you give us the word they've been arrested."

"I'll let you both know as soon as I can. Meanwhile, I'd also ask you, please stay well clear of the suspects."

"I've got a brewery to run," Jones assured him.

"And *I'll* be busy doing additional background research," she added.

Howard nodded. "I'd appreciate it if you'd forward to me anything else you feel might be helpful."

"Always happy to be of assistance to the Bureau," she said before he ushered the two of them out of his office.

"That seemed to go well enough," she told Jones once they had taken the elevator downstairs and exited to the bright spring sunshine. "I can't tell you what a relief it is when I meet a Fed smart enough to actually listen instead of blowing me off because I'm *'just'* a lowly PI." She rolled her eyes at the memory of past frustrations.

"Well, your presentation was first-rate," he said, "and I'm sure your reputation has preceded you—which is great, as long as it gets the two killers off the streets."

"I'm with you on that, but you have to understand, Jones. The FBI's methodical. They won't make an arrest until they have an airtight case, and there's no telling how long that could take."

He pulled out his keys. "But what if, in the meantime, these two decide to play round three of their game, or even to up the ante by taking out a greater number of victims at one time? I can't stand the thought of any more families having to live through what mine did.

Maybe we should keep an eye on them, just in case they—"

"Forget it," Allie said, clamping down on the idea with a shake of her head. "I know you have the best of intentions, but you heard what Special Agent Howard said. We're not jeopardizing the case by getting within a mile of those two guys. Besides, I'm sure the FBI'll get surveillance on them as quickly as possible. With all the speculation in the news about these murders, there's no way they're going to want another incident in the area setting off some kind of panic."

Jones quit walking, as did Allie, to allow a landscaping truck to cross the drive into the parking lot in front of them. As the breeze tousled the fresh, green leaves of a row of nearby trees, he said, "This doesn't sit well with me, just waiting."

"I know it's hard, believe me," she said. "But let's give this a little time to play out, and in the meantime, I'll keep working to make sure these two aren't showing any signs they're about to strike again."

He nodded in agreement. "You do that, please," he said as they headed toward his car. "But first, how about some lunch before I have to head in to the brewery? I didn't think I'd ever want to eat again, but for some reason, I'm suddenly starving."

"You should be, after skipping breakfast."

He used his fob to unlock the car as they approached it. "It seems to me, it's time to introduce you to another Chicago specialty. Ever hear of an Italian beef sandwich?"

It was on the tip of her tongue to tell him that he didn't have to play the gracious host with her, but in his face she saw that he needed the simple comfort of a good meal and quiet conversation even more than he needed to satisfy his hunger.

"I've never heard of it," she said, "but I'm game to give it a try."

He slapped his hands together. "Trust me, after you taste this, you're never going to want to leave this city."

She laughed, raising her hands in mock surrender. "Between last night's dinner at True and all of your temptations, I'm going to have to double the distance of my runs—and you have no idea how much I *hate* the thought, Jones."

"I'll make it worth the extra miles, I promise."

Sometime later, they were finishing their meal, which Allie had talked Jones into splitting after seeing how huge the gravy, spicy veggie blend and sliced beef sandwiches were, when her cell started buzzing. Wiping her hands on her napkins, she frowned down at the screen. "It's Detective Joe Parker from the Chicago PD."

Concern flashed over Jones's face, though they had both just been laughing over her futile efforts to eat her portion of the messy, but utterly delicious, sandwich without getting it on her face and in her hair. "Why would he be calling you, unless Agent Howard's already contacted him about us going in to see him?"

But Allie had already answered to find out for herself. "What can I do for you today, Detective?" She hoped she hadn't stepped on the man's toes by bypassing him to go to the special agent, since Parker had been the one to initially bring her up to speed on the homicide investigation. Police, in her experience, could be sensitive to slights over turf.

Instead of complaining, however, the veteran detective surprised her by asking how she was feeling. "I heard you had some trouble last night," he elaborated, "in the form of an assault outside of a North Center area restaurant. I saw in the patrol report that you'd sustained a knife wound."

"It only amounted to a few stitches and a sore shoulder." She kept the fainting part to herself, embarrassed about an aversion to the sight of blood that she'd hoped she would have long since gotten past. "I'm feeling pretty good today."

"I'm sorry you were injured. Can you tell me, do you have any idea what it might've been about?"

"What do you mean, what it might've been *about*? Last night, we were told that my attacker, this Curtis Stubbs, is a frequent flier in the prison system, with a history of violence against women in particular."

"So you're telling me you believe that this assault was random?"

She glanced at Jones, who'd looked in her direction, her stomach tightening.

"Are you telling *me*, Detective," she asked as dread ran an icy finger along her backbone, "that you have information that it wasn't?"

"That's exactly what I'm saying," he said. "I'm going to need you to drop by my office. We have some issues to discuss—and I have something you need to see right away, preferably you and Jones both…for your own safety."

Chapter 5

As Allie ended the call, she pinched the bridge of her nose between her thumb and index finger.

"What's going on?" Jones asked as he returned to their table after disposing of their trash. "What did Detective Parker tell you?"

She went a little paler. "Apparently, last night's attack on me *wasn't* random."

"How could he know that?"

She shook her head. "I presume that's what he means to show me. He wants us both to head over to the station. But I know you need to head in to the brewery, so maybe I could get a car and go on my own—"

He waved off the idea, frowning. "Of course, I'm coming with you. You think I'd just *leave* you with this?"

She gave him a worried look. "Maybe you should, before you're in too deep. It seems to me you already have plenty on your own plate without worrying about my troubles."

"Hey, c'mon," he said, pulling out the chair to sit beside her and offering a smile. "We defeated that monster sandwich together, didn't we?"

She faltered through a smile of her own. "That was mainly you, but yeah."

"Then we'll get through whatever this is, too, so we can get back to the business of digging up dirt on those two slimeballs who killed my dad and Uncle Alfie. Do we have a deal?" he asked.

"Let's hear what the detective has to say first," she said. "Then I'll give you another chance to figure out whether you're still down with the idea—or would rather see about finding yourself another private investigator to wrap up this case."

"I hired the best there is because that's what my family needed and deserved," he insisted, "and I have zero intention of letting anybody change that, as long as you're still willing."

She didn't answer, but the look she gave him, filled with both uncertainty and apprehension, spoke volumes. Depending on what Joe Parker told them, she might well be on the next plane...and out of Jones's life forever.

He told himself it shouldn't bother him. Despite the swift and sure connection he'd felt with her after learning that they had shared the same calamity, the murder of a parent, they scarcely knew each other.

I do know she's brilliant, if a little shy, but caring with my family.

I also know she's tough enough to face down criminals and stand up against a cop who'd crossed the line but soft enough to pass out at the sight of her own blood.

And I know that I felt something I've never felt be-fore when I pressed my lips against hers...

It was a feeling Jones didn't want to let go of with-out exploring further, even if they both understood it could only be a temporary thing.

The drive across town to Detective Parker's station took longer than it should have, thanks to an unusually heavy midday rush. As they headed in the direction of the lake, Jones noticed that Allie had fallen silent, her eyes glassy as she stared into the middle distance.

"You holding up okay?" he asked her. "How's the shoulder feeling?"

"Not bad at all," she told him before admitting, "I'm just wound a little tight right now, that's all, and trying to piece together where I might've gone wrong cover-ing my tracks just lately."

"You said you'd talked with Detective Parker, didn't you, sometime before the two of us met."

"Yes. After he vetted my credentials, I found him quite helpful."

"I checked out some of your references, too—called around to people you've worked with in the past, in-cluding a Sheriff Hadley in West Texas."

She shook her head as they inched forward. "Ah, Sheriff Hadley. A true prince among chauvinists."

"He did come across as something of a dinosaur, but he told me you did good work—even if you didn't 'smile real pretty' often enough for his taste."

"I can't imagine why."

"Finally," Jones said as they made it through the backed-up light at last. "But here's what I *can* imagine, since all the cops I've ever known seem to socialize a lot within the wider law enforcement community. I see them hanging out with each other over at the brewery a lot."

"They do tend to stick together," she agreed.

"What if one of those references that either Detective Parker or I checked you out with happened to mention it to someone else, someone with a connection to that Arizona police detective who was put out to pasture because of his misconduct after your arrival? What was his name?"

She gave a little groan. "Oz Sullivan—and I never considered that possibility. You could be right, even though it makes me sick thinking that anyone who's ever worn the uniform could be so far gone that he'd actually conspire with the scum of the earth to get even with me."

"It's horrible to think of, yes, but it sounds to me like this guy's blaming you for wrecking his life," Jones said, "even though he did it to himself."

"Sullivan probably finds it easier than admitting he tossed his ethics out the window over a massive ego issue," she said. "And this way, he can keep his alibi rock-solid while he relaxes back in Arizona and lets the traffickers settle his vendetta for him."

"I'm so sorry this is happening," he told her. "And I'm doubly sorry if it's anything I did or anyone I might've called who ended up leading these criminals on your trail to find you."

"There's no way you could've known," she said. "And I *invited* you to check me out with some past clients. I even gave you names and numbers. I should've thought about something getting back to Sullivan via word of mouth."

For the rest of the short ride, the two of them fell silent, and soon, Jones was forced to focus his full attention on the challenges of parking. Once that was managed, the two of them walked toward the police station, which in contrast to the sleekly modern FBI field office was a utilitarian brick building that made Jones feel depressed and anxious every time he came within a mile of it. But since the only times he'd been here had been in reference to his father's and his uncle's killings, he supposed the place would always hold negative associations for him.

Apparently, he wasn't doing the greatest job of hiding his discomfort because when Allie glanced over at him, she said, "You look like you're heading in to have a root canal. You okay?"

"The truth is," he admitted, "the last time I spoke with him, Detective Parker warned me to quit interfering in the investigation. I may've been driving him a little crazy with my efforts to look into the murders on my own before I hired you—not that I was having any luck, but—"

"Caring too much is no crime," she assured him, taking his hand, "especially when you've waited so long for justice. But if you'd rather wait for me in the car—or I could grab a ride-share to take me home…"

"Thanks, but no. I need to hear this." He squeezed her hand. "And I want to be there for you."

An African American man in his midforties with serious, dark eyes, Detective Joe Parker greeted Jones with firm handshake. A shade shorter but more solidly built than Jones himself, the veteran officer maintained his grip a beat too long while another passing officer paused midstride to watch their interaction. "Glad you could make it in today, too, Jones. It's good to see you… *this time.*"

It was a firm reminder that his presence hadn't always been as welcome, but Jones held his ground as always.

"I *will* want to speak with Mr. Colton," the detective said, nodding toward Jones, "but first, Ms. Chandler, I'd prefer to begin our discussion in private."

"Mr. Colton's with me at my request, and as a witness to last night's assault. As you're also aware," she reminded the detective, "I'm here in Chicago at Jones's behest, so anything you have to say to me, you can say in front of him."

The second officer moved on to go about his business, while Parker shifted his regard to Allie. "You're sure you want your current employer hearing whatever might come out here?" he asked, his expression hinting that it might not be the sort of information she would care to share.

With a sigh, she nodded. "If it's what I think it is, it's for the best. He needs to be aware of the situation before he makes a decision about whether he still wants to keep me on."

"All right, then. If you'll both come this way..." The detective escorted the two of them to a small, spartan room set up with a long table containing a plain manila folder and surrounded by four chairs.

He chose the one next to Allie, the two of them seated across from Parker, who dragged the file folder closer to him before spinning it around, his wedding band glinting in the light.

"I'm at a loss, Ms. Chandler," he said, plucking out a photograph, stained and creased but still recognizable as a very becoming head shot of a smiling Allie, though it looked to have been taken several years before, at least. "How is it that one of our patrol officers would come to find this photo of you, a private investigator who's only just arrived from Southern California, hidden on the person of the recently released criminal who attacked you here in Chicago last night?"

"Stubbs had my college graduation photo?" she asked, nose crinkling.

"Inside that grimy raincoat he was wearing," Detective Parker said.

"Ugh." She shuddered, rubbing her arms, and Jones could hardly blame her.

"And I'm afraid that's not the only picture we've recovered," the detective continued, pulling out a copy of the same shot, also dog-eared and wrinkled, from the folder. "Another officer found this one lying on the ground outside a homeless encampment not far from where Stubbs often stayed."

"So you think there may be more?" she asked, eyes widening.

"It stands to reason. Look at the back, Ms. Chandler. Go ahead."

She flipped over the photo, and her hand flew to her mouth to cover a cry of pure dismay.

When Jones looked down, he saw why, for there, hand-printed in a spidery script were three brief lines, each more chilling than the last:

Allison "Allie" Chandler—$5K cash
May be in company of Jones Colton
No witnesses—or no pay!

Before either of them could recover, Detective Parker rapped sharply on the table with his knuckles, asking her, "So what is this? Please tell me, Allie. Who is it that wants you either hurt or dead?"

* * *

As the two of them walked out of the station an hour later, Jones's disappointment in Allie was given away by his tight silence and the waves of suspicion rolling off him as he eyed everyone they passed.

"You're going to have to try to relax, at least a little," she warned him, her own anxiety tightening her stomach. "Otherwise, you'll make everyone suspicious— or terrified—that you're a threat with the way you're glaring at them."

"For all I know, any one of *them* could be the threat," he said before admitting, "Well, maybe not *any* of them," as a frail-looking white-haired woman shuffled past using a walker. "I just wish you'd told the detective everything so he could help you."

"Well, for one thing, I kept waiting for him to bring up that stun gun I had. I assume, in all the confusion, the police found it last night?"

Jones managed a smile. "You'd be assuming wrong, then. Micah and I thought they might give you trouble over it, so he tucked it away for safekeeping for you."

"Thanks for the quick thinking." She nodded in approval. "But getting back to Detective Parker, I told him everything that I can *prove*, which is to say that I've had a threat from an unidentified source. Anything else I might have mentioned to you is strictly conjecture."

"You sounded pretty sure last night about who's stalking you," he said.

"I might *believe* it's those sex traffickers based on the timing, but I'm not about to level that kind of explosive allegation without hard proof to back it up. Especially when I know that the powers-that-be in Sullivan's department won't support me if Detective Parker calls Phoenix to confirm my story."

"So you're telling me this disgraced detective has that many powerful allies?"

She nodded. "Oz could be a swaggering bully at times, but apparently he made a lot of friends and closed a lot of cases. Worse yet, the chief who forced him into early retirement is out of a job herself now because of local politics, and the assistant chief who took her place is the very man who blocked my payment, claiming my methods violated department policy—even though he was only too happy to look the other way and claim credit for the case closure when it went down."

Jones's sigh was heavy with frustration. "I guess you're right, then, about not naming any names yet. But who knows who might be out there even now distributing those photos of you, or just how many of these pictures might already be in circulation around Chicago?"

Allie didn't like to think about it, so she just shook her head. "We'll just have to keep as low a profile as possible and hope, like Detective Parker suggested, that that picture could've been an extra copy Curtis Stubbs dropped, since it was found so close to the tent where he had his belongings stashed."

"Maybe Parker will get something out of him during questioning," Jones said hopefully.

She shrugged. "It's always a possibility, but I wouldn't hold my breath."

On the way back to the house, Jones said, "As soon as we make it home, I'm calling Yolanda to let her know I won't be in today or this evening. I can't leave you home alone, not after this."

Though part of her was touched to think he cared for her well-being, she was a PI, not a helpless damsel in distress, whatever his hormones might have informed him as a result of their kiss. "Don't change your plans for my sake. I'll be fine at the house, working."

"Maybe *you're* sure of that, but who's to say someone won't dig up my address online and come looking, now that my name's out there in connection to you?"

"I know this stuff is scary, but I don't need or want a babysitter," she said as they reached the car.

Unlocking it, he frowned at her. "*Don't* you? Because last night, when you were lying on the pavement— you know, after you'd been *stabbed* and *fainted*—you seemed like you needed my help plenty."

Grumbling under her breath, she climbed into the passenger side and slammed the door. Once he was inside as well, she shot a narrow-eyed look in his direction. "Low blow, Jones, but while we're dishing them out, allow me to also point out that your manly presence failed to prevent either one from happening."

"Maybe *that* time, but from now on I'll be on guard."

"You and me both," she assured him. "The thing is, though, I work best alone, without somebody breathing down my neck. Also, I know how to dial 911, or, if it really makes you feel better, you could always leave your gun at home with me."

"My *gun*?"

"Why not?" she asked. "I'm surely better trained than you are. I would've brought my own if it weren't for all the restrictions with air travel. I *am* licensed to carry—well, at least back in California."

"I'm sure you're fine, but—"

"You just might want to call me before you come home from the brewery so I know it's you who's walking in."

He started up the car and then turned to look at her. "You're really serious? You'd rather I went in to work?

Because after the news you gave me this morning, I'm not so sure I can—"

"After that news, *especially*," she said, her heart twisting as she recalled how gutted he'd been after hearing about the senselessness of the crime against his family members. "The sooner you get back into your routine, the easier it's going to be for you to deal with it, I promise."

"You really believe that? Because every time I think about my family not knowing yet and how it's going to crush them—"

"That's why your work matters so much now," she assured him, knowing he would need the distraction to keep from succumbing to the temptation to confide in at least one of them, "just like my work matters to me."

Jones knew Allie had imagined that getting to work would take his mind off things. For the first few hours he was at the Lone Wolf Brewery, she was almost right, since a bartender had called in sick and he was forced to pitch in until another employee could come cover. It was a reminder of how much he relied on Yolanda, who was off today, to handle the constant stream of staffing and supply issues that cropped up, especially since he'd been so distracted following the murders.

Though he knew she was happy to pick up the slack—partly out of appreciation for all he'd done for her last year following the loss that had left her so devastated and mostly because she was a good employee and a better person—he made a mental note to offer her a raise.

But as busy as he was, splinters of memory kept needling at him, reminders that there were two murderers out there—killers whose names and faces were now branded painfully on his consciousness—living their lives while his family struggled every day with grief. More painful still was the realization that there had been no rhyme or reason, that to those two sick SOBs, his father and his uncle had been nothing but convenient targets.

Those bastards had better damned well hope the Feds take care of them before I do, he thought before the customer across from him, a man in his midthirties with wire-rimmed glasses and a hipster's goatee and beanie, asked, "Is it something I said, man, or do you just have a problem with my looks?"

"What?" Jones asked, startled from his thoughts.

"You've been staring a hole in me, like, glowering for the last five minutes instead of asking what I needed. I gotta tell you, dude, if you're working for tips, this is *not* the way."

Laughing at the blunt, but absolutely correct advice, Jones said, "I'm so sorry. I'm afraid my mind's been on a personal matter, but that's absolutely no excuse for forgetting I'm in the business of hospitality." Extending his hand, he said, "I'm Jones Colton. I'm actually the owner, and if you'll forgive my rudeness, I'd love to offer you and your friends over there a free round and an order off our bar bites menu, on me."

Shaking his hand, the customer smiled and thanked him, assuring him that everybody had their off days.

The trouble was, Jones had been having way too many of them lately, and this new wrinkle, along with his incessant worry over what the beautiful woman working at his house might be doing at the moment, wasn't helping a bit. So when the employee he'd called in arrived, with more scheduled help on the way, he decided he would knock off earlier than usual. Better that, he reasoned, than scaring away customers with his lousy attitude.

Before he could leave, however, his brother Heath surprised him, his tie loosened and his jacket missing after what must have been a rough day at Colton Connections, given the lines creasing his forehead and the worry in his dark blue eyes.

Meeting him at the bar, Jones said, "Hey, brother, buy you a drink? Looks like you could use one."

Raking a hand through his short, blond hair, Heath said, "That'd really hit the spot."

"Everything all right? You and Kylie still good?" Even as he asked the question, Jones dismissed the thought that something might have gone wrong with his older brother's relationship with his fiancée, who was also the company's vice president, since the two had looked so happy at last night's tasting dinner.

"We're great," Heath assured him, "never better. What about you, though? I heard from Carly about last night."

Glancing around, Jones noticed that some other customers nearby had paused in their conversation, as if they were listening in. "Let me grab a couple of beers," he suggested, "and I'll meet you at that table over on the far end."

After letting the bartender know he needed some private time so they wouldn't be disturbed, Jones thanked him and then headed over, where he set down a mug of the dark brew he knew was his brother's favorite, along with his own current preference.

As he sat down, Heath thanked him before picking up where he'd left off. "I understand you and your date had some trouble after the tasting dinner. Is she all right?"

"She's going to be—and she's my marketing consultant, not my date." Jones felt a twinge of guilt, repeating the lie about Allie's purpose in coming to Chicago, but he knew that sticking to that story was the best way to ensure he didn't give in to the temptation to break his promise to keep his mouth shut about the suspects under investigation.

Heath's brows rose. "You sure there's not more to it than that, because I saw you laughing together at one point, and I have to tell you, you two were looking pretty tight. Kylie thought the same thing."

"You know me." Jones shrugged it off. "I like to laugh with beautiful women."

"Not lately, you haven't been."

"Yeah, well, I've had a lot on my mind these last few months."

"I know you've been beating yourself up about— you know—the way things were with you and Dad for so long," Heath said, his expression serious, "unnecessarily, as far as I'm concerned. You two might've butted heads a lot, but underneath of it all, I know you cared—and that he absolutely would've wanted you to be happy."

Jones looked away, not used to such direct talk from the brother who had always been pointed out to him as a role model to be emulated, the son who never disappointed. For a long time, he couldn't help resenting Heath, who'd so effortlessly moved up the corporate ladder at Colton Connections, making their parents proud at every turn. At some point, however, Jones had realized that his rock-solid brother had never set out to create a competition—or taken a professional role from him that he would have ever wanted for himself.

But what Heath was hinting, about him and the

woman he'd only met for the first time yesterday, wasn't possible. No matter what he'd felt when he'd kissed her for the first time and held her in his arms.

Pushing the memory from his mind, Jones said, "You're just saying that because you're getting leg shackled soon—I'm better off keeping my options open, keeping things casual until things are more settled."

"As *casual* as the way you punched that guy out— the one with the knife?" Heath asked.

"Anybody would've done that to protect the woman with him," Jones said. "Or at least any man brought up the way our father raised us."

Their gazes locked, unspoken sentiment passing between two brothers who were more comfortable discussing sports scores or local happenings than the landscape of their grief. Then, at the same moment, each lifted his mug. As the edges clinked together, Heath said, "To our dad and Uncle Alfie and the men—and women—they raised."

For a few minutes, they drank in silence, each lost in his own memories. Jones, as usual, was the first to give in to his natural restlessness and break the silence.

"It was nice to see most of the family last night, but I was wondering, have you heard from Simone? I made a point to invite her personally, and I'd really hoped that she might actually show up this time."

The eldest of their uncle Alfred's three daughters, Simone, a psychology professor at the University of Chicago who'd been especially close to her father, had taken both his and her uncle's murders particularly hard—to the point that she'd withdrawn from the rest of the family lately.

"Tatum said she'd reached out to her, too. She and January are both a little worried."

Jones nodded, hoping this didn't drive a wedge between the sisters. "She probably just needs a little space right now to work things through in her mind. I know that was true for me."

With a murmur of agreement, Heath drank from his beer.

Sensing there was something on his mind, Jones said, "I know you didn't show up here before your usual knocking-off time just to check in on me, so let's have it. What's this visit really all about?"

Setting down his half-full mug, Heath sighed. "I got this letter in the mail today. A letter from a lawyer, marked *personal* so it would be directed to my attention only instead of being routed through any secretary or assistant."

Even more than the words, Heath's tone touched off a cold chill of premonition.

Jones leaned forward on an elbow. "You certainly have *my* full attention…"

His brother cleared his throat before glancing at the bartender, who was heading in their direction.

Jones waved him off, mouthing the words, *We're good, Esteban.*

Once he was out of earshot, Heath finally let the other shoe drop. "This lawyer was writing as a courtesy, he told me, letting me know that the client he represents is laying claim to half of Colton Connections."

The cold chill froze Jones to the marrow. "*Half?* On what grounds?"

"He's not saying yet, and he won't name the litigant or litigants involved either. But I've got our corporate attorney looking into this. We both think it sounds awfully sketchy."

"I have to agree," Jones said. "Probably scammers

coming out of the woodwork since the murders have come back up in the news after these more recent killings."

"That's what we figured, too," Heath told him. "Just you wait. This so-called 'lawyer' will turn out to be nothing but some two-bit lowlife looking for a quick and dirty settlement, thinking the grieving family will roll over to avoid any more trouble."

"I'm sure you're right," said Jones. "Nothing will come of this."

After that, Heath let the subject drop, moving on to surprise him with the news that Carly had mentioned she and Micha were talking of a setting a wedding date next year. "I think they want to keep things low-key, take time to make sure they've worked through any lingering issues they may still have—"

"She seems really happy to me," Jones said, "and I'm sure they're both committed to getting this thing right. I like their odds."

"That's good." Heath grinned. "Because I've already given them my blessing."

"Look at you, playing the paterfamilias, now that you're the oldest male Colton." With the jest, Jones offered a pained smile, which his brother returned.

By the time they walked out together a short while later, Jones was left with a feeling that things were finally at ease between the two of them. But when he thought back to the mysterious warning Heath had received, Jones's earlier misgivings returned to haunt him, clinging like the memory of a particularly disturbing dream.

Chapter 6

Eyes burning after hours at the keyboard, Allie grumbled under her breath as yet another attempt at cracking Leo Styler's social media account password failed. Her difficulty with Jared Garner's didn't surprise her as much, but she refused to believe that the poster child for angry young men everywhere could be *that* smart and careful.

Still, she wasn't about to give up on either suspect. Once she cracked the first password, experience had taught her she would be able to use it like a key to unlock multiple doors to expose more and more of her targets' private information. Though neither the police nor the FBI would officially approve her methods, she knew they wouldn't look too hard for the source of any anonymously transmitted information that helped to put away the suspects in a series of shootings that had struck terror in the Greater Chicago area.

Now all she had to do was find a way to deliver and help bring Jones and the rest of the Colton family one step closer to healing.

Years ago, she'd come up with a system that worked for her in at least eight out of ten cases. After harvesting as many of the personal data points most users turned to in order to help them better remember their own passwords—things like dates of birth and graduations and present and past addresses, all of which were readily available on legal public databases—she input the information into a hacker tool she'd personally developed, along with a host of commonly used password fodder she'd gleaned from the two young men's social media postings. These included names of family members, past and present pets, favorite sports teams, hangouts—and even one high-end dream car that Jared had posted dozens of photos of after last year's auto show.

Frowning at her screen, she thought for a few minutes before altering the parameters and giving it one more shot. But this time, the system locked down completely, booting her for too many failed attempts.

She groaned in frustration, knowing this could only mean one thing. The cybersecurity team working for the system she was attempting to breach had once more upgraded the system, escalating the ongoing arms race designed to keep bad actors—and nosy but well-intentioned PIs—out of their users' business.

As she mentally scrambled for some new workaround, Allie ignored her stomach's growled reminder that she should probably at least grab a granola bar or something. Her sore shoulder added its own twinge to her body's litany of reminders that it was well past time for a break. Then the ding of her cell phone derailed her train of thought completely.

Conceding defeat, she took off her computer glasses and stood up to stretch. She snatched up her cell, then strolled into the living room, stretching her legs as she checked her messages.

Stuck in traffic on the way home, read the text from Jones. Try not to shoot me when I walk in.

Smiling at his last line, Allie glanced at the pistol sitting near her elbow—a gun she hadn't ventured more than a few steps from all afternoon, though the home alarm remained set.

In spite of the safety precautions and her usual ease with working on her own, she felt relief washing over her at the idea of Jones returning. As hard as she'd tried to push last night's attack from her mind, several times during the afternoon, she'd found herself reacting to the creak of a settling board somewhere upstairs or a complaint from the old house's pipes after she had used the bathroom. At one point, at the sound of a siren passing on the street outside, she'd found herself straining her ears, heart pounding as she sat on the edge of her seat listening for some unseen footstep on the front porch or a hand trying the doorknob.

Ridiculous, she told herself, shaking off her uncharacteristic jitters. Instead, she focused on the far more pleasant thought of Jones walking in through the door, smiling as he asked how her day had gone.

She found herself caught off guard by the rush of anticipation she felt at the thought of his company. Maybe it was working in his space, among his things, that had kept his masculine presence planted so firmly in her mind throughout the afternoon.

Or maybe it was the giddy rush of pleasure she felt

each time she thought back to their kiss last night… along with a few daydreams about what might have happened if he hadn't decided it was rotten timing. Though Jones was technically right about that, she conceded, even if she still felt the sparks from their brief contact from her fingers to her toes.

Breezing back through the dining room and then into the kitchen, she scanned the place to make sure she hadn't left any of her absent-minded messes around to shock his sensibilities. Though it was seven in the evening, she'd been too full from that filling sandwich earlier to bother with so much as a snack, so thankfully, even his kitchen remained as neat and organized as he'd left it.

But it really didn't have to stay pristine, did it? She thought about how kind he'd been to her these past two days, and what horrendous news she'd laid on him this morning. News so difficult that she suspected it might be the reason he had cut his workday short.

If left to her own devices, she probably would've gone for one of the frozen meals Jones had stockpiled in his freezer so she could get back to work more quickly. Thanks to her mother's insistence on teaching her basic cooking skills, however, Allie was perfectly capable of doing better. And she would, she decided, because both of them deserved a decent homemade meal.

After redoing her ponytail and washing up, she went to the fridge and considered for a couple of minutes before making her choices. Though it took her a little longer to get going than she'd hoped, due to the unfamiliar kitchen, she had things well underway by the time she heard the chirp of the alarm system as a side door opened.

She strained her ears for his footsteps or perhaps a

friendly greeting. When neither came, her pulse ticked faster, her thoughts flying to Detective Parker's warning that others beside Curtis Stubbs might have had her photo given to them. *What if it's not Jones coming inside?*

In an instant, every fond memory of making dinner with the mom she missed so dearly that had played through her mind as she'd chopped veggies for the salads and started sautéing the chicken breast cutlets abruptly gave way to a jolt of apprehension. Turning off the stove, she moved the skillet to an unused burner, the back of her neck prickling as she grabbed the pistol, which she'd left sitting on the countertop.

Gun in hand, she crept back toward the doorway, her heartbeat picking up speed as images from last night's attack flickered through her mind like the frames of some old horror movie. *Has Stubbs been released already for some reason and gotten the idea to come looking for me at Jones's place before somehow figuring his way around the security system? Or is it someone else this time? And who's to say there's only one of them, out to collect that five grand for hurting me? Or might there even be a bonus if she ended up dead?* The photo hadn't been specific about the payer's end game.

Seeing the side entry door standing slightly open, Allie stopped short, her mind teeming with warnings, along with scores of questions. Before she could decide whether she'd be better off bolting through that exit and running for help or staying, the hinges creaked, and a figure filled the doorway, eliciting her startled yelp as she lowered the gun.

It was only Jones, a couple of cardboard delivery boxes in his arms and a look of horror on his face.

"Allie—what the devil? Didn't you get my text that I was coming home?"

"I did. But when I heard the door and you didn't answer… I thought it might be— I—" Erupting into tremors, she blinked back a heated haze. "I might've—"

Stomach turning, she put the gun down on the table. "Get that away from me, please."

After dropping the two boxes onto the nearest chair, he said, "It was my fault. I'd just hit the code to undo the security system when I remembered that my neighbor had texted to let me know he'd accidentally gotten some hinges and fasteners I'd ordered for one of my handyman projects. So I ducked back out to pick my stuff up next door before I—"

"Without saying a word to me?" Allie demanded, her face burning with anger—though it was mostly at herself. "You're aware as I am of my situation—and that I was here, armed. When you didn't greet me, and I saw the door standing open, I thought you might be—"

"I can see that now," he said, his dark blue eyes stricken. "I'm really sorry I didn't stop and think of what you've been through. I'm just too used to being on my own, I guess."

She blinked, but not fast enough to prevent a single tear from spilling. "I almost *shot* you, Jones—which really would've put a damper on the evening, not to mentioning trashing any chance I might've had at getting one of those Employee of the Month certificates I saw back at your office."

He managed a wry smile at her lame attempt to lighten the mood. "You *think*?"

She laughed a little too hard, trying to cover how shaky she still felt from her fright. "I certainly do. And I *am* sorry."

"Well, if it makes you feel any better, I promise not to scare you like that again. But how about if maybe we put the gun away for now? I have to admit it's making me a little nervous."

She nodded in agreement. "Please. You cannot get that thing out of my sight fast enough."

After disappearing into his bedroom with the offending weapon, he quickly returned and laid a hand on her shoulder. "You still look like you could use a stiff drink. You okay?"

"I will be," she said, looking up into his face, "but I wouldn't say no if you were to offer to open that bottle of rosé I saw chilling in the fridge while I finished making dinner."

"I'm happy to—and I wondered what was smelling so good in here. I can't believe you're cooking." He followed her into the kitchen, where she'd left out a cutting board, knife and small pile of scraps and veggie peelings.

"I—I'd just got to thinking, after last night's big dinner and that filling lunch, maybe we'd both enjoy something on the lighter and healthier side this evening."

"You did all this for me?"

He looked so amazed, she wasn't sure whether to laugh or be insulted. Choosing the former, she said, "For *us*. It's just a simple, fresh tossed salad, with seasoned chicken breasts and some Dijon vinaigrette dressing I mixed up—"

"You made the dressing from scratch?"

"Believe me, I'm no Tatum. It's so simple, anyone could do it." She looked him over, wondering if she'd blown it by picking out a menu for them. "You aren't one of those guys who hates all green things, are you?"

"If I were, do you really think I would've had all that

fresh salad stuff in my refrigerator?" He shook his head. "I try to balance out the beer, pizza and occasional Italian beef sandwiches with as much low carb and clean eating as I can when I'm at home."

"Good deal," she said. "Let me just check on this chicken."

As she did, he came up behind her, feathering his fingertips along the outside of her arm as he spoke near her ear. "I may be used to coming home to my empty, *perfectly neat* house alone." His breath, along with a hint of gentle humor, warmed her ear, putting her body on high alert as his words drew her attention to the mess she'd made of his kitchen as she'd begun working on the meal. "But this feels really nice, too."

Feigning annoyance, she said, "You're just saying that because I didn't shoot you before the first course."

Laughing, he gave her a quick squeeze around the waist. "Yolanda'd better watch her back. That's starting to sound a lot like Employee of the Month talk."

"You might want to hold off on that judgment until you've tasted my cooking," she said, hoping that the chicken hadn't gotten chewy sitting on the stove.

Once she'd put the finishing touches on her preparations and they were seated at the table with their meals a short time later, Jones was quick to compliment her effort, interrupting her rundown on her earlier attempts to crack the suspects' passwords.

"Thanks," she said, "but don't get too used to it because I'm warning you, my attacks of domesticity are incredibly sporadic."

"Well, let's honor the effort then by making a pact. No more talking business," he said, "at least 'til dinner's over. Deal?"

She nodded, promising, "I'm in," though she hoped

she could manage to think of something, anything non-work-related to talk about, since dazzling conversation had never been her strong suit.

She needn't have worried, for Jones made it easy. As they each enjoyed their meal with a glass of wine, he started asking her about the various places she had worked or hoped to visit. Soon, he had her laughing as he shared a couple of amusingly offbeat stories from his travels during his younger years.

After waving off his offer of a refill on the rosé, she said, "I'm half surprised to see you drinking that, too. Does it feel a little like you're cheating on your beer?"

"Not a bit," he answered before a grin spread across his handsome face. "Though I do find myself wondering if this meal—which really was delicious, thank you—might've paired even better with a pilsner."

Pushing back from the table, she stood, meaning to help him clear the table, since he'd decided to forego a second glass, as well. "Just can't help yourself, can you, Mr. Brewmeister?"

"Not around you, I can't," he said, maneuvering himself so that as she came to her feet, she found herself standing so close, she was looking straight up at him.

"I like you having you at my house, Allie Chandler," he added, slanting a look down at her that made her heart bump harder. "I like talking with you, eating with you and looking at you across a table. And the view only gets better the closer that I get."

"Jones…" she said, all her previous sensible objections to any involvement with this gorgeous man rising and scattering like a flock of doves startled from cover. Because feeling his heat this close to her, smelling the scent of him, she couldn't recall a single reason why she shouldn't rise up onto her toes to breathe him in.

Acting on the impulse, she did exactly that, her sensitive lips scraping the light stubble on the underside of his jawline—tasting a hint of the salt on his skin as she reached up to wrap her arms around his neck. "I like you, too," she whispered, close enough to his ear to let him feel the warmth of her breath. "A lot."

He shivered lightly, groaning, and she could almost feel his restraint creaking like a huge oak in a heavy wind. She imagined it cracking as he reached to pull her into his own embrace, the fingers of his big hands splaying to sending electrifying waves of pleasure from her ribs to her hips.

"These last few months have been so damned... everything's felt twisted around wrong, hollowed out and empty. But this—*you*—right now," he said. "It's the first thing that's felt right to me in so damned long."

It was her turn to shiver now, as the throaty rumble of his voice sent the past two years' worth of repressed desires into overdrive. Had it been last night's brush with death, the way he'd come to her aid—or the way they'd bonded over Jones's family situation that was responsible for her out of control hormones?

Whatever it was, she found herself answering, "I didn't plan to, didn't mean to—not with somebody that I'm working with, because I never allow myself to do that. But I feel it, too, with you, Jones. I won't deny there's something..."

"I'd never want you to think, not even for a moment," he said, his dark blue eyes turning serious, "that any kind of expectations come with the territory, with you working for me and staying here."

"Never...crossed...my mind," she said, only craving more of exactly what she shouldn't, which was to feel him touching her *everywhere*, without the barrier of so much clothing between them. Her breath hitched with the imagining and with the wanting of this connection that she felt arcing into life between them… with the hunger for this man to be a part of her life, at least for whatever brief span of time they had together.

Lifting her head, she raised her arms to pull his head down. Their mouths found each other, their kiss hot, deep and probing—nothing a bit tentative about it. Her body melting with the pleasure of it, she found the hem of his shirt—and slid her hands up underneath it, needing to feel the heat of his skin, hard muscle and the drumming of his heart.

Cupping her breast with one hand, he squeezed it through her clothing, and she whimpered, not with pain, but her own fast-building excitement.

She knew it had been a long drought for her—since before her mother's death, and then some—but she tried to think back. Had she ever felt like this before, so utterly caught up, so consumed in spiraling sensation?

No, never, she thought as Jones took her by the hand and led her—or was she leading him?—to the big sectional in the next room. *But then, you've never been targeted by criminals and stabbed either, have you?*

But she didn't want dwell on all that right now, couldn't—not with Jones pulling her hair loose from her ponytail and trailing kisses down her neck. Wanting more, she helped him peel off her top and unhooked her bra, then nearly came apart when his mouth found an aching nipple…

Soon, she lost all track of time and every other obligation—barely hearing as first Jones's cell phone and then her own, a short time later, rang a few times before falling silent around the time the remainder of their clothing hit the floor. After that, there was no room for thought or worry—no room for anything but experiencing his lips, his clever tongue, the thrust of a finger inside that had her crying out his name as her awareness splintered into a thousand white-hot shards of pleasure.

"You had enough yet?" he asked her, kissing her sweat dampened temple as she lay back panting. "You look a little—"

"I'll tell you when I've had enough, Jones. But right now, I need *this*. *You*." She smiled up at him before pulling him down to kiss him thoroughly, her hand stroking the length of him as he rubbed against her hip. But it wasn't enough. Not nearly, and she found her legs parting.

Jones rolled off her, asking directly, "Shall I get a condom? Because if you'd rather we backed off now, or at any point, I'm perfectly okay with—"

"Get the condoms," she insisted, needing to feel him moving inside her.

"On it," Jones said before seeming to reconsider and surprising her by scooping her up in his arms.

"What are you doing?" she laughed, her feet kicking as he carried her toward the bedroom.

"The condoms are in my nightstand," he told her, "and I didn't want to waste a single step—or have to run back for another—because something tells me we'll be needing more than one."

On some level, Jones understood that they'd both been using not only sex but one another. Allie, in order to escape whatever fear and trauma she carried from last night's attack, and him to try to shunt aside the rage eating at him over the idea that his father's and his uncle's deaths had been so pointless.

Even so, their connection had felt real to him, more immediate and truer than anything he'd known in the past. So much so, that when he woke, he was deeply disappointed to reach for her and find her missing from his bed.

Had she retreated back upstairs to the guest room? Some paranoid corner of his imagination pictured her there, packing up to flee his house before things between them crossed the line from hot and steamy sex to the trickier landscape of expectations and emotions. Because despite his glib suggestion about keeping whatever happened between them casual, they'd already verged into the danger zone...

Or maybe it was only him...

Now fully awake, he rolled out of bed before donning a fresh pair of boxers and a T-shirt and heading toward the kitchen for a glass of water.

"So this is where you went," he said, more relieved than he should be to find Allie sitting at a barstool at the counter, her face illuminated in the darkness by the bright screen of her phone. "Everything okay?"

"I woke up asleep on my sore shoulder," she said, frowning. "Guess I was so relaxed I didn't notice, but I thought I'd better take a couple of over-the-counter tablets so I wouldn't wake up too sore."

Turning the kitchen light on, he saw that she, too, had pulled on a tee with a pair of panties. Her bare legs and appealingly tumbled hair served as further reminders of what they'd been doing—and just how enthusiastically they had been going at it.

"I hope I didn't hurt you, earlier—your shoulder."

She smiled. "Did those sound like cries of *pain* to you?"

He grinned back at her, aroused anew by the reminder.

"I hate to change the subject," she said, gesturing with her phone, "but that call I received while we were occupied? It was from the FBI."

Jones's smile faded as he thought back to their earlier visit to the field office. "Don't tell me they have news for us on Jared Garner and Leo Styler already?"

"Actually, there is, and I was shocked, too, since it's way more like the Feds to spend months investigating a lead before deciding whether to act than it is getting on anything this quickly. But clearly Special Agent Howard didn't want to risk those two taking out more victims if they delayed bringing them in."

His pulse accelerating, he said, "You're telling me they've been *arrested*?"

She shook her head, the sympathy blooming in her light brown eyes warning him he wasn't going to like whatever came next.

"According to his voice mail, no. When the Feds sent agents to question them at their homes, their parents were all over it, advising their kids not to talk and calling in family attorneys so fast it would make your head spin."

"Sounds like the families have money," Jones commented.

"And some legal savvy, too," she agreed before hitting the play button on the message.

After the special agent methodically outlined the same information Allie had just told him, he added, "Later this afternoon, both attorneys showed up with statements, signed by the parents, attesting that their sons were at both at home with them during the time frames of the murders. And Jared's parents claimed their son was with them and other family members at a restaurant dinner celebrating their wedding anniversary on the date that Ernest and Alfred Colton were killed."

"They're lying," Jones blurted, "circling the wagons to keep their killer kid safe."

But Special Agent Howard was still speaking, apologizing that he didn't have better news for Allie. "I'd like to tell you we could break those alibis and build a case against those two, but I'm not seeing it, especially with the Garners' relations corroborating the parents' story and swearing that the boy was there. The evidence was paper-thin in the first place, and there's really nothing more to go on."

After thanking Allie again for the lead, he invited her to call him back if she had further questions—or came up with additional information she felt inclined to share.

"So that's it?" Jones asked, once the message ended. "We're right back where we started—all because two privileged families chose to lawyer up and lie about it?"

Covering his hand with hers, she shook her head, her eyes blazing with a look of fierce determination. "The FBI might have to pull back, but I can promise you one thing for certain. I'm just getting started—and if those two are guilty, they are going down."

"Whatever it takes," he said. "I'm there to help."

"Even if it means looking the other way when I ask, so you're not an accessory to anything…questionable?"

"In my mind," he said, "there *is* no question. Whatever needs to happen to bring my family peace and keep those two from hurting anybody else, you can damned well count me in."

Chapter 7

Jared Garner's account was the first to fall to Allie's password-cracking efforts. When it finally gave way, she gave a loud whoop, bringing Jones running from the kitchen, where he'd been making breakfast for them.

Laughing to find her doing a fist-pumping victory dance in front of her computer, he asked, "So what's up, crazy lady? Did you get something good?"

She turned her most dazzling smile on him, appreciating for a moment how flat-out sexy he looked with his blue eyes alight with amusement. After insisting it was his turn to cook for her this morning, he held a large spatula in his hand and a streak of what looked like pancake batter smeared across the navy T-shirt he wore with his boxers.

"Only the keys to the kingdom," she explained. "I've just managed to download Garner's e-calendar and a slew of his text messages."

"That's amazing—and kind of scary at the same time, to think that anybody could get into all your private information like that."

"Hey," she chided him. "I'm not just *anybody*. And you'll have nothing to worry about if you change your password once a month or so and don't use super-easy information like the names of childhood pets, favorite sports teams and key dates that anyone could figure out from public records."

Face reddening, he avoided her gaze, prompting her to challenge, "You're making a mental note right now to change some passwords, aren't you?"

He gestured at her with the spatula. "One more word about it, and you'll get the pancakes from my first batch—the ones with the burnt bottoms."

"I *thought* I smelled smoke a little bit ago," she said. "Are you sure you don't need my help in the kitchen— maybe to man a fire extinguisher or something?"

He shook his head. "Very funny. But I was just distracted, listening to a voice mail from a friend who's been acting as my business adviser and finance guy."

"Everything all right?" she asked him, vaguely recalling having heard his phone ring.

"I guess you could say so." A smile spread across a face she couldn't get enough of. "One of the critics who attended the beer tasting the other night, a really influential local writer, apparently had some pretty amazing things to say about my beers in particular. Her write-up called me a *'rising star'* in the industry, and already, other restauranteurs have been calling to see if they can get it on the action."

"That's wonderful," she said, spontaneously throwing her arms around him. "So I guess this morning's off to a great start for both of us."

He kissed her, giving her a quick squeeze before saying, "Any morning where I get to wake up to a beautiful woman like you counts as a great start for me."

This time, she felt her face heat, recalling how, in the darkest hours, he'd awakened her to another slow and sensual round of lovemaking. And how her body had opened to pleasure like the petals of a night-blooming flower unfurling in moonlight.

But now, for whatever reason, she felt abruptly self-conscious to be complimented. If she started believing that he really meant it, and that these feelings bouncing around inside her could mean something more than a short-term fling, she'd be setting herself up for nothing but weeks or months of pain.

Better to hold back now, she decided, reminding herself that she was here to do a job and right an injustice. Not to ease the nagging loneliness she'd been unable to silence lately, for all her efforts to remind herself that she was better off on her own.

"So what're you hoping to find in his calendar and messages?" Jones asked her.

Once more banishing the memory, she said, "I'll know it when I see it. I can hardly wait to dive in."

"Well, I know how single-minded you get once you get wrapped up in your work," he told her, "so how about you hit the pause button on that for now, just until we've finished breakfast. I had something else I wanted to run past you anyway, to get your take on."

Curiosity piqued by his serious expression, she closed her laptop. "Sure thing."

"Why don't you come over and we'll talk while I do this new batch of pancakes," he suggested, nodded back toward the kitchen.

While he turned the burner back on, she sat on the

barstool across the kitchen island from him. "So what's up?" she asked, feeling a flutter of apprehension in her stomach. "You look worried about something."

Was he feeling as awkward as she did in the wake of this lovemaking? Suddenly self-conscious, she blurted, "If you need me to try to find another place to stay today, I'm happy to call around to see—"

His forehead creased, confusion blooming in his blue eyes. "What? Why would I want that, especially after—"

"I just thought you're probably used to women leaving afterward, for their own places. Maybe you feel trapped, inside your own house, with me, now that we've..."

He shook his head. "How can you think that? Have I said anything, done anything to make you feel unwelcome? Because you're definitely not."

"Your manners have been first-rate." She shrugged. "But both of us—we're more used to operating independently, and I don't want it to feel weird for you, stuck in your place with me."

He tested the pan's heat by sprinkling a first drops of water off his fingertips onto the cooking surface. As they danced and sizzled, he insisted, "I'm not *stuck* with you, Allie, and I'm not just saying so to be polite. I'm happy—make that damned delighted—to have you staying with me."

Still feeling skeptical, she sized him up. "Then why are you scowling down at me?"

"Because it hacks me off, listening to a woman with so much to offer selling herself short. And it makes me wonder, Allie—who was it who did such a number on your confidence?"

"Who was it?" She snorted a laugh without a trace

of humor. "You don't know me very well if you haven't realized that you're looking at her."

He ladled out the pancake batter onto the hot surface. "Then you need to give that side of you a rest, because I definitely want you here, but only if you're still comfortable with the idea. Will you stay here with me, Allie? No strings attached, I promise. Anytime that you decide you want to redraw boundaries, I'll respect your wishes."

She let it sink in what a good man he was, to remind her of that option, when a lot of men would take her consent as a given now that they had slept together. But in his tone and his expression, she saw that if she put the brakes on their intimate relations, he wouldn't be the type to slam drawers, stomp around or sulk over what a lesser man might take as an intolerable rejection.

"I'd like to stay," she said, adding a small shrug. "It's a great workspace—and the company's not bad, either."

He nodded his approval. "I'm glad. Then I won't be tempted to inhale all these carbs on my own."

"And do I smell bacon in the oven?"

"You do."

"Then I'm *definitely* all in," she confirmed before offering to set the table.

Once they'd been seated and were finishing their breakfast, Allie set down her coffee and admitted, "All earlier fire extinguisher cracks aside, you're not a half bad cook yourself."

Snagging another strip of bacon, Jones waved it at her. "Don't let it get around though. I'd hate to ruin my rep as the helpless bachelor and lose out on any delicious homemade pity offerings my cousins, my sister, or my grandmother might decide to drop by with every now and then."

"That's pretty sexist, you know."

"I prefer to think of it as a classic rogue move," he said with a wink.

Allie bit her lip to keep from laughing, thinking that he was *such* a youngest sibling. Not that she'd ever had siblings of her own, but she could easily imagine him as the charming prankster, always skating out of trouble—and infuriating his older siblings for getting away with what they never could have.

Remembering his more serious mood earlier, she asked, "So are you going to keep me in suspense much longer? What *was* this thing you wanted to run by me?"

"It's something my brother Heath stopped by the brewery to tell me about yesterday," he said. "It reminded me a little of the anonymous threat sent to your house."

As he shared the details with her, she was relieved to hear that Heath's letter, at least, had not involved a threat of violence or any photos marked with crosshairs.

"I tend to agree with you and your brother," she said, "about it sounding like a prelude to an attempted shakedown. You said the lawyer didn't reveal the name of his clients in the letter, but do you have the attorney's name?"

Jones shook his head. "Heath didn't mention it, but he did say he's having the corporate attorney do some digging on this."

"If you can get the name out of your brother, pass it on to me, why don't you? Then I'll see if I can get something to pop in places Heath's company guy won't know where to look."

"Thanks," Jones said.

"And if I were you," she advised, "I wouldn't mention my involvement to your brother…just in case he needs to be able to deny any knowledge later of how certain information happened to fall into his hands."

Rather than leaving her to work at home alone again, Jones talked Allie into joining him at the brewery for the afternoon.

"Ordinarily, I'd put up more of a fight about giving up my private work time," she said as she slid her laptop into her backpack after both of them had cleaned up and dressed for the day. "But I suspect that if I didn't, you'd only drive me crazy calling to check in every hour anyway."

"I'm not usually the hovering type—" he stopped his pacing to explain, more relieved than he wanted to admit "—but between worrying over your staying here alone and wondering what you're finding in Jared Garner's files, there's no way I'd be able to stop myself. Sorry."

"Don't be because I get it." Compassion warmed her gaze. "Solving this case may be important to me, but it's *everything* to you and your family. If I'd had someone doing the digging into my own father's death, I'm sure I wouldn't have given them a moment's peace until I had my answers."

"But you didn't have anyone to help you, did you?"

She shrugged. "At first the police just assumed he'd only run off. They didn't take anything my mother was telling them about his issues with his business partner seriously—the old friend he'd run a nightclub with for years. Their theory was he'd left with one of the women he'd met there. By the time his car and body were finally pulled out of the river, the remains were in such a state that no one could even say for certain whether he'd been murdered or ended up there accidentally."

"And they never looked into the business partner?"

"They did," she said, the words edged with bitterness, "but by then, that double-dealing sleazeball had had plenty of time to cook the books to tell the story that he wanted…which turned out to suggest that my father had been embezzling funds—and maybe even drove his car down that slope to end things."

"I'm so damned sorry," he said, thinking how painful it would be if someone were to try to smear his own late father's reputation. "I can't imagine dealing with all that, especially as a helpless child."

"I didn't stay helpless," she insisted as she zipped the backpack. "For one thing, someone had to keep my mother going, to make sure she actually swallowed the food in her mouth and had clean clothes to wear—and to follow up with the police on the days she couldn't bring herself to."

Reaching out, he caught Allie's hand in his, unable to imagine how frightened and scared she must have been, struggling to keep the remainder of her world from collapsing. "You've made me realize that, as tough as things have been just lately, how damned lucky I am to have the family and friends I do so we can help see each other through this. Compared to what you had to go through, I've had it so easy—"

"Don't do that." She shook her head at him. "Don't try to rank pain, or minimize what you're still going through. There are no Suffering Olympics."

He smiled at the way she'd put it. "I guess you have a point there. And who really wants to end up standing on that podium anyway?"

"Personally, I've found it way more satisfying to deal out some suffering to those who have it coming."

"But who gets to decide that?" he asked lightly. "Who has it coming, I mean?"

"The people they've hurt—*we* have that right," she insisted, removing her hand from his to hoist the backpack over her shoulder. "Or in a perfect world, we ought to. Speaking of which, let's get going, please, because I'm getting really antsy to start digging into Garner's secrets."

But as tough and determined as she seemed, as the two of them drove back toward the more commercial West Loop area, Jones soon noticed Allie growing very quiet, her body tensing every time he slowed for traffic or stopped at a light. As she watched a small group of pedestrians waiting at a crosswalk along a street crammed with shops and other businesses, a pair of young men came up from behind them to roll past the passenger door on their skateboards, their shouted conversation causing her to jolt forward against her seat belt, gasping.

"Easy there," he said. "The doors are locked and it's broad daylight, in the middle of a crowded street."

"I—I'm fine."

"C'mon, Allie," he said as the light changed, allowing him to continue. "We both know you're nervous about going out again, and that you have every right to be."

"I'm so sick of this," she blurted, making a slashing motion with their hand. "I'm supposed to be the hunter here, not anybody's prey. And maybe I'm getting worked up over nothing, but I can't stop wondering how many more photos there might be of me floating around out there. And whose hands they've fallen into, and what they're up to right now."

"We can't change that part," he acknowledged, "but

maybe we can make things a little tougher, in case anyone is out there looking for you."

"How's that?"

"For one thing, I'll switch vehicles this afternoon. I have a friend who's headed out of town this week, and if I tell him I'm having an issue, I'm betting he'll let me borrow his ride and leave my car in his garage."

"That's not a bad idea," she said, before giving him a puzzled look. "You have a lot of good friends, don't you?"

He nodded. "I'm not the type that gets super tight with any one person, but yeah, I do count myself lucky that way, especially since I haven't been the greatest about reciprocating lately."

"I'm surely they understand you're going through some things now."

He grimaced. "So how long did it take you to get back to normal…after your father?"

"I'll let you know," she said dryly, "not that I was ever exactly a social butterfly in the first place. It used to drive my mother crazy."

"Used to?" he said, catching the disclosure. "I didn't realize that you'd lost your mother, as well."

Allie murmured in the affirmative. "To cancer, a couple of years back. She wasn't sick long, which I suppose is a blessing, but—there's never enough time to say goodbye."

"I'm sorry."

"Thanks," she said.

"And you don't have any other family?"

"None worthy of the name," she said, before surprising him by elaborating. "They weren't there for us after my dad's disappearance—not even when I called and tried to tell them that she needed help."

"Sometimes, family's where you find it."

"We were each other's family. It was enough, as long as it lasted."

But who's there to watch out for you now?

"At the brewery today," he told her, vowing he would be there for her as long as it was in his power, "I want you to keep out of sight. Since we're heading in to open up this morning, I can set you up inside my office before anybody gets there."

"I was planning to work in there anyway," she said. "But whoever gave Stubbs my picture knows I'm hanging out with you. It's making me worry I could be responsible for getting you hurt, too."

"I can handle my own safety," he assured her. "If anybody comes into the bar, we have security measures in place. Behind my desk, you may have noticed the CCTV set up with a split-screen view of what our security cameras are seeing in the bar area and out the front and back. There's another screen behind the bar, along with a panic button in case of a robbery. And if we happen to see trouble coming, the exterior doors can be electronically locked, too, with the touch of a button."

"Sounds like a good system," she said. "You haven't had problems in the past, have you?"

He shook his head. "Not in this neighborhood, no, and honestly, a craft brewery's not the kind of place your everyday criminals would normally target for a robbery. But considering some recent incidents in the news, I decided it made sense—and my insurance company gave me a break, too, for building in sensible precautions and taking care of my customers and employees."

"It definitely makes me feel a little better about being here," she told him.

"I'm thinking, too, you might also want to try out a different clothing style and doing something with your hair—or even get yourself a hat or maybe a big pair of sunglasses—anything to throw off anyone who might've seen that picture."

"A disguise?" Brightening, she nodded. "I kind of like that. Hacker-PIs never get to do nearly enough of the cool stuff like they show in all the movies."

As they pulled into the Lone Wolf's currently empty parking lot, he grinned. "So you're saying that sitting in dark rooms, tapping away at your computer isn't that exciting?"

"I never *said* it doesn't have its high-octane moments," she said lightly, "only that the hours of scanning, sifting and coding that go into them are about the least sexy work you can imagine."

"If you're doing it, I beg to differ," he argued, "but I'll tell you what. If you find something useful for us today, I can at least offer you a celebratory beer once you get finished."

"What if I *don't* get anything on him?" she countered. "Or worse yet, I uncover something that complete rules out both him and Leo Styler as our suspects?"

"Then we'll call them consolation beers and drown our disappointment in them," he said, as he put the car in Park and removed the keys from the ignition. "Either way, we still get beer."

"Way to look on the bright side," she said, smiling, "but getting back to your disguise idea, where am I going to come up with what I need to pull it off if I can't risk showing my face out in public?"

"Why don't I call Carly?" Jones asked. "She mentioned she has today off, and since she knows that you're here investigating the murders for me, I'm betting she'd be willing to help out. And if anybody could give her good ideas on disguises, her fiancé, Micha Harrison, is the right man."

Allie shook her head. "How's that?"

"He's former Special Forces, and the kind of guy you'd expect would know a half-dozen ways to make himself invisible if he got into a jam."

"Sounds like a good person to keep on speed dial, in case we do run into trouble."

"Absolutely," Jones agreed as he opened his car door to step outside, "but let's hope, for all our sakes, it never comes to that."

Chapter 8

After locking the door to Jones's office to avoid the possibility that any of his employees might interrupt her, Allie wasted no time claiming the big desk and getting straight to work on the files she'd downloaded using Jared Garner's password. First, however, she glanced over at the CCTV screen, watching it cycle through views long enough to spot Jones pacing near the still-unopened bar on his phone, most likely talking to his sister.

Turning back to her laptop, she began by opening Garner's text messages, which she hoped would prove a treasure trove of incriminating information.

The first exchanges, between himself and each of his parents, were innocuous, along with a conversation she quickly realized was with a professor who seemed to be his academic adviser, urging him to be sure to turn in all his papers and study for his finals to get his grades up before the end up the semester.

"What's the matter, Jared?" she asked, remembering those dead eyes from his more recent photos. "Are you finding your little murder hobby's interfering with your education?"

But Jared had sounded supremely confident as he had sought to quell the man's concerns. No need to worry. I've got everything under control, now that I've quit the paintball team that was wasting so much of my time.

Of course he'd quit the team, she thought. League play would've come with rules and offered nothing like the thrill of hunting human targets.

Scrolling farther, she found another set of recent texts to a "Nana," whom she soon realized, with a sinking feeling, lived somewhere overseas and was inviting her grandson to fly over to visit her this summer.

I've told your parents you can even bring along a friend if you like, too, she'd coaxed. And I'll have a car available for you two fellows to enjoy exploring the coast.

"And that'll be the last that investigators see of Jared and his good friend Leo," Allie said aloud, instinctively understanding that this would be the next step the young men's protective parents would take to keep the pair safe from the FBI's investigation. It only made it more imperative that she find more evidence against them before they were able to make the arrangements.

Delving further into the texts, Allie found that Jared's conversations with what she assumed to be his peers were far sparser. Whenever anyone reached out, rather than responding, he instead directed them to look him up on an app called SelfDestrukt, including a link and his username in his reply.

In one particular text, he'd explained to a female friend named Kyrie Rae, who had sent a flirty message asking if he might want to party: Gotta make sure Big Brother isn't getting all up in our business.

Allie sighed, having come up against apps like Self-Destrukt before, which allowed users to send encrypted messages to one another. Within a set period—often five to ten seconds—of being opened by the reader, the message vanished without a trace. Though this sort of self-erasing messaging was increasingly valued by young people looking to safeguard their privacy and future reputations, the apps had become favorite tools of those engaging in bullying and sexual harassment, along with cyberstalking and planning illegal transactions, since they couldn't be recalled by authorities to be used as evidence for prosecutors—unless the person being harassed took a screen shot, and even then, it was nearly impossible to prove the message's origin.

Seeing no contact between Garner and Leo Styler within the messages she'd downloaded, Allie made a note of Jared's username and used her tablet computer to download the SelfDestrukt app, where she quickly found Garner's user profile.

Sure enough, Leo was listed there among his connections, though he was calling himself *Lee-Oh-No!* on this application.

Though he'd attempted a smile for this particular profile picture—perhaps in an attempt to meet some of those women he'd professed interest in on his other social media page—it looked mean-spirited to Allie, like the lip-curling sneer of a bully who'd just tripped a younger child and caused her to fall face-first into the box of birthday cupcakes she'd been carrying. Or maybe she only thought that because of the assault-style weapon he had posed with.

But sure enough, when she checked Lee-Oh-No's page, she found that, here, too, he had very few female friends, especially for a guy who described himself as a "playa with the ladies."

Rolling her eyes, she decided that unlike the popular Jared, Leo's clearly delusional tendencies gave her an opening—one she couldn't ignore, even though she was certain that Special Agent Howard wouldn't appreciate her going anywhere near either of these suspects, even on social media.

But he wouldn't even *have* suspects if not for the work she'd done already, so she decided not to allow his potential anger to stop her. Soon, she was setting up her own account under the false name Lexi Hartz and looking through her photo files for a picture to represent her alter ego.

Choosing a photo of herself wearing a fedora hat and leather vest over a microskirt and platform shoes, she felt her face heat at the memory of the day that her friend Mistie, who lived to attend cosplayers' conventions in the guise of various fictional characters and was always trying to convince Allie to come out of her shell and "live a little," had talked her into playing dress-up at her apartment. Though Allie, suffering from a near-fatal attack of shyness, had hated every second of it and flatly refused to set foot in public, her friend had snapped a series of photos in a vain attempt to convince Allie that, in the anime-inspired look, she was "just about the cutest thing that ever lived."

Though Allie thought that was highly questionable, she'd nonetheless hung on to a few of the shots, thinking they might come in handy—and she decided that this picture would be the perfect bait to go catfishing for a young guy like Leo Styler, since the laced-up vest made the most of her modest breasts. And thanks to Mistie's expert makeup application, Allie knew she could easily pass for twenty, or even younger.

Frowning with concentration, she tapped out a request. So I just transferred into Western this semester and still don't know a lot of people, she wrote, referring to the junior college he and Jared both attended. But my friend Kyrie told me I should say hey. I think I saw you both with Jared G. at the student union last month?

After hitting send, she held her breath, half expecting Leo to come back with, *Who the hell is this?* Or worse.

But he didn't reply as all, meaning he was most likely offline at the moment, so she put the message—and the angry young Leo Styler—out of her mind for the present before going back to examine Jared Garner's calendar.

Searching for recent entries, she soon huffed out a sigh of frustration. It seemed that, as had been the case with text messaging, he rarely used his phone's default calendar application. During the past few months, the only entry she found marked was for the upcoming end of the college's spring semester, two weeks from today.

Deciding that he must mainly rely on some other program to organize his social, family and school appointments, she nonetheless continued scrolling backward through the calendar she had access to, first checking the dates surrounding the more recent sniper-style murders. Finding the entire month of the double homicide devoid of any entries, she grimaced but kept going, scrolling all the way back to January, the month of Alfred and Ernest Colton's murders. There at last, she was surprised to find a several entries—including one for the very afternoon the brothers had been killed.

"Well, isn't that convenient?" she said, clicking to expand the details for the date.

Mom & Dad Anniversary Dinner @ Bianchi's, it read, followed by the time 5:30 p.m.

Her heart fell, realizing that this entry served as confirmation for the Garners' family function story. No wonder his parents had been so certain about the particular date, if it had been their wedding anniversary.

Or was it really? She frowned down at the screen, thinking about the near-total lack of calendar entries in other months, before or after January.

Opening her notes file from her previous day's research, she pulled up the full names of Jared Garner's parents, which she had looked up the previous day, while researching some basic background data on both him and Leo Styler. Deciding it was time to dig in deeper, she logged into one of several databases she subscribed to and typed in the Garners' information.

Soon, she'd unearthed a wealth of information on the couple, who enjoyed an excellent credit rating, were members of a local country club and donated regularly to the campaigns of various candidates for public office. In addition to their own home, in what appeared to be a very nice Oak Brook neighborhood, they were also listed as the owners of the building that housed their specialty furniture store. But it took a deep dive into the county clerk's online portal for Allie to find the confirmation she'd been looking for: a marriage certificate showing that the couple had been wed not in January but during the month of June instead, twenty-three years prior.

"So there's the first lie," she murmured, wondering

where else a couple eager to clear their son of suspicion might have slipped up.

After checking the source code of Jared's calendar entry, Allie quickly discovered that the scheduled event had originally been added via an email invitation. The email, sent from an address that appeared to belong to Jared's mother, had been sent out last night at 8:34 p.m., nearly five months *after* the likely fictitious anniversary dinner.

"And there's strike two," she said, before going to the restaurant's website, which had a link to a reservations portal…

"Hmm," she said, setting her mind—and her total concentration—to the task of breaking into the system to try to find out whether there had actually been any reservation for the Garner family on the date in question.

She spent the better part of an hour working her way into the system, only to face more disappointment when she learned the reservations were only saved for a period of ninety days. As she struggled to think of what to do next, her gaze strayed to the CCTV screen, which showed the bar area now bustling with customers as Jones, Yolanda and a waitress worked to serve them.

That was when it hit her. The Italian restaurant where the Garners had allegedly "celebrated" with their family would likely have a similar camera system, not only to safeguard against outside threats but to help monitor employees, who often handled cash and credit card transactions, and protect themselves from potential false accusations.

Which meant the digital footage was stored somewhere, possibly in such a manner that someone with the right skill set could get to it. Smiling in anticipation of the challenge to come, she fell down the rabbit hole of the task…until sometime later, a knock came at the door.

"You forgot to ask me for the secret password," Jones teased as she let him without hesitation.

"I saw you heading this way," she said, hooking a thumb in the general direction of the CCTV monitor screen. "Sorry to keep you from showing off your cloak and dagger skills."

A roguish grin slanted across his face. "Humor me, will you? We brewmeisters get so little opportunity to flex that muscle."

She couldn't help but smile back. "So what brings you back here, Mr. Bond?"

"Just checking in to see if you'd like something from our kitchen. Or I could order out if you'd like?"

Confused, she looked at the clock and blinked hard. "I can't believe it's midafternoon already. But I'm just getting into something good at the moment, so I'll pass on eating."

"What do you have, Allie? I can see on your face that you've found something big."

"It's something, all right, but not the smoking gun we'll need to blast Jared Garner's alibi to pieces and get him and his friend Styler put away forever."

She briefly brought him up to speed, from her disappointment over learning Jared apparently did most of his messaging using an app that left no footprints to the discovery that his supposed alibi had only been added to his e-calendar *after* he'd been alerted that the FBI was looking at him.

"The date's not even his folks' real anniversary," she said.

"Isn't this all proof enough that they're a bunch of liars?"

"It's a good start," she allowed. "What I'm hoping is, the restaurant's security video will prove that he was never there at all."

"Wait a minute? How did you get into their CCTV footage?" he asked her.

She pinned him with a look until he held up his palms in mock surrender.

"You're right. I don't need to know that," he said. "I just want to see whether Jared and his family are anywhere in that footage. What do the parents even look like?"

Clicking a tab on her screen, she pulled up a photo she'd found on the web of both of the Garners together in front of their furniture store—the father a prosperous-looking, suit-wearing version of his handsome son, though the older man had thinner hair, and the mother a well-dressed blonde whose makeup showcased the smile of a born saleswoman.

"Here they are, Rob and Marilyn Garner," Allie said. "But you may want to pull up a chair, Jones. It could take a while for me to get to the correct camera view and the right time."

"If it's all the same to you, I'll hover," he said, obviously too wound up to relax as he moved in behind her once she'd reclaimed the desk chair.

"Sure thing," she said, returning her attention to the files, where she quickly began opening video files until she found one that gave a view of every customer entering the restaurant.

"Looks like a pretty swanky place," Jones commented, laying a hand on her uninjured shoulder, a subtle reminder of their connection.

Too wrapped up in what she was doing to properly enjoy it, Allie continued fast-forwarding to within thirty minutes of the reservation time. "They did claim they were there to celebrate."

It wasn't long before Jones pointed at the screen. "Right there—there's the mother. Hair's a little different, but I swear that's—"

"I don't think so," she began to argue, squinting at the video in time to see the woman in question rise from a bench where she'd been waiting and go to greet what was clearly Jared's father with a kiss.

"That's definitely the two of them. You called it," she affirmed. "Now we wait for the rest of the family to arrive."

They continued watching, only to observe the couple going to the hostess stand, and then leaving the camera range with a young woman as if to be seated.

"They have to be alone," Allie told Jones. "Did you see that? They never looked around or glanced behind them on their way to the table, the way you would if you were waiting for another party."

"Let's keep going, though, with this camera," Jones suggested, "to see if Jared ever does show up."

But there was no sign of him at all when Allie sped through the video. Instead, they watched multiple people come and go before the Garners themselves left as a couple.

"So this proves their alibi was garbage," Jones said. "Maybe now Agent Howard can put those two behind bars, where they belong."

Hearing the excitement in his voice, she advised him, "You need to understand, nothing I've gotten today can be used as legal evidence."

"Because of how you got it?"

"Right. It's only to help make certain we're definitely on the trail of the right people—and to maybe help guide any anonymous tip we might leave Special Agent Howard about where he'll want to direct his investigative efforts."

"And then he'll arrest them?"

"Eventually," she said, "but only after they come up with concrete evidence directly linking both Garner and Styler to the crimes. Now that those two have lawyered up, the Feds will have to work slowly, methodically to make sure they have every *t* crossed and *i* dotted."

Scowling at the idea, he asked, "How slowly are you talking?"

"To be honest, it could be months before they're arrested—if they ever are."

"What do you mean, *if*—and I can't just sit around and wait for months, or keep all this from my family that long."

"I understand completely," she said, rising from the chair so she wouldn't have to keep craning her neck to look at him. Besides, she decided, it was critical, for this part of the conversation, that she look him directly in the eye. "That's why I've put another plan in motion."

"What kind of plan?" he asked her.

"The kind of plan," she said, drawing in a deep breath as she prepared herself for the objections she knew she'd face when he heard about the friend request she'd sent to Leo Styler, "that I'm very much afraid you're not going to like."

"You're not planning on leaving already, are you?" Jones asked, thinking it would be bad enough, being forced to wait in silence, unable to speak a word of this while the investigation slowly dragged on, but doing so without her guidance would qualify as a torture. While she might argue that she had fulfilled her contract with him by finding two suspects and turning their names over to authorities, he needed more, much more to bring him the closure he'd imagined.

"It's an option," she admitted, "and one that could save you quite a lot of money, if you want to let the authorities take it from here."

"And if I don't?" he asked, his gut contracting at the thought of losing his direct link to the investigation so soon. Or maybe it was the idea of losing touch with Allie herself that scared him most—especially since he feared that, because of the threats against her, she would disappear to someplace where he'd never again be able to make contact. As the reality of it hit him, he quickly added, "Because costs be damned. I definitely don't want you leaving yet, not until we—"

The chiming of his cell phone interrupted. Grimacing, he said, "I'd better check this. Carly's supposed to be dropping off some things I asked her to bring over for your new look."

Allie nodded. "That'd be perfect—and even better if I got the chance to thank her in person for all her help."

After reading the text, which was indeed from Carly, Jones said, "She couldn't stay, I'm afraid. Apparently, she has some appointment across town, but she dropped off the bag with Gina—that's the waitress on duty—who said she'd run it back here to the office as soon as she gets a minute."

"Oh, okay," said Allie before a jingling tone had her turning to look at her tablet computer. "Oooh, yes! I've got a bite."

"A bite?" he asked. "What exactly are you up to?"

"A little fishing expedition," she said.

She turned the screen to show him a photo of the sneering face of the younger man Jones recognized as Leo Styler, which was connected to a cartoon-style speech balloon containing the message he had just sent Allie: *Hey there, Sexy Lexi! Next time you see me over there, say hi and I'll def buy you a smoothie or whatever. Especially if you've got that vest on.*

Accompanying the message, he sent an icon featuring a lecherous cartoon wolf with drool dripping from his unspooling tongue.

"You—you're trying to meet up with this guy?" Jones demanded, his heart battering his rib cage. "And what on earth's this Sexy Lexi—"

A tiny bomb icon in the upper right-hand corner of the screen counted down 3, 2, 1 before an explosive sound effect heralded the disappearance of the message.

"What happened? Where'd the message go?" Jones asked, more confused than ever.

Allie explained the nature of the app. "I set the timer for as long as possible, but the whole point is not to leave any kind of trail."

"Got it." Jones nodded, familiar with such applications. "But I still don't understand what you think you're doing here—and why on earth you'd want this creep slobbering after you."

"Collecting evidence to help out Special Agent Howard, I hope," she said, "and if it helps to get a couple of stone-cold killers like Leo and Jared off the street, I'm only too happy to set a little honey trap online."

"What exactly did you use for bait?" he asked.

"Meet my alter ego, Lexi Hartz," she said before pulling up a photo of a young woman—or maybe a teenager—giving the camera a come-hither look from beneath the brim of a fedora with her heavily lined cat's eyes. Along with a tiny skirt, she wore a lace-up vest—with no top underneath it—that acted as push-up bra.

"Wait a second," he said, giving it a double take. "Don't tell me that that's really *you* in that?"

Shrugging, she said, "If you want to go catfishing for an emotionally stunted nineteen-year-old, it doesn't hurt to have the right lure."

"Or the *wrong* one," Jones said, his stomach turning at the idea of Styler ogling her photo, "if he's trying to meet up with you in person. Surely, you're not thinking of taking him up on it."

"It wasn't my original intention," she said, "but think of it, Jones. On the app, the only thing I could hope to capture would be a screen shot of possibly incriminating statements—which he would totally know I was getting because the program sends the user an alert, shutting down the conversation."

"I can see how that would be a problem. If he has even half a brain, he'd be bound to get suspicious."

She nodded. "Exactly, but in a one-on-one situation with a female he's bent on impressing, I can't imagine that a guy like Leo could possible resist bragging about the things that he'd been up to—especially if I play him right."

"No way, Allie," Jones said, his heartbeat picking up speed at the thought of her getting anywhere near one of those killers. "It's far too dangerous. We already know what this guy is, and who knows how far you'd have to go to gain his trust before he'd—"

"I could handle it. I'm sure of it," Allie assured him. "I'll just go hang out at the school this week and—"

"Forget it. I couldn't—"

A knock came, and he went to the door and greeted Gina, a curvy redhead in her midthirties who was well-liked by both customers and her fellow workers. But as she passed him tote bag from Carly, Jones couldn't help but notice the tension in her normally friendly gray eyes.

"Thanks for bringing this back, Gina," he said as he passed off the bag to Allie, "but is something wrong? You look a little worried."

"I think you might want to come out front, Jones. Yolanda's having an issue with a customer—and things are starting to get a little heated."

"What?" Swiveling his head to glance at the CCTV monitor, he noted that Yolanda—who was a pro at diplomatically cutting off those who'd had enough, switching them to coffee or water before quietly calling them a cab or ride-share to safely get them home —had come out from behind the bar to deal with a large male who appeared to be getting in her face. "Oh, boy. Yeah. Let me go deal with this."

"Do you want—" Allie said, pulling something from the tote bag. "It looks like Carly's returned that, um, *item* her fiancé was holding for me for safekeeping."

Jones understood that she had to mean the stun gun. But he was already heading for the door, shaking his head as he told her, "The day I need a weapon to toss a troublemaker out of my bar is the day I'll close my doors. Wait right here, and I'll be back in just a few…"

He couldn't recall the last time they'd had a serious issue with a customer at the Lone Wolf Brewery. It wasn't the kind of place people went looking to get wasted, but any business dealing with the public, particularly any business serving alcohol, had to be prepared to deal with the occasional unhappy—or flat-out belligerent—patron. Confident in his own experience in handling such customers in previous places he'd worked,

as well as Yolanda's good sense, and the bar's other patrons—who could normally be counted on to help calm
such situations—Jones had little doubt the interruption
would be a short one.

Before he made it halfway to the bar, he got his first
inkling that the situation wasn't what he'd assumed.

"I damned well know he's hiding in here somewhere," a male voice shouted, sounding angrier than
he did intoxicated. "And I already told you, I'm not
going nowhere 'til I see the sorry son of a—"

"Come on, man," said a regular, a plaid-shirted retired engineer named Dave, who came in for lunch with
former coworkers a couple of times a week and often
hung around to talk craft beers with Jones and other
regulars. "The lady's already asked you nicely to take
it elsewhere. Be a shame if we had to spoil everybody's
afternoon calling the police about this."

Wheeling to face the older man, the belligerent
visitor—a thickset bodybuilder type in a ball cap and
navy sweatshirt—grabbed a handful of Dave's collar
and yanked him so close the two of them were practically eye to eye. "Did I freaking *ask* for your opinion, old man?"

"You let go of him this instant," Yolanda ordered,
turning to nod toward Gina, who had her cell phone
out, as if to indicate that it was time to call in the dis-
turbance.

But by that time, Jones was already across the room
and clamping a restraining hand on the rock-hard arm of
the aggressor, a complete stranger who turned to glare
at him, his heavy, black brows angling downward between a pair of eyes so dark they resembled a pair of
holes punched through to midnight.

Realizing he was a fraction of a second from throw-

ing a punch, Jones tried to strike a friendly but concerned note as he asked, "You wanted to see me about
something?"

Releasing his grip on Dave, the stranger shoved the
older man roughly aside to turn his full attention on
Jones.

"Hey!" Thrown off balance, the far smaller Dave
staggered forward—and would have fallen had Yolanda
not managed to grab him.

"You never mind that bullying fool," she soothed
him, steering him away from the trouble and toward a
barstool. "Let's get you off your feet now."

A muscle twitched in Jones's jaw from the adrenaline surging through his body as he fought his initial
impulse to wipe the floor with this aggressive jackass.
But since his opponent, though half a head shorter, had
a good sixty pounds of pure muscle on him, along with
the misshapen nose and cauliflower ear of someone
who fought both viciously and often, he kept his temper in check.

"So what's it going to take to get you on your way?"
Jones asked him. "Because I'm sure I don't need to tell
you, your last call's come early, brother."

"I'm not your freaking brother, Colton," the stranger
said, his voice a low growl of menace, "and nobody
wants your crap swill anyway."

"I'm sure Yolanda here knows how to make a
Cosmo," Jones said, tossing out the name of a drink
most macho types wouldn't be caught dead ordering,
"or maybe you'd prefer a Shirley Temple?"

The stranger's light-olive-complexion darkened a
fraction, but he ignored the insult, saying, "I need to
know where you've got her stashed. I need to know

right now or there's gonna be some trouble. With that pretty face of yours."

"I wouldn't be so sure about that," Jones told him, not giving an inch as it came to him that this thug, like the man he and Allie had encountered last night, likely was in possession of her photo—and the promise of a reward for doing her harm. "But regardless of how that turns out, it doesn't matter, since I have no idea who you're talking about."

"We both know you're lyin', so where is she?"

Praying that Allie wouldn't happen to choose this minute to ignore his directive to stay inside the office, he shook his head and said, "She's skipped town."

Before the thug could respond, Gina called over in a shaky voice, "The police will be here any minute!"

When Jones glanced her way, he noticed Yolanda coming from behind the bar, where she'd retrieved her old wooden baseball bat—a legendary accessory that she jokingly referred to as The Equalizer but had never been known to actually wield.

Looking fiercely determined, she strode in Jones's and the troublemaker's direction, gripping it as if she meant business. "That means you'd better shoo now. But if you decide you mean to get in a few licks for the road, I mean to tell you, mister, we don't fight fair when it comes two-bit bullies here at the Lone Wolf."

"No, we don't," said Dave, who was backed up not only by his three silver-haired friends, but several younger and fitter male customers, all of whom stood glowering, their arms crossed and their faces uniformly stern. "So maybe you oughta move along—unless you want to have to tell your buddies how you got yourself stomped by a gang of angry old men and a very formidable lady with a Louisville Slugger."

Scowling as he took in the evolving threat, the stranger pointed a thick finger at Jones and said, "Don't think I haven't been tossed out of better places," before spitting on the floor and stalking toward the exit.

Emboldened by their success, Dave and his friends, along with the other customers, jeered after the man, hooting and whistling and then cheering loudly when he finally vacated the premises.

"Thanks, everybody, for the timely assist," Jones called to them once the noise had died down. "It's good to know you have my back."

"You know it was just that pretty face of yours we were all protecting," Yolanda called, to general laughter.

"In that case, this round's on me," Jones told them, prompting a cheer and some backslapping and hand-shaking, along with a flurry of well-intentioned comments.

"Just so you know, my money would've been on you, man."

"Hey, Jones, seriously. You'd better watch your back. That dude looked like trouble."

"You haven't been running around with that guy's old lady or something, have you?"

By the time he'd gotten everyone settled down, a patrol officer arrived. After thanking her for coming, Jones were outside with her to check around the parking lot and the immediate vicinity.

When no sign of the unwelcome guest was found, the officer, a woman with a salt-and-pepper pixie cut, whose been-there, done-that attitude more than made up for her small stature, said, "Seriously, you should be fine. In ninety-nine cases out of a hundred where the troublemaker gets embarrassed and run off like this, he stays gone."

"And in the hundredth?"

She grimaced. "He shows up later packing heat and tries to shoot up everybody in the place. So maybe assign an employee to keep an eye on that monitor you showed me for the next couple of days. And don't be afraid to hit the locks and call us back out if you see any signs of trouble coming."

Nodding, he said grimly, "Don't worry. If he shows up again, you'll be the first to hear about it."

Chapter 9

Allie rushed over to the office door to let Jones in the moment that she heard his knock, so on edge that she nearly bumped her laptop off the desk in her hurry.

"Yolanda came back and filled me in like you asked her to," she hastened to explain the moment he stepped inside, "but she's *definitely* suspicious about why anyone that sketchy would come here looking for a brand and marketing consultant."

"So she's figured out it's you that guy was after?" Jones asked.

"Oh, yes," Allie said, "and between that and last night's mugging incident, which was apparently the hot topic of conversation among your friends and family today, I'm afraid our cover story's blown—with her at least."

"Since I'll need her to keep an eye out for any more trouble at the brewery, I'll have to tell her why you're really here," Jones said. "If it's all right with you, I'll also tell her you may have a problem related to a former investigation that's coming back to haunt you."

"That's fair enough," Allie said. "But I hate the idea that my being here could be endangering the people who work and come here. None of them signed up for that."

Pacing the room, she rubbed her arms, wound up again at the thought of what Yolanda had told her. *That lowlife might've been asking for Jones, but he was looking for you—no doubt at all about that.*

"You're right about that," Jones said, "which is why we're leaving right now."

"For where? Because these people—they won't stop coming by here. It'll be your house next. They'll never quit coming and coming as long as they believe you're their ticket to tracking me down."

"I don't give a damn about that. I can handle whatever—"

"That's easy for you to say now," she argued, "but how're you going to explain it to Roderick if Yolanda ends up getting jumped going to her car after a shift? Or that little red-haired waitress? Because you don't know these killers like I do, Jones. These guys fight dirty."

"I'll hire security—or even shut the bar down if I have to. And when I talked to my friend who's going out of town about switching the cars, he suggested we should just stay at his place while he's gone. He left a key for me."

"What a great friend," she said, impressed, but not surprised, that Jones was the kind of person who'd inspire such unquestioning generosity.

"Seriously," he agreed. "I need to be sure to buy him a bottle of his favorite whiskey and maybe a gift card for a nice steak dinner for him and his girlfriend."

"Do you know how long he plans to be away?"

"Five days," he said.

"That should be enough," she said.

"Enough for what?" he asked.

"Time enough me to get everything I need out of Leo Styler so I can—"

"Wait a minute." He was shaking his head. "I thought we'd already agreed that that catfishing plan of yours was way too dangerous."

"No, *we* didn't agree," she said. "*You* voiced your objections, which were duly noted before I wrote Leo back."

"Wait—what?" he asked, clearly confused. "When could you possibly have done this?"

"While you were talking with the officer, I had quite a conversation going with Mr. Smooth." She rolled her eyes. "And I'm telling you, if I *ever* thought I had issues socializing, this poor guy's beyond pathetic, with absolutely zero game when it comes to women."

Bristling visibly, Jones said, "You make him sound like some kind of joke, not a stone-cold killer."

"Believe me, no one's laughing—and I'm not losing sight of what he is, even for a moment," Allie promised. "But my point is, for all his tough talk online, this guy's so desperate for female interaction—and an actual girlfriend who understands him, that he's absolutely ripe for spilling secrets."

"So why not get him on the phone and record it? You could even dress up if you had to and do some kind of video chat with him."

She shook her head. "If I thought for a minute that would work, I'd be all over it, Jones. Believe me, I don't love the idea of getting face-to-face with this creep any more than you do."

"Don't you?" Jones argued. "Because it pretty much seems like that's what you've been aiming for."

"Only because it's obvious I have to leave soon. It's not safe for me to stay here—not for me or for anyone around me—and I don't want to go off leaving the job half-done...unless that's what you'd rather I do."

His jaw clenched, he averted his gaze. "Of course it's not," he admitted. "But maybe that's because I can't stand the thought of you dealing with these people who're out to hunt you down all on your own."

"You don't need to worry," she assured him. "I can bug out just about anywhere on my own and work remotely until I figure out how to deal with this issue on a more permanent basis."

It was one good thing about not having family or close friends to tie her down. She could even have the contents of her condo packed up and put into storage if need be—or even sell the place at a nice profit, since her once down-at-the-heels neighborhood had recently become trendy. Creating a new identity would be trickier in this day and age, but she had the skills—along with a sizable nest egg socked away in online accounts—to resurface as nearly anything and anyone she wanted...

Except as California Private Investigator Allie Chandler. Her true identity would be lost to her, along with any future chasing criminals at the behest of law enforcement agencies.

And whatever future she built for herself, it would be completely impossible for her to ever again make contact with anyone from the life she had abandoned. Including a client from Chicago she'd once slept with, on a night both of them had desperately needed to feel something besides grief or loneliness or fear.

"I don't want you to go," Jones said, their gazes con-

necting in the memory of what they'd been through together and how they had connected, before he added
quietly, "Not yet."

She swallowed. "Then we're agreed. I'm heading
back to school tomorrow morning."

"To school?"

She shrugged. "Just to the student union over on the
campus of Western Community, where I've agreed to
meet with him for coffee after his early class releases
at 10:25."

"So this is in a public building, where I can keep an
eye on you?"

"Yes, it's in a public building, but you're absolutely
not going to be there."

"The hell I'm not," he insisted. "You aren't getting
within a mile of that murderer without me there to watch
your back."

"Like I said, forget it. I'm going to need you elsewhere, for several reasons."

"Allie, please—"

"Just hear me out," she said, before holding up one
finger. "First off, I'm going to need you off-site, to test
out the effectiveness of the wireless mic and recording equipment we're going to purchase this afternoon."

"Then we're going shopping?"

"We are," she confirmed, knowing, after having
looked through the disguise Carly had brought her, that
she would still need a few more items to pull off her
transformation. "Second, your physical presence would
prove a huge distraction. Not only would it increase the
chance I might be recognized and followed by anyone
looking for me, I'd also be tempted to look at you instead of focusing on Leo."

"I understand your concerns," he said, "but I'm sure

if we put our minds to it, we could come up with some way to make it work for me to be there, too."

"But I still haven't gotten to the most important reason."

"What's that?" he asked impatiently.

Crossing her arms over her chest, she looked up at him. "Because I don't want to have to explain to your family why you're in jail for beating Leo within an inch of his life the second you lay eyes on one of the two men you believe responsible for your father's and your uncle's deaths."

After picking up a few things from his house and driving around long enough to determine that they weren't being followed, Jones took Allie over to Sergei's place, a sleek, modern condo located only a few blocks from True. Happy to see the garage was monitored and that his friend had already informed the guard he would be staying, he parked his own vehicle as directed before grabbing Allie's and his bags and heading for the elevator.

"Let me help with that," she offered. "I have one good arm, at least."

He handed off the tote from Carly along with another of the lighter bags.

Once they'd stepped inside the car, she seemed both surprised and delighted to find the elevator opened directly into Sergei's living area.

"Wow, you run with a swanky crowd, Jones," she said as she eyed the large format, modernistic paintings that punctuated the otherwise coolly austere decor. "Or does every guy in your crowd have a decorator in the family?"

"Sergei's a design architect, so I'm pretty sure he's

about a million times better at that sort of thing than I am."

"Yes, but does the man know his way around hops like you do?" she asked, slanting a smile his way.

Jones laughed and touched her shoulder. "I knew there was a reason that I liked you. Well, other than the fact that you're straight-up gorgeous, fun to be with and a wizard at what you do."

"And you're not half bad at flattery. So where should I go change?"

"Change?"

"Sure," she said. "If we're going to head out shopping in your friend's car, I'll want to change into the outfit Carly brought me. She even included hair extensions and sunglasses, so I should be able to pull off a whole new look."

"She told me she had some of that stuff from one of those murder mystery parties she and January were both invited to last year. She had to dress up and pretend to be a Hollywood starlet, who was one of the prime suspects." Jones smiled to imagine his sister getting into the playacting. "I think January, of all people, turned out to be the killer."

"That actually sounds like fun," Allie said, "and you know how I feel about parties…"

"Maybe you've just been attending the wrong parties. If you're hanging out with people who're fun to talk to and you're doing things you want to do as opposed to things you're being forced to, they can be a good time."

"I'll take your word for it," she said, "but only because the beer dinner wasn't awful."

"*'Wasn't awful,'*" he echoed. "We'll be sure to quote you on the advertising posters for next year's event."

Grinning back at him, she said, "Oh, all right. Since

it's for charity, I'll change my online reviews to, *'Absolutely to die for, from the hors d'oeuvres to the after-dinner stabbing!'"*

"Harsh but fair," he allowed before showing her to the master bedroom. "We'll change the sheets in here later, and I'll take the guest room."

"You don't have to—"

"It's fine," he said, not wanting to make any assumptions that what had happened between them last night would become a regular event. But as tempting as the thought was, the incident at the bar today had put him on notice of just how strong his need was to protect her. Worse yet, the feelings had only intensified, making him feel downright *possessive* at the thought of her going anywhere near Leo Styler or his murderous friend Jared.

How much more unmanageable would his emotions grow if he got in any deeper with her? Would he be able to let her do the job he'd brought her here to do at all, or would he abandon his efforts to get justice for his family? And how would he bear seeing her leave alone, knowing she had no one else to watch her back?

But with his life, his still-grieving family and his business all here in Chicago, he knew the situation was impossible—as impossible as continuing to pretend that he could wall off the sex from his personal feelings for this woman. So as difficult as he knew as it was going to be, he told himself the best thing, the only fair thing for both of them in the long run, was to back off now, while there was still a chance of getting out of this thing with his heart intact.

In the parking lot of Western Community College the following morning, Allie sat inside the tiny silver hatchback she had rented earlier and pretended to re-adjust the pale-pink flutter-sleeved top she'd picked out last night while surreptitiously switching on the tiny mic she'd carefully stitched to her bra strap.

"If you can hear me, text back, and I'll make sure I can feel the vibration in my pocket," she said.

While waiting for Jones's reply, she fluffed the long, bright blond-streaked extensions Carly had given her, which she'd curled and sprayed into loose, beachy waves this morning. Along with the breezy, summery top, she wore rose-tinted sunglasses, distressed-denim cropped jeans and trendy platform sandals, bangle bracelets and hoop earrings—but according to Jones, it was the sparkly lip gloss and eye widening false lashes that guaranteed she wouldn't be able to buy beer anywhere inside the city without being carded.

"Seriously," he'd said, looking surprisingly troubled. "I'd never take you for twenty-one. It makes me feel a little weird that we ever…"

"Oh, knock it off, old man," she'd teased, elbowing him in his ribs.

Now, the phone in her back pocket buzzed, reminding her that she'd forgotten about shutting off the ringer. As she did so, she looked down at Jones's message on the screen.

Be careful and say the code words if you need me.

Shaking her head, she pocketed the cell again, gri-macing at the reminder of his insistence on waiting in his friend's SUV in a parking lot on the other side of the campus, just a few minutes away, where he would be both recording the conversation and monitoring for any signs of trouble. If she felt endangered for any reason, he'd told her that she need only mention Wrigley Field and he'd come running.

His insistence on it this morning had taken her by surprise, considering how he'd cooled toward her throughout the latter part of the previous day. Though he'd continued being as polite and helpful as ever as the two of them had run their errands and later shared a takeout dinner, he'd quickly refocused the conversation whenever it began straying into personal territory, and he'd made no move at all to touch her again that evening.

Was he upset about her using her sexuality to bait Styler? Certainly, Jones had seemed disturbed after seeing the first catfishing photo she had sent the nineteen-year-old. Or maybe, the incident with the thug showing up at his bar looking for him had made him realize that being involved with her was likely to end up causing him far more trouble than a short-term fling was worth.

Either way, she swallowed back the sour taste of what felt like a rejection, reminding herself that she needed to keep her full focus on the real reason she'd driven here this morning: to wrest a confession from a killer, by any means necessary.

Checking the dashboard clock, she saw the time had come to head in for her meetup. "Time to shine," she told Jones via the microphone. "Let's both hope the creep shows up."

Grabbing the smaller daypack she had picked up on their shopping run, she slung it over her shoulder and left the car, stepping out into a morning whose early chill was quickly giving way to another day of vibrant May sunshine.

The campus itself, she soon found as she started down a sidewalk that an online map had indicated would take her to the student union, was quite attractive, its groomed, landscaped areas bright with spring flowers and a series of small reflecting pools and fountains. After passing a redbrick library, followed by a more modern-looking academic building, she peeled off from a group of students she'd been walking with and headed for the two-story, semicircular student union, which she recalled from the website housed financial aid and student housing offices, along with a bookstore, coffee shop, ATM and a couple of food kiosks. Leo had suggested meeting at one of the latter, but she'd arrived a little early, eager to observe his arrival—and to familiarize herself with the location. With the latter in mind, she flipped her sunglasses to the top of her head and took a bit of time to stroll, getting a feel for the building and its layout.

During her exploration, she found other areas as well, including the offices for various campus activities, arranged in a ring around the large second story lounge–game room, with its casual seating clusters, table tennis, pool table and carts with video gaming systems that could be checked out from one of the student attendants sitting at one end.

"If I really were attending this school, I'd *never* want to graduate," she commented in a voice low enough for Jones to hear but not the other students who were chatting, sitting and playing with their phones, or engaging in any of the other nearby activities. "Heading down to the coffee shop."

This had been the spot she had agreed to meet Leo at 10:30, and it was now 10:22 a.m.

Jones didn't text an acknowledgment, but she didn't think much of it until she'd taken the stairs and channeled her inner coed with the purchase of a foamy indulgence of a hazelnut latte. After finding a seat at a table for two, she set her daypack on the other chair to save the spot and then looked around for any sign of Styler.

Not seeing him yet, she pulled out her phone and saw that she hadn't missed a message. "Jones, if you can hear me, text something, will you?" she said. "Even a thumbs-up, just so I know we're still on."

With every second no reply came, her stomach grew heavier, until she finally texted, Are you hearing me at all?

But no matter how hard she stared at the phone's screen, she saw no sign that a reply was in progress. Heartbeat accelerating, she wondered, had Jones received her text at all, or was she in a dead zone? But her cell showed excellent reception, which made it highly likely that, since he was so close by, he would have decent coverage, too.

Despite the fact that he'd grown more emotionally distant, there'd been no mistaking his seriousness about this morning's operation. He knew his role in it was critical, so she had no doubt that he would respond if there was any way he could.

So what had gone wrong? Could his phone have died or the app malfunctioned for some reason, leaving her no witness to independently corroborate her testimony or the recording she planned to make with her own cell phone? Or could the campus police have spotted him waiting in his car and stopped to ask what he was doing there, without a student parking permit? Although she had little doubt that Jones was capable of coming up with a reasonable explanation, any such delay could reduce the evidentiary value of any information she might collect.

Disquiet rippling through her, her instinct whispered,

Maybe I should bail now, get over there and check on him, just in case.

Deciding to use SelfDestrukt to let Leo know that something had come up and she would catch him another time, she opened the app. But when she happened to glance up, her breath caught at the sight of the shaggy-haired young man making a beeline directly toward her—and the awful realization that it was too late to back out now.

Chapter 10

Jones had been sitting in his borrowed SUV, a white Range Rover that still looked and smelled brand-new, for about ten minutes in an otherwise-empty section of parking lot on the far end of the college's administration building. As he pretended to read through a folder full of random junk mail, he flipped on the vent, a rising feeling of foreboding raising his body's thermostat even faster than the morning sun was heating up the temperature outside.

Between his body's clamminess and his thrumming pulse, he was sorely tempted to pull out his cell and text Allie. Or better yet, he'd call her, so she could hear the urgency in his voice as he pleaded with her to forget this whole insane idea. Leave Styler and Garner to the federal agents, no matter how long their investigation took them.

At least they, unlike Allie, would have competent,

trained and well-armed backup in case something went wrong. And at least whoever faced down the stone-cold killer inside the student union would not be the woman Jones couldn't help but care for, deeply, no matter how hard he'd been fighting to close the tap on his feelings.

He pulled the phone out, but before he could hit the button to connect, he frowned, reminding himself that as an experienced private investigator who'd put away any number of desperate criminals, she'd surely faced down equally dangerous situations for years and lived to tell about it. She was smart and capable, and he could all too easily imagine his sister and his female cousins demanding to know if he would pull a *male* investigator off the case if the circumstances were similar.

Maybe not, he answered the accusing stares that he imagined, *but if Allie had been a male investigator, I damned well wouldn't have slept with her—or let my emotions get entangled.*

If feeling that way made him old-fashioned, Allie would just have to deal with it. He was the one paying her fee, after all, so he had the right to call the shots on what he could or couldn't live with.

As he raised his phone, however, her voice came through the speaker.

"Jones, if you can hear me, text something, will you?" Though little more than a breathy whisper, her voice was easily audible, since they'd turned up the volume and sensitivity to the highest levels so that nothing would be missed on his recording. "Even a thumbs-up, just so I know we're still on."

He clicked the messaging screen, but before he could send any response, a sharp rap at the window made him jump.

Reflexively turning his head, he froze, the phone

dropping from his hand as he came face-to-face, not with the burly male in the navy sweatshirt who'd walked up to the vehicle slightly behind the door beside him, but with the barrel of the gun pointed at the side of his face, on the other side of the glass.

As with most people one encountered after meeting them online, the reality of Leo Styler was different from the image he presented in his social media photos. For one thing, his complexion had cleared, and his dark brown hair, though longer and spikier, was actually clean-looking. She noted, too, that the army-surplus camouflage and torn denim he was wearing might look distressed, but the clothing fit well and smelled freshly laundered, making her wonder if he'd made an effort on her account this morning.

But there was nothing squeaky-clean about the double length of chain draped around his neck, which, with the heavy lock hanging from it, looked thick and heavy enough to double as a murder weapon. Nor did she miss the edge of a knife handle, quite a wide one, clipped to the top of the pocket of his jeans.

Yet instead of the glowering tough guy she might have expected, he smiled at her. "Sexy Lexi, right?"

"Just Lexi will do." She slanted a coy look up at him. "Although I *suppose* I won't hate you too much if you find me low-key cute in this outfit."

"I guess you couldn't show up in that hot vest—" Leo's grin bordered on a leer as he ogled her, or more specifically, her breasts "—not without causing some kind of a riot."

She rolled her eyes, her skin wanting to crawl off her body and exit the building on its own. But despite her distraction over Jones and how odious she found Leo, she reminded herself that it was crucial to remain in character and get this job done as efficiently as possible. "*Hardly*. So, are you done with classes for the day?"

"Nah, I've got a break until twelve fifteen and then an exam in Western Civ."

"You ready for it?"

He shrugged. "I'll pass that class, at least. It's that algebra class that has me worried. I fail that one again, I'm gonna shoot that professor." Anger flashing over his face, he said, "I can hardly understand a word that foreign bitch says."

Taken aback by the eruption of sexism, xenophobia and the casual threat to take another person's life, Allie was glad she'd had the chance to switch on her phone's recording app. But she knew, too, that there were, unfortunately, many—including no small number of criminal defense attorneys—who would defend what he had said as "just another young guy harmlessly blowing off steam."

Except that she knew all too well that Leo Styler was in no way harmless.

Needing to encourage him, she forced herself to play along, nodding in feigned agreement. "I know *exactly* what you mean." Removing her backpack from the seat, she patted it. "Here, why don't you take a load off? Or did you want to grab a drink first."

"I think I will," he said. "Want anything else?"

"I'm good," she answered, raising nearly full drink. "I'll save the seat for you, though."

"Glad to hear it." Touching his neck, he smirked and added, "I wouldn't want to have to get my chain all bloody whaling on the competition this early in the day."

As he turned and walked away, she said quietly,

"Gross, gross, gross. I hope you're hearing this," to Jones.

But she still had no way of knowing if he was picking up her microphone on his app, and a quick check of her cell showed that he still had not texted or attempted to call.

A chill swept over her, raising the fine hairs along her arms as she recalled the thug who'd confronted him yesterday at the brewery, the man who'd clearly considered Jones the easier path to her. What if, in spite of all of their precautions, someone like him or the goon who'd stabbed her had caught up to him on campus?

Raising her cup to her lips, she fought to swallow back her rising panic, reminding herself the problem was far more likely to be a technical issue and she'd be a fool to squander the opportunity she had to collect and record evidence that might help Special Agent Howard make an arrest. To bolster her conviction, she pictured Jones's disappointment if he learned that she'd backed off now, when things were going so well and his own situation turned out to be nothing.

Besides, Leo was already heading back her way with coffee, looking pleased as he could be as he claimed the seat next to her.

"I keep thinking it's so weird I haven't run into you here before," he said. "I'm sure I'd have remembered a babe like you hanging around."

"I was putting in so many hours at the café where I was working, I've hardly had the chance—until just last week," she said, deciding to toss out another piece of juicy bait to see how he might react by dropping her gaze and squirming in her seat.

Sure enough, Leo asked, "So what happened? You get fired or something?"

She shook her head. "Quit. I had to. That creepy manager couldn't keep his perverted comments—or his grabby hands—to himself. And the guy was really *old*, like almost forty, with a wife and kids and everything." She faked a shudder.

Leo scowled, his brown eyes burning with outrage. "Probably one of those Chads who's gone through his whole life thinking he can just have any pretty girl he wanted when he's just another loser rando that any real man could teach a lesson any time he wanted."

A thrill of horror ran up her spine at his use of the term *rando*, so she leaned in, making and holding eye contact. "How would *you* teach my boss a lesson, Leo?"

"Trust me," he said, his voice dropping to a whisper that sent a flurry of shivers racing up her backbone, "you don't want to know…"

Jones reached for the lock, but before he could hit it, the navy sweatshirt guy yanked open the SUV's door.

"What the hell?" Jones shouted, alarm whipsawing through him.

Before he knew what was happening, he found himself roughly jerked out of the Range Rover. He started to fall as he resisted, but his assailant slammed him backward. His head banged against the top edge of open doorframe, hard enough that spangles of white-hot pain burst across his vision and blue sky and parking lot seems to spin around him.

Stomach threatening upheaval, he struggled to get his feet underneath him.

"Hold still, damn you," yelled the dark-eyed man in the watch cap from the bar. "I just need to know where she is, and then we're done here."

As the gun rose toward his head, Jones acted on pure

instinct, bowing his head and allowing his knees to sag as if he were collapsing.

"Hey, man, don't you dare pass out on me," the gunman said, stepping in even closer—so close that when Jones used his powerful leg muscles to spring to his full height and headbutt him, he heard the satisfying crunch of bone and cartilage, along with the sharp cry of the man whose nose he had just unmistakably broken.

Next came the impossibly loud explosion of a gunshot and a searing sting across the left side of his neck below his ear, but Jones couldn't stop to wonder if he'd been shot—didn't dare stop fighting to grab the thug's right wrist to see the source of the shouts he'd heard from across the parking lot.

Instead, he focused on his still-armed opponent, who was vowing, "You're dead!" and struggling desperately to keep Jones from twisting the gun out of his hand.

Half choking on the blood running from his mashed nose, the man yelled, "Let *go* of it, right *now*!" Finally, his thick finger, still threaded through the trigger, squeezed off two more rounds just as Jones was pushing the muzzle away from his own body.

The gunman got in a hard shove, throwing Jones off balance enough for his assailant to scramble back a few steps and bring the gun around to take aim. This time, there would be no missed shot—and from the look in those coal-black eyes, no mercy, either—

The horn of a small car sounded, an insistent toot-toot-toot that rose in volume as the tiny silver hatchback rocketed across the parking lot, barreling straight toward them. Realizing that the driver—Allie—was not about to stop, Jones took another step backward, flattening himself against the side of the Range Rover, while the bloody-faced thug, recognizing the threat at last, tried to throw himself out of the path of the threat.

He nearly made it, but the small car clipped his leg and sent him sprawling, the gun flying from his hand. As Jones ran to grab it before his assailant could recover, Allie braked hard, leaping from the hatchback.

"Are you all right?" she asked Jones. "Your neck."

"I'll be fine," he said, so flooded with adrenaline he was aware of nothing but the pounding of his own heart and a buzzing sound in his ears. "Thanks for showing up at the right moment. Otherwise, I'd be—"

Still writhing on the pavement, the gunman struggled to rise before falling back. "You broke my leg!"

Sending a fierce look in his direction, Allie said, "Point a gun at my friend again, and I'll break the other one, I promise—or maybe even worse."

Giving her a double take, the thug said, "Wait a minute. You're *her*, aren't you? That girl from the picture. You're worth a lot of money," he added. "Double if you turn up dead."

As Allie stared at him, dumbfounded, Jones recovered first to ask him, "Where'd you get that picture? And how many more of them are out there?"

"I'm not tellin' you a thing. If you'd only talked when I asked—but no, you had to go'n bust my nose and fight me."

"Because I knew you were out to hurt her," Jones said. "You really think I was about to let that happen?" He couldn't bear to imagine what such a tough and utterly merciless thug would do if he ever happened to catch Allie off guard, but Jones was sure of one thing—he'd take a bullet if he had to, to prevent it.

"Listen," Allie told the man, "I can pay—and pay you well—for information."

"Cash'll do me no good when I'm dead and buried," he said, "which is exactly where I'll be if I go'n run my mouth on people like this—"

"People like what?" she demanded. "Who gave you that picture? Or was there more than one of them? Were they American or—"

Instead of answering, the injured man only cursed them both before demanding, "Can't you see I'm in pain here?"

Jones turned toward the sound of approaching sirens just as the first of a pair of campus patrol cars roared up. An instant later, a female officer emerged with her gun drawn, pale gaze sweeping the scene to train her full attention—and her aim—on Jones, who now held his attacker's pistol—and both hands—pointed skyward.

"I want you to put down the weapon," the officer ordered, an athletically built woman with her blond hair knotted at the base of her skull, "and then slowly and carefully back away with your fingers interlocked behind your neck."

"Yes, ma'am," he told her, as he complied. "I just picked up this gun to get it away from this man, who assaulted me—"

"Do it look like *I* assaulted *him*?" bellowed the injured man on the ground before pointing furiously at Allie. "And she ran me down on purpose!"

Allie turned her palms up. "I was coming to a man's aid—since you were clearly about to shoot him." She pointed toward Jones.

"That's enough, all of you," the officer said firmly as the second patrol car pulled up and two male officers left their vehicle. "You'll all get the chance to tell your stories—and get medical attention if you need it."

"Before you get too far into this, though," Allie advised her, "I'd suggest that you contact Detective Joe Parker of the Chicago PD. He has relevant information that I can assure you is going to save us all a lot of time and trouble."

Chapter 11

As the injured gunman was loaded into an ambulance, the older of the campus officers strolled over to his female colleague, who'd been speaking with Allie while Jones was having what appeared to be a graze wound looked at by a second EMT unit nearby. Though he'd insisted that his injuries were superficial, Allie still felt light-headed each time she thought of how close the gunman's bullet had come to doing catastrophic damage.

But she didn't dare to think about that right now—or how close she'd come to intentionally running down the shooter. She never would've imagined she had that kind of violence in her until the moment she had mashed down on the accelerator, intent on taking out the threat before he could kill Jones...

She pushed aside her horror to better focus on what the big-bellied graying officer was saying.

"Jimmy's riding in the rig with the suspect in case he gets testy again," he told the blonde woman. "I'll follow them over to the ER and wait for Chicago PD detectives to arrive to transfer the suspect to their custody then try to figure out who he is."

"Did you get a chance to check out the van's interior?" Officer Handler asked, referring to an older, white cargo vehicle a witness had seen the thug exit after parking it nearby.

"Not yet," said the male cop before passing her a set of keys, "but the suspect had these on him, so here you go."

"He have anything else, like a driver's license or a cell phone?" Allie couldn't stop herself from asking.

The older officer, whose name tag read R. D'Amico, gave her a look that let her know she'd overstepped her bounds.

The blonde officer she'd been talking to was quick to reassure him, "It's okay, Ted. She's a working PI, vouched for by the Chicago PD detective I reached out to."

D'Amico's brushy brows, a shade darker than his salt-and-pepper hair, rose as he eyed Allie in her outfit. "*She's* a real PI? You're kiddin' me."

"Licensed by the state of California," Allie assured him. "You need to see my ID, too?"

"I've already check it out," Officer Handler assured him. "Can you believe this one is twenty-seven?"

The older cop made a harrumphing sound and muttered something about having pairs of boxers that were older.

"No offense, Officer," Allie said, "but I'm more interested in finding out whether that suspect had any ID on him than hearing any more about your drawers."

"That makes two of us," put in Handler, whom Allie was liking better by the minute.

"Unfortunately, our suspect didn't have any ID on him," D'Amico said. "No phone or other devices. Only the gun, an extra clip and a little cash, but that's all."

"Maybe we'll get lucky and find something in the vehicle," Officer Handler stated.

"Probably just plumbing equipment," said the older man. "I just ran the plates on my computer in the car there, and it turns out the thing was reported stolen a few days back, with a bunch of tools inside it."

"Owner'll be lucky if he hasn't hocked 'em for cash and dope yet," Handler told her colleague.

D'Amico grunted his agreement. "You're probably right about that."

"I'll wait for the detective Chicago PD's sending over, and then we'll check it out together, let them bring in an evidence team so we can tie him to the auto theft, too."

"What about the two of us?" asked Allie, gesturing from herself to Jones, who looked to be finished with the EMT.

"I'll need the two of you to stick around while I deal with some paperwork in my vehicle," Officer Handler said, "since I'm sure whoever's investigating will have plenty of questions for you."

While they waited, Allie walked up to Jones, who had a clean, white bandage taped to the side of his neck and was holding an icepack to the back of his skull.

"What did the EMT say? Did she try to talk you into going to the hospital?" she asked him, still wondering if she should have called up Carly to browbeat him into getting checked for a concussion.

"Not very hard," Jones said. "The graze wound

barely broke the surface of the skin, and apparently, my vitals, pupils and answers to her questions all convinced her I hadn't cracked my skull *that* hard against the doorframe. Besides, even Carly would have to concede I'm the most hardheaded member of the family."

Crossing her arms, Allie frowned at the macho act. "You have to take this seriously. You could've been *killed*, Jones."

"I might have, if you hadn't nearly run him over," he said. "Thanks for that."

"I'm not really sure you should be *thanking* me for that, seeing as how it's my being here that's put you in danger in the first place," she said, "but anyway, let's go sit in the Range Rover while we're waiting. We may be across campus from the student union, but anything that reduces the chances of Leo spotting me out here with you is a good idea."

"Speaking of Leo," Jones said, once they'd signaled their intention to wait inside the SUV to Officer Handler before climbing in, "did he ever show up?"

"In all his creepy glory." Allie rubbed at the gooseflesh rising on her arms at the thought of the menacing vibes that Leo had given off.

"What did he say?" Jones asked eagerly. "I didn't get to hear any of it before that thug interrupted."

"He said enough to unnerve you or me, given what we know, but definitely nothing that would be legally incriminating," she allowed. "He for sure got off on hinting that he's Mr. Tall, Dark and Dangerous."

"Do you think you can get more out of him?"

"Let's put it this way. I'm a human female who's given him a measure of attention. My prediction is he'll be harder to get rid of than a bad rash, and twice as nasty."

Jones made a face. "I'm not sure I need the combination of Leo and bad rashes crawling around inside my brain—especially in relation to you."

She laughed. "Point taken. What I'm getting at is I can see already he's the bragging type, and the more encouragement I give him, the more tempted he's going to be to boast, especially if he imagines he's competing for my affection."

"So you're planning to continue this conversation on the app?"

"As much as I can, but what I'll really need is to record him while I'm wearing a wire."

Forehead creasing, Jones frowned. "Listen, Allie, catfishing is one thing, but what you're talking about sounds really dangerous. As your employer, I'm not comfortable with you deliberately inflaming him in a way that's going to get you hurt."

"But don't you see?" she argued. "We're running out of time here. We have no way of knowing when the next thug or the one after that is going to succeed where the last two've failed. Or maybe the sex traffickers are going to get tired of waiting for one of the local lowlifes to score and send actual pros here to take care of business. And I can promise you that when they do, Jones, we won't get as lucky as we have with these amateurs." She thought of the photos she'd seen in the Arizona police files of their handiwork, stomach-turning testaments discovered in remote mine shafts and sun-bleached stretches of the desert...when they were found at all.

"You're calling this *lucky*?" Jones asked her, staring in what looked like disbelief.

"We're both still *alive*, aren't we?" she asked grimly. "Even after they've tracked us down twice."

"Speaking of which," Jones asked her, "I've been racking my brain, trying to figure out how that guy found me. There's no way he followed us from the brewery yesterday. First off, we would've made that tail, as carefully as we were watching for it."

"I agree. He wasn't back there."

"And second, if he'd trailed us to Sergei's condo and then followed us here this morning, he would've surely spotted us leaving the garage to pick up your rental car, or he would've likely targeted you from there."

She thought about it for a moment. "Your phone…"

He shook his head, looking confusion. "What about my phone?"

"Of course…" she said, mostly to herself as an idea formed in her mind. "I'm betting someone's tricked you into clicking a link over the past few days. It could've come inside a link or email."

"There was this form from my business adviser— or I thought it was a form. When I clicked the message in the note he sent me, it just led to a blank page. I've been meaning to ask him about it," Jones said.

"It might've looked harmless," she said, "but I'd bet my bottom dollar it was malware sent from a cloned address. Someone's basically introduced a program to your phone that utilizes its GPS capabilities to send your location to a third party."

"But who? If this thug didn't even have a phone on him—"

"Maybe there'll be something inside the stolen van. Look, that must be the Chicago police detective right now," she said as an unmarked sedan pulled up beside the campus officer's car.

Moments later, as the man inside left the vehicle, she

said, "Hey, isn't that your cousin's fiancé?" The short, light brown hair and athletic build both looked familiar.

"That's Sean Stafford, all right," Jones said, sounding unhappy about the development. "Prepare for some tough questions, Allie. He's bound to want to know what's brought us here—and I have the feeling he's not going to be very happy with our answers."

Just as Jones had feared, Sean wasn't pleased to learn that he'd initially been lied to about Allie's reason for coming to Chicago in the first place.

Dressed in a dark sport jacket and tie, he cast a disappointed look at Jones once they'd filled him in, somewhat reluctantly, on what they'd been up to here today after the campus officer had been called away to deal with another matter. "You know, you *could* have trusted me enough to tell me that Allie here's a PI working on the murders instead of giving me that line about being a marketing professional the other night at the beer dinner."

"I'm sorry that was necessary," Allie said simply, as all three of them stood in the shade of several oak trees at the parking lot's edge, not far from the stolen white van.

But Jones wouldn't have her taking the blame for the deception. "I was the one who insisted on the cover story." He didn't mention that Carly had been the one exception. "I didn't want to get my family's hopes up again, not after everything they've been through. If things end up not working out, I can't bear to be the cause of any more heartbreak."

"I can respect that," Sean admitted, lines creasing his forehead. "January's only now starting to sleep halfway decently at night again, and she really needs her rest now. With her job and everything."

At his hasty addition, Jones recalled the possibility that his cousin might be expecting—a theory it certainly wouldn't be appropriate to bring up at the moment. But it was one more reason not to want to cause January any more worry than he had to.

Allie looked up at Sean. "You're comfortable with keeping this from your fiancée?"

"January and I both have lines we can't cross when it comes to professional confidences. I'm sure she'd understand."

"This is no ordinary line, though," Jones pointed out. "It's about her father's and her uncle's murders. So you're sure about this?"

Anger flashed through Sean's green eyes. "I told you I'd keep it confidential, didn't I? Now tell me, both of you, what do you think you're doing, interfering in an ongoing FBI investigation? Because this idea you had about coming here to try to meet up with one of the suspects under investigation—" he gave Allie an accusing look "—I shouldn't have to tell you what a terrible idea that is."

Bristling, Allie insisted, "First of all, the Feds wouldn't even *have* any suspects under investigation if it weren't for me handing them over on a silver platter, and we're not doing anything to interfere."

"I doubt they'll see it that way when I tell them."

"Tell them *what*?" she asked with a dismissive shrug. "That I tried to gather more intelligence on one of these guys via an in-person meetup, but he didn't show?"

An uncomfortable silence followed…or uncomfortable for Jones, anyway, who was in no way used to lying to police. Especially to a detective he not only knew and respected but was beginning to consider family.

It had been Allie, though, not Jones himself, who'd told both the campus officer and Sean that same story about their potential suspect's failure to show up today. It was a stark reminder that when she was on the trail of what she considered to be true evil, there were lines she had no compunction about crossing. It was a price that he, too, would have to live with paying if he wanted to take down two killers before they could strike again.

"Whether or not your quarry showed up," Sean said, "it was still a terrible plan. Worse, when you both knew that Allie here has a serious problem, courtesy of one of her past clients. After this call came in this morning, Detective Parker filled me in on your previous visit to the station. By the way, he's currently en route to question this new suspect at the hospital where he's been taken."

"Here's hoping this creep proves more talkative than the last one," Allie said.

"What about you, though?" Sean asked her. "Surely, you must have *some* idea who could've put this hit out on you? A recent job, perhaps, that's been especially contentious, or a particularly dangerous criminal you've worked to track."

Allie was quiet for a few moments before confessing, "As I told Detective Parker, I get threats from time to time online, but three weeks ago, I received one at my home through the mail, with another photo, but of course there was no way to pinpoint its origin."

"If you had to guess, though?"

"Over the past year, I've worked to disrupt organized pill mills, child sex traffickers and a particularly nasty set of con artists who'd been scamming seniors out of their life savings, so, honestly, you could take your pick."

"You're sure about that? The part where you're being honest with me, I mean?" Sean asked, his gaze as sharp as it was serious. "Because we'd have a lot better chance of keeping you safe here in Chicago—not to mention anyone who happens to be too close to you the next time trouble comes calling—if you could give us something more to go on."

"If I knew something I thought would help, I'd be the first to tell you," Allie assured the detective. "Risks are part of my work, and I accept that, but the *last* thing I want to do is put Jones or anybody else in danger."

"She made it clear to me earlier, she was willing to cut the job short and leave town early," Jones explained to Sean, "but given how much progress she's made already in the case, I didn't—and I still don't—want her to leave."

Frowning at him, Allie said, "I don't know, Jones. This is starting to get really scary."

"But if they've been using my phone to track my location, can't we just—" Jones started, not wanting to get into another discussion of her leaving.

"What's this about your phone?"

Allie explained her theory about the malware sent to him via a cloned address. "You don't even have to be much of a hacker to pull it off," she said. "I'll need to check Jones's phone out and debug it."

"Speaking of phones," Sean said, pulling out a packaged pair of nitrile gloves out of his pocket. "I'm going to take a preliminary look inside the van now. Maybe we'll get lucky and find something that leads to an ID—or better yet, to whoever's sending low-level street thugs after you here."

"Mind if we watch?" Allie asked.

"You'd better both stay back here. If we end up needing to process the vehicle, I don't want to have to explain how any stray prints or hairs or whatever came to be there."

Once Sean had walked away, Allie asked Jones to unlock his cell so she could download another app that would scan for and eliminate malicious programs.

"Before you clean it," he said, "is there any way to trace back where the program's sending the information?"

"Theoretically, it's *possible*," she explained, "but in practice, the senders are almost all using relays of virtual private networks to forward what they're getting to untraceable throwaway accounts. It could be worth a shot at trying, but the problem is, as long as you're carrying this phone around, it's like a homing beacon for more trouble."

"What if we used it to set a trap, then? Sean could help us catch the next guy who shows up and—"

She shook her head. "Don't you see? It's useless. Since whoever's doing this is outsourcing their hit job, the guy's likely to be as unwilling to talk as the last two—and these lowlifes have probably been given no real information that'll trace back to the source. Plus, with the reward still in play, the parade of thugs will just keep coming."

He sighed. "I take your point. Just get rid of the malware, if you're able. If you have to, wipe the phone entirely. There're no important files I don't have backed up to the cloud."

"I'll be sure to run a sweep on those, too," she said, "so we don't just end up reinfecting your phone when you reload it."

Stepping out the side door of the white van, Sean waved both of them over to where he was putting down an unzipped nylon duffel. When they walked over, he straightened, his expression grim.

"I don't want you touching any of this," he warned, "or even leaning too close, but I think it's important, before you go playing cops and robbers anymore—or whatever the hell the two of you are really up to—that you see get an idea of what the real stakes are here."

"We're not *playing* at anything," Allie argued, her cheeks flaming at the way he'd put it. "I know what I'm doing, Detective, when it comes to investigating dangerous criminals."

"I don't mean to in any way to diminish the important work you do," Sean told her, "but aren't your hunting grounds normally online, Ms. Chandler?"

"Please call me Allie," she said, "and that's my expertise, yes."

Squatting, he pulled open the sides of the duffel and said, "Well, the virtual world is one thing, but as you can see, this threat against you is absolutely as real as it gets."

When Jones reached to take Allie's hand, he found it cold and shaking. Both of them stood staring down, shocked into silence at the sight of the coiled rope, the roll of duct tape, the black plastic garbage bags and short handled shovel that made up the thug's kit.

A kit that had been clearly assembled for only one dark purpose. Their murders and the subsequent disposal of their bodies.

Chapter 12

Though the sky was a perfect bottle blue and the early-afternoon sun pleasantly warm, Allie broke out in a cold sweat as they drove back to the condo after returning her damaged vehicle to the rental car company for repairs.

Her hands shook as she worked to restore Jones's cell to its original factory settings, wiping every shred of data from it. "If we had more time or the stakes weren't so high," she explained as he drove, "I'd finesse this job to save you the trouble and potential data loss, but—"

"Right now, I'd beat the damned thing to pieces with a hammer if I thought it'd make us one bit safer," he said. "But do you really think wiping it will do the trick? What if the guy who came after us today had a chance to report to whoever he's working with that I'm driving this vehicle instead of the BMW?"

She shook her head. "We won't know for sure until

Chicago PD's IT department takes a crack at accessing the phone." Surprisingly, for a cheap burner, the thug had had it password protected. "But I'm not sure he would've necessarily shared that information. Since these creeps are all vying for the same bounty on me, why would this particular lowlife choose to pass along a detail that could help his competition?"

"That's a good point," Jones said as they slowed behind a bus when traffic blocked them in the right lane. "And I can't imagine him making bail, considering the kind of charges he'll have stacked up against him, so anything he knows might stay with him for the time being."

"There's no guarantee he won't try to get the word out through the jailhouse grapevine," she said. "Even so, I suspect this vehicle's safer than your regular ride."

"What about the condo, though? Do you still want to head straight back there?"

She nodded. "I don't see a lot of other choices. For one thing, all my equipment's there," she said, and she was dying to get out of these unfamiliar clothes and wash off this makeup, too. "We'll have to trust to the building and the unit's security to keep us safe until we can come up with another plan. But we'll have to be extra careful coming and going, just as we will if we go to the brewery or your home."

"If you want," he offered, gesturing toward a cluster of chain restaurants, "we could stop and pick up lunch first. It could be something quick if you'd like."

Stomach turning, she shook her head. "I couldn't eat right now, but if you're hungry…"

"I'm a lot more concerned with finding us another place, a safe place," he said as traffic eased enough to let them thread their way through the busy shopping and dining area. "I'm just not sure where to go."

"There *is* no place in Chicago you can be safe," she reminded him, chilled by the horrifying memory of the thug taking aim at Jones's chest, "not until I leave town—or one of those goons catches the brass ring by finally wrapping me up in one of those black trash bags."

"Don't even joke about that, Allie," he said sharply. "Not after what we've seen today. This is serious business."

"Don't you think I know that?" she fired back, with far more heat than she expected. "I saw the same murder kit that you did, and I nearly watched you become collateral damage, all because I've been a fool."

"What do you mean?"

"If I'd had any sense at all, I would've left town the moment I realized my presence here was going to be a problem."

"You didn't leave because I asked you to stay."

"I didn't because—because I couldn't bear to leave before you and your family had some answers about the killing of your father and your uncle."

"Since it reminded you of losing your own father," he suggested, his words somber.

"*Every* victim's someone's something—a father or a mother, a lover or a child. I didn't get caught up in it because of who *they* were," she admitted, shaking her head. "It's who *you* are that's kept me from leaving like I need to. You're a hard man to say no to, Jones Colton... at least for me."

"I'm glad to hear it."

"Don't be," she said, her eyes shining, "because it's a mistake I intend to rectify—by leaving town today."

"What are you talking about?" he asked, a note of

panic in his voice. "Didn't you tell Sean you were coming into the station this afternoon to give him background on those previous cases you'd worked and names of the various departments that've employed you this past year?"

"That was just to buy time," she admitted. "I'd like you to drop me at the airport this afternoon, or I can get my own ride."

"In other words, you were lying to him—*and* me." When she said nothing, he angrily accused, "I thought we'd both agreed that you were staying long enough to finish this—to make sure Leo Styler and Jared Garner were both put behind bars."

"That was before I nearly watched you die and almost killed a man to stop it," she said. "And as for your father's and your uncle's killers, I *will* finish this, remotely—or at least I'll do my best to."

"But you said before, leading on Leo in the cyberworld will only get you so far."

"Even if I tried to stay here," she admitted, "we both know it could take weeks or even longer before Leo trusts me enough to spill anything worthwhile. Meanwhile, every *hour* I stay brings another chance of bringing a new tragedy to your family's doorstep. They *can't* lose you, too, Jones. They can't—and I won't be responsible—"

"And so you'll do what? Keep running, to the next place and the next one? Hiding from these guys forever?"

"I'll find another way," she promised, "figure out who's stalking me for sure and go to the Feds—or maybe find some way to turn the tables."

"You don't sound very convinced of that yourself," he pointed out, "so how am I supposed to buy it?"

"You don't have to buy it," she insisted, more adamant than ever. "All you have to do is stay alive. If I accomplish nothing else, I promise you, I'm going to see to that much."

"How?" he challenged. "For all you know, they'll keep on coming for me, even after you're gone."

"I guarantee you that won't happen," she said as the pieces of the plan slowly spun together inside her mind, "because I plan to leave them a very long, convoluted, difficult-to-follow trail far away from here…but one so obvious that even a blind man could sniff out the bread crumbs. The trick is being somewhere else entirely by the time they finally get there with all their guns and their plastic bags and shovels."

As Jones pulled into O'Hare International two hours later, he said, "Let me park, at least, walk inside with you to say goodbye."

Wrung out from trying to change her mind for the past ninety minutes, his voice was hoarse, and he was feeling desperate.

But Allie didn't waiver. "Let's not make this any harder than we have already. Don't miss the exit up ahead for departing domestic flights."

"So I'm just supposed to drop you off at the curb, not even knowing where you're going?"

"Like I explained before, it's safer this way…at least for the time being. If anyone asks, just tell them that I flew back home to Southern California."

Both of them knew she wouldn't go there, that it would be as good as suicide to do so right now.

"But eventually, you'll reach out?" His throat thickened as he grasped at the slimmest of threads. "Let me know when you're safe?"

"Only if I can do it without exposing either of us," was the most that she would promise.

When he pulled into the busy drop-off area, which was packed with crawling shuttle buses, passenger vehicles and travelers wheeling luggage, he thanked her again for coming and for pointing the FBI to Jared and Leo. "We might never have had a clue what happened without your help."

"I only wish I could've stayed long enough to nail down that confession," she said, their gazes connecting as he reached out to lay his hand atop hers. Outside the SUV, a security announcement played, reminding travelers of various precautions, while behind them, a car honked and an airport security officer motioned for him to move forward.

After pulling up as far as he could, he felt a stab of grief, the loss of something he could only guess at. But he knew enough to understand it might not come his way again for a long time, if ever. "I won't forget you, Allie Chandler."

As her brown eyes found his, he saw her lashes were clumped and damp.

"I'd better go now," she said, dipping toward him to brush his cheek with her lips before bailing out to grab her bags from the back.

The security officer gestured emphatically and shouted, refusing to let Jones linger, as she disappeared into the crowd. So he drove away, regret sitting like a leaden weight in his gut.

About fifteen minutes later, from the short-term lot where he'd parked, Jones finally—if somewhat reluctantly—reached out to Sean, catching him at the station.

"It's about time you got back to me," Sean complained. "I've left messages for you and Allie both, trying to figure out when she's coming in since I need to go and interview a witness on another case I'm investigating."

"Allie won't be coming in to see you." Jones still felt hollowed out by loss as he broke the news. "I hate to tell you, but I just dropped her at the airport. I'm over in the lot at O'Hare right now."

"What the hell? And you couldn't at least give me a heads-up and a chance to talk her into letting us try to help her?" Sean said, raising his voice so that Jones had to hold the phone away from his ear.

"I have talked and talked until I'm blue in the face," Jones told him, recalling how cold she'd grown, how distant—though he'd seen glimpses of the pain behind the mask. "But she's absolutely convinced that if she stays here, she's only going to get me killed. It really shook her up, what happened this morning. She's used to shifting for herself, but the idea of someone else—"

"She may be right about one thing. You're definitely safer keeping your distance from her."

"I damned well don't *want* safer," Jones argued. "I want Allie, right here beside me, helping to finish what she started." *What* we *started*, he thought, unable to forget how it had been, the night they'd spent together, or to imagine ever growing restless with a woman who was made of such surprising contradictions.

"Are you sure that's all you want her for...or has... has this gotten personal, between you?"

When Jones failed to respond, Sean said, "I was afraid so."

"I was the one who insisted we keep things casual," Jones confessed, "but she's like no one I've ever met before, brilliant and shy, but as tough and fierce as they come when she's fighting for something she believes in."

"Have you tried telling *her* this?"

"It wouldn't make a difference," Jones said. "People are still out to kill her—people who have it in their heads that the best way to get to her is through me, so she's determined to get the word out that she's heading home."

"She's not, though, is she?"

"No. She's booked another flight."

"Where's she's really going? When's her flight leave?" Sean asked. "Maybe I can catch her, talk some sense into her while we arrange for some kind of protection."

"If I knew, I swear I'd tell you, but she wouldn't give me the first clue—except that I dropped her off at domestic departures."

"If she's using her own name—and in this day and age, it's damned near impossible to fly anywhere using a false ID—I may be able to get a bead on her if I hurry," Sean said.

"Call me if you figure out anything," Jones said. "I can hang out here if you want."

"I don't want you waiting in a lot alone right now, Jones. Why don't you head home—or better yet, over to the brewery, somewhere that's plenty secure, where you're around lots of other people."

"I'm not feeling much like company."

"Are you feeling much like giving the next thug or the one after that the chance to try to force you to take them straight to Allie?" Sean said darkly. "Because they won't know she's gone yet—and until she finds a way to get the word out, you'll still be a target. Or do

I need to call Cruz on his day off or maybe Micha to come and babysit you?"

Sighing, Jones conceded. "You don't have to do that. I'm heading over to the Lone Wolf. You just worry about Allie—and if you *do* reach her, please tell her I'm willing to take any safety measure she wants—whatever it takes, if she'll only reconsider."

One of the few luxuries Allie splurged on every year was membership in an airport lounge network, which allowed her access to various semiprivate areas where she could work, rest and enjoy a complimentary snack or drink with little risk of being bothered or having her belongings stolen. Since she flew often and her work was highly confidential, she considered the expense a worthwhile investment, but considering the four hours she had to kill before this evening's flight and the possibility that someone might show up looking to kill her, this well-appointed—and sparsely populated oasis— might today prove to be a literal lifesaver.

Besides, she had a lot of work ahead of her if she wanted to be certain that her pursuers caught wind of the fact that she was leaving Chicago. To do so, she logged in to Twitter, where she posted a smiling selfie she had taken near the ticket counter of the airline on which she had purchased a return ticket to Los Angeles International Airport.

It's been real, Windy City, but I'm happy to be heading home, she tagged it, though she had no intention of ever taking the expensive, last-minute return flight. Instead, she'd booked another ticket, on a different airline, to the opposite coast—and that would be only the first leg a three-part journey involving a train, a rental car and ultimately, a tiny mountain cabin, where she could hole up and hide out until she figured out some way out of this mess—or they somehow hunted her down. This, however, she judged to be low-risk, since she'd secured both of the latter two reservations using the name on the fake Missouri driver's license she had sewn into the lining of her purse.

Still, she understood that it was possible that she might be stuck there, in that remote New Hampshire cabin, isolated and alone for an extended length of time, separated not only from her home and her belongings but any chance to experience the kind of companion-ship she'd barely begun to understand how badly she'd been missing until she'd spent time with Jones and his friends and family.

If she'd been able to stay here for a while longer, to get to know him better, might she somehow have found a place inside that supportive circle? Or something even more miraculous: a man as loyal and as passionate as anyone she'd ever known?

But it was too late to fantasize about impossibilities now, or to second-guess a decision that had been made already. The only possible decision that would keep both Jones and herself safe.

With that in mind, she returned to the task of mis-leading whoever had been feeding her pursuers infor-mation. Moving on to her only other public social media account, she "liked" a few friends' postings and then made lunch plans for tomorrow in her Los Angeles sub-urb with another "friend"—actually a fictitious account that Allie herself had previously created—in a posting that anyone could see, making both the time and the lo-cation of the supposed meeting public, as if she hadn't a worry in the world.

Would her pursuers really imagine she would be so

stupid? Probably, she decided, knowing from her own experience tracking quarry in the cyberworld how careless people often got when hurriedly responding to their friends online. She'd located missing persons, suspects, even felons in the past, all because they'd momentarily forgotten they were using a public forum rather than responding via a somewhat more secure text message or email.

Once she had finished, she tried to focus on the backlog of work-related messages she'd been ignoring while drinking a water from the lounge's cold case. But no matter how hard she fought to concentrate on mundane matters such as online bills, spam that needed to be discarded and even inquiries regarding future jobs, she kept finding her thoughts returning to the events of the past few days and especially the time she'd spent with Jones.

When she happened to look up to see a tall, dark-haired man entering the lounge, she was halfway to her feet, heart swelling with joy, before the realization hit her that of course, it wasn't him, coming to reclaim her. She'd already seen Jones for the last time, just as she'd insisted—and he'd reluctantly agreed.

Blinking back the bitter sting of her disappointment, she swallowed hard and reminded herself she should by now be used to the fact that none of her jobs were long-term. For the longest time, she'd been able to convince herself that was a benefit, that it was fun and exciting, always getting to meet new and different people, unraveling short-term relationships the way she did other new challenges. In her heart, she'd been relieved, too, to escape before her colleagues got to know the real her. The person they surely wouldn't like much, once they figured how painfully awkward she made social interactions.

But Jones had glimpsed the real her and had actually liked the woman he'd seen. Enough to risk his safety to be near her… Enough that she knew she would miss him for a long, long time to come.

A pinging noise from her phone made her jump, alerting Allie that she had a new message from Lee-Oh-No! on SelfDestrukt. On opening it, she felt her brows rise as she read his declaration.

If I flunked that exam today, it's all your fault, he'd written. *Couldn't think of anything but how freakin' hot you are the whole time I was supposed to be keeping straight who fought who in what damned world war.*

She made a scoffing sound at that, loud enough for a well-dressed older woman with neatly coiled micro-braids working at her own laptop a few seats down to cast an annoyed look in her direction.

After mouthing an apology, Allie muted the phone before the message detonated and then vanished and then replied to Leo, *Don't blame me for your craptas-tic study skills! LOL! I have enough bad grades on my conscience!*

Proofreading her own message, she backspaced and misspelled *conscience* and deleted one of the punctua-tion marks to make it slightly more plausible that "Sexy Lexi" might have any interest in pursuing a friendship with someone like Leo Styler.

Encouraged by her quick response, Leo continued to flatter and flirt, so haplessly that she might have felt sorry for him were it not for the creepy, antisocial edge to far too many of his messages—the most alarming of which suggested that if his algebra prof would "just choke on her own puke and die" before the semester's grades were posted, that would be all right with him.

As Allie read, she couldn't help but wonder if, some-day very soon, Leo would find some inexperienced young woman, a virtual girl with such low self-esteem that she would allow his over-the-top gushing about her appearance to drown out whatever alarm bells his more horrifying comments set off.

You know he will if you don't stop him, just like he'll keep escalating the thrill-killing until he's either caught or killed.

Those truths—and most of all, her own promise to Jones to finish what she'd started in terms of putting Leo and Jared away—were the only reason she didn't delete the messaging app and leave the monster and his equally murderous friend to the FBI.

But how much damage could a guy like this do, in the span of time that might take? Might Leo even feel emboldened enough, after getting away with four homi-cides, to go after a target he really had a beef with, such as the math professor he'd already mentioned wanting to see dead twice?

As Allie tried to think of how she might track down and privately warn this innocent woman or perhaps the college's administrators without creating a mass panic, another message came through.

Hey, there's this party tonight, starting over at Bow-man's off the Quad. It's gonna be lit. U wanna maybe meetup?

Stomach sinking, she glanced down at the bag that held her boarding pass. Though this morning she'd been hoping that such an invitation might come about, she'd never dreamed that it might happen so quickly—but what about the bounty still on her head and the pair of tickets aboard outgoing flights she'd purchased for tonight?

Could simply making her pursuers—and Jones himself—*believe* she'd left Chicago be enough to keep him safe? Or would she be a fool to risk staying in the city long enough to go to this Bowman's on her own, with no backup whatsoever?

What good will getting a confession do if you end up murdered—if not by Leo himself, then by whatever fortune-seeking thug might happen to spot you—before you can report it?

Really nice of u to ask, she wrote back to Styler using the app. But I have this huge paper to get in by tomorrow. She added a crying face emoji. It's already 2 days late and I'll fail for sure if I don't hand it in tomorrow morning!

Oh, come on! Leo pleaded. My a-hole friend Jared's acting like I made you up— I showed him the vest picture and he said no way. Can't wait to see the look on his face when he gets a load of you.

Chills running up her spine, she thought, *Could I really get this lucky—to meet both of them at once?* How could she possibly pass up such a golden opportunity?

Still, she already was well aware that, however tempted to boast Leo might be if she somehow played him off against his better looking, more sociable friend, the two of them together were known to be a lethal force. Even if she weren't caught out by the men the sex traffickers had bribed to harm her, if the two of them turned on her, would her risk turn out to be for nothing?

Still, she took a moment to look up Bowman's and found it to be a dance club near the campus—the kind of place that allowed entrance to patrons between the ages of eighteen and twenty-one, although their hands were supposedly marked to prevent them from ordering alcoholic beverages. Snorting at the idea, she shook her head, imagining that drinks were often passed from those twenty-one and over to the supposed teetotalers while the club's staff looked the other way.

But even if she'd imagined for one moment that the rules were consistently enforced, Leo dispelled them when he messaged, I know a guy who works there, and he can get us ANYTHING! In addition to the all caps, the final word arrived in a multicolored, flashing blaze of glory before its countdown to detonation.

What time u gonna be there? Allie asked him, deciding she could use the time between now and then to set up a fail-safe system to record the data from her wire online.

After he replied, she said, Can't stay super long but will try to swing by—if only to show your jerk friend and chill with a couple of hard seltzers before I get back to my work.

Will hook you up for sure! Leo promised. See you soon!

After sending another of the "Sexy Lexi" vest shots—this one cropped to make it look as if she'd taken a flirtatious selfie, heaven help her—superimposed with the word Later! Allie wrote out a detailed email to Special Agent Howard. An email that made her heart skip a beat, as she knew it was going to deeply upset him— and probably make him furious, as well.

"But what do I care?" she mumbled to herself, since if he actually *received* this message it would mean that she was either dead or in big trouble. Otherwise, she would cancel the delayed delivery of the link she was emailing that would lead him to the recording she planned to upload from her file.

Impulsively, she added Jones's email address into the address box, thinking that if anything really did go wrong, she owed him the chance to know the real truth rather than whatever edited version the authorities might choose to give him. But imagining how tortured he would be, potentially listening to her distress—and possibly even her murder—at some later point without being able to do anything about it, she frowned before deciding she couldn't do that to him. After deleting his email address, she went ahead and wrote the message to the special agent explaining her undercover gambit.

Dear Special Agent Howard,
If you're receiving this, I've miscalculated. Badly. Sorry about that—for lots of reasons—but you may still be in luck...

Once she'd finished with the message, she set the delayed delivery option for 2:00 a.m. Afterward, she took her backpack with her into the lounge's semiprivate restroom and did the best she could, using her makeup kit, to re-create the more youthful look she'd affected earlier. Unfortunately, she'd already checked in the suitcase containing her other clothing and hadn't brought Carly's hair extensions with her, which caused her a momentary panic, since she couldn't very well show up looking like a different person.

Venturing forth from the lounge, she felt her skin prickle with unease as her gaze darted around the busy terminal. A terminal where she'd publicly announced her presence, although since she'd already cleared security, that meant it would be difficult for some low-level criminal type to come in off the street in search of her unless he wanted to cough up the price of an expensive last-minute ticket. Even if he chose to do so, he'd have to go through the same X-ray machines that she had, which made the likelihood that she would face a gun or knife low.

Deciding that she liked those odds, she went to check some of the airport's many shops. At the third one she ventured into, she was able to purchase a low-cut hot pink T-shirt, a bunch of bangle bracelets and some bejeweled hairclips. Inside another restroom, she reaffixed the wire from her backpack to her bra—something she was seriously grateful had gotten past the screening—and changed her clothing. To disguise the missing extensions, she gathered her hair into a fun-looking updo before adding enough bubble-gum pink lipstick to effect a final transformation.

"This'll have to do," she told her reflection in the mirror. Next, she considered what to do about the flight she was about to miss—not the one she'd intended to skip but the one where she had actually checked through luggage. While she could attempt to find a ticket counter and reschedule now, saving herself the cost of the ticket, less a rebooking fee, she realized that simply noshowing had the advantage of confusing anyone who might be tailing her. Since the time was by now growing short, she decided to write off the extra cost and figure out what to do about her luggage, which should be automatically pulled from the flight when she failed to board, later.

Decision made, she thought about what to do about her backpack, which was both too heavy and too valuable to lug with her, loaded as it was with computer equipment. Since airports no longer had lockers for rental due to security concerns, she thought about it briefly before leaving the screened area of the airport and then making her way to an airport hotel across from the terminal. After waiting in the bell check desk line, she was able to pay a fee to have the backpack stored in a luggage room there. Though not an ideal solution, since she had a tracker on her laptop and her essential data way backed up to the cloud, she would have to take the chance.

With nothing to carry other than her small purse, she felt light as a feather as she walked out of the hotel. She could head over to Bowman's now, but a quick check on the time on her phone told her it was still a little early. Though her stomach was too jangly with nerves to register hunger, she decided that she ought to grab a bite to eat someplace, if only to kill another hour.

With her mind ticking off various menu options, she reentered the terminal, never seeing the tall man who'd spotted her from some distance away crossing the concourse on a diagonal to come up rapidly behind her. And never looking around until he reached forward to grab her.

Chapter 13

Out of breath from his rush to catch up with the woman he had initially spotted from some distance, Jones said, "Hold up, please. I need to—"

She wheeled on him, the white blur of terrified eyes and sound of her choked cry leaving him terrified that he had, in his desperation to find Allie, mistakenly accosted some strange young woman.

"Allie, no! It's me." Releasing his grip, Jones prayed that he wasn't about to find himself explaining his error to airport security.

But instead of either screaming her lungs out or taking a swing at him, as he'd more than half expected, the woman—who was unquestionably Allie—froze to study his face before abruptly launching herself into his arms.

"Are you crazy?" she cried, evidently not caring about the stares they were attracting. "You scared me half out of my skin."

"I can well believe it, from the way you're shaking," he said, holding her tightly out of the fear that she might vanish like smoke in a high wind if he released her. "And I'm sorry for startling you. I would have called your name if I hadn't been winded from trying to catch up. I've been from one end to the other of this airport looking for you."

"Why would you—" Her head shaking in confusion, she pulled away to stare into his face. "Couldn't you have just *called* if there were some emergency?"

"I knew what you would say, and I didn't want to hear the arguments," he admitted, steering the two of them out of the main flow of traffic and toward a small bank of seating in front of a small bookstore, though they were both too wired to do anything but stand. "But the truth is, I didn't make it halfway to the Lone Wolf before I called Sean back."

"Called him back?" Allie's eyes widened in alarm. "What do you mean?"

"I informed him I was turning around and heading straight back to try to find you instead of going to the bar like I'd promised after telling him you weren't coming in to see him."

"So you've been looking for me ever since then?" she asked.

Blowing out a breath, he shrugged off the insanity of trying to find a needle in a haystack in the country's largest airport. "I even went to the gate of the LA flight you'd booked a ticket to fly out on. I heard the gate agent call your name, but of course you were a no-show."

"Wait a minute. What?" She shook her head. "How did you figure out I had a ticket on that flight?"

"Sean told me he'd found out about both your bookings. And I got past TSA by buying myself a ticket to

Milwaukee that I don't intend to use so I could get past the security screening."

"Look at us—" she managed a wan smile "—single-handedly bailing out the airline industry by buying expensive cover-story tickets."

"I'd buy a first-class ticket to the moon for one more chance to see you."

She frowned at him before shaking her head. "I should be absolutely furious with you right now—fouling up my best-laid plans, sneaking up on me when you had to know I'm half expecting some sleazy wannabe murderer at any second, and blabbing to Sean about where I'd gone."

"He's one of the good guys, Allie. He only wants to help you."

Shaking her head, she said, "He *can't.* And the only thing *you* have going for you at this particular moment is that what you just said about the first-class ticket's probably the sweetest thing that anyone's ever told me, and not by a small margin."

Jones smiled to hear it. "After what I've been through these past few hours, I'm not taking any chances that you'll misunderstand me."

"Misunderstand you? About what?"

Pointedly looking over her new top and hairstyle, which would have thrown him off had he not known her chameleon-like tendencies as well as he did, he said, "I need you to get it through your head that whatever the dangers, we're in this together. Whatever you're *really* planning on, with this ruse about the flights out when you're clearly going nowhere and this new look that I'm betting has everything to do with Operation Catfish, it's long past time you fully dealt me in—because I care about you, deeply."

"Jones," she said, her eyes filling, "I don't want to fight you on this…"

"Then don't, because I promise you, you haven't begun to meet my stubborn side. I'm not leaving you alone."

Blinking back tears, she tried to answer, her beautiful face flushing as she fought to get the words out. "But you don't really *know* me."

"I know enough to know that I've never felt this way for any woman in my life," he told her. "And you don't really know *me* if you believe I'd walk away from that."

Apparently too choked up to say more, she blinked back tears and then surprised him by standing on her toes to wrap her arms around him and let her kiss express all the emotions locked inside her.

The alarm on her phone buzzed, vibrating urgently in her pocket, reminding Allie that she didn't have all evening to stand here making a scene inside the airport. Were it not for the noise, she could have gone on kissing him forever, lost in the protective circle of his arms around her, the warmth and passion of his lips, and whatever wonderful insanity had overtaken them both…if only temporarily.

But the insistence of the alarm, which she had set to get her moving toward her planned rendezvous with Leo, reminded her that they were drawing unwanted attention. Mindful that in this part of the airport unscreened passengers moved freely, she broke off the kiss reluctantly, silencing the cell phone before realizing she no longer needed to kill time by stopping for a meal.

But that made little difference, as butterflies now filled her stomach, excitement jostling with nerves as she thought about the coming evening. "If I want to make my rendezvous with Leo, we should probably get moving. There's still time enough for me to explain along the way."

"So you *are* meeting up with him?" Jones's blue eyes narrowed. "Please don't tell me you've had this planned all along."

She shook her head. "I'd honestly intended to be on that flight to Boston, but when the chance came up and I found out Jared was going to be there, too—I couldn't let my promise to take those two down slip through my fingers, not without giving it this one shot."

"You meant to take on those two murderers *alone*? Are you out of your mind?"

"It's in a public place, a little club near the campus called Bowman's."

"I know the place," Jones told her before shrugging. "I went there a few times when I was a lot younger, because a buddy'd told me the markers they used to put the X on the backs of underaged patrons' hands came off with a certain brand of hand cream."

At her look of disapproval, he shrugged and chuckled. "This wasn't long before I dropped out of school and took off for Europe, so I wasn't exactly making the most solid of life choices at the time."

"Since I was probably being hauled before a judge at about that time, I won't bother with the lecture," she admitted with a dismissive wave. "Now, can we head for the car and talk more there, please?" She looked around to see if anyone was watching them too closely. "I basically outed my location online, thinking I was in a secure spot and about to leave town. But now I'm worried that trouble might track me here, just the way that you did."

He nodded. "Let's go, then. I'm parked in one of the outside short-term lots. This way."

She hesitated. "I'll have to come back later to get my backpack and suitcase."

"We can do that," he assured her, "unless you'd rather take the time now."

She shook her head. "There may not be time to wait around—and I think my stuff's as safe here as anywhere for the time being."

"Sounds like a plan."

With both of them mindful of the potential danger that might be stalking them, they buried their emotions, along with any further conversation, for the time being. Making their way outdoors, they walked for what felt like forever before Jones finally unlocked the white Range Rover.

"Thank goodness," Allie said, slightly out of breath from trying to keep pace with his longer steps. "I was beginning to imagine that you'd parked in Peoria."

"You're only about a hundred fifty miles off there," he said dryly as they climbed inside.

Shrugging off the criticism, she said, "My sore feet beg to differ with you."

"Hope they have something left in them to trip the light fantastic with your new friend Leo," he said wryly. "As I remember, Bowman's has a dance floor with the flashing lights and fake smoke—"

"Not happening," she said. "I'll claim a twisted ankle or whatever—because I'm only there to talk. Or mainly to record him talking and see if I can play him off against his buddy Jared. It sounds like there's something of a rivalry between the two, at least when it comes to women."

She filled him in on the SelfDestrukt exchange she'd

had earlier with Leo, along with her plan to record their conversation later.

"Without any backup?" He started up the engine, but didn't put the SUV in gear. "*That's* what you were planning?"

She decided that telling Jones about her worst-case-scenario planning, with her delayed email to Special Agent Howard of the recording from her wire, would only serve to freak him out. Intent on projecting more confidence, she said, "According to their website, Bowman's employs security. And there'll be tons of people all around us. I can handle myself."

"First of all, their bouncers can't be everywhere, and if they're anything like the ones I remember, the one thing they were best at is looking the other way. Which is why I'm coming inside with you."

Alarm surging through her, she shook her head rapidly. "No, Jones. You'll spoil everything. You need to wait inside the car and use your phone app to listen in just like we planned the first time."

"I'm sorry. I can't do that."

"But if they see you walk in with me—"

"I'll wait until you've been inside about ten minutes before I head in. Then I'll pick a place where I can nurse a drink from across the bar and keep you in my line of sight."

"What about the audio? I expect it'll be really noisy in there."

"I have my noise-canceling earbuds on me. I'll link them to my phone so I can hear what's streaming through the app you set up while it's recording."

She nodded, though now that she'd thought about the noise level, with the music inside, she worried that her wire might not pick up all the conversation. At the moment, however, she needed to stay focused on directing Jones, as this would be her only chance.

Grasping his hand, she asked the question that most concerned her. "Are you going to be able to just sit there watching when they walk in, suspecting what we both believe those guys did to your dad and uncle?"

His jaw clenched, but he nodded, blue eyes solemn. "I gave you and Special Agent Howard both my word, so I won't attack them on sight, if that's what you're thinking."

"And you can promise me that you won't make a move, not even if they say or do something really sleazy around me?"

"That," he said, "is a promise I can't guarantee—"

She removed her hand. "If you can't, you'll need to stay out here, then, because we only get one shot at this, and I won't have you messing it up trying to be chivalrous."

"I'll make you a deal," he told her. "As long as they aren't physical, I'll hold back. But if they're doing anything I reasonably believe puts you in real danger, I promise you I'm going to pound the two of them into sick little grease spots right there in the bar."

Deciding that was the best she was going to get without pushing him to lie to her, she nodded. "That's fine, but just so you know, I do have my stun gun in my purse. And I've been looking out for myself for a very long time."

"I can't help remember how that worked out in the parking lot outside of True."

"I was taken by surprise that night. I won't make that mistake twice."

"I'm glad to hear it," he said.

"Good." She nodded. "Now please, Jones, watch your back inside there."

Leaning toward her, he cupped her face with one large hand. "I'll be watching mine and yours both, Allie. You can count on that."

Chapter 14

Bowman's owed much of its popularity—and its business—to the fact that it backed up to a quadrangle on the grounds of Western Community College. Between that and the club's marketing outreach to other local universities, the place was always packed during the semester. This evening, though a Thursday, was no different, with plenty of foot traffic along the street front, which was also home to a popular pizza joint, a hot dog stand and a coffee shop, along with other stores that had already closed their doors for the night.

After a stroke of fortune allowed him to find street parking only half a block from the club's windowless facade, he asked Allie, "Do you have a fake ID that shows you as being younger?"

"A fake ID, yes, but it still has me as over twenty-one," she said. "I was just going to pretend I'd forgotten my ID, figuring they'd mark my hand with the X assuming I'm in the eighteen-to-twenty set."

More familiar with the regulations that governed such establishments, he shook his head. "They won't let you in at *all* if you're without an ID, in case you were actually under eighteen. The whole bar could lose its license. Just show them your actual ID and tell them you plan to be your group's designated driver, so you don't wish to be served. Here's a ten for the cover charge."

She waved away the folded bill. "I don't need your money."

"Just take it," he insisted. "Chances are, they won't even charge you anyway and will serve you all the free nonalcoholic beverages you can drink, seeing as it's a draw having gorgeous young women in the house."

"If I run across any, I'll be sure to let them know," she said dryly, still ignoring the offering.

"My mother always taught us, the correct response to a compliment is a simple 'thank you,'" he corrected.

"You're welcome," she said brightly, clearly intentionally misunderstanding to be stubborn as she finally snatched away the ten and tucked it into the front pocket of her formfitting jeans. "Now let's say we get this show on the road before our audience of two spots us together?"

After looking around to be certain no one on the street was watching, he grasped her hand and leaned in for a quick kiss. "That's for luck…and to remind you not to take any chances. If anything feels off, I want you to promise me you'll trust your instincts and get out of there—and I'll be right behind you."

She took a moment to reapply her lipstick before nodded and telling him, "You've got yourself a deal. Here goes nothing…"

He watched her as she walked down the sidewalk to join the short line of other young men and women waiting to show their IDs to get inside the club.

True to his word, he set a timer on his watch for ten minutes so he could follow and then started the app on his phone to listen in on her wire just as she was giving the bouncer at the door her designated driver story.

Jones smiled at the gravel-voiced reply: "It's ladies' night. No cover for you," though he knew very well that the bar's actual ladies' night was on Wednesdays.

"Told you, gorgeous," he said, though he knew Allie couldn't hear him. He then settled in to listen as she headed inside.

Almost immediately, he was nearly deafened by the thumping beat of the music being played inside the club. Lowering the volume, he heard Allie speaking, as if to herself, "Let me just get a little farther from the blasted speaker and—wait. I think I see them, over on the left side as you're coming in."

After that, she made no more attempts to speak to Jones himself, thought he heard what sounded like jostling movement and Allie excusing herself as she tried to get past people in the crowded area.

As she moved to a somewhat quieter section of the bar, he heard a male voice, excitement unmistakable: "*There* you are. I *told* you she would be here. This is Jared Garner, Lexi. This is my friend Lexi Hartz, so pay up, jackass."

"What?" asked Allie, clearly confused.

"Hey there," the other male voice said. "You know, I just lost a twenty on you. So you owe me already. Oh, and you've got some white stuff on your chest there. Let me brush it off for you—"

"That's okay. I've got it," Allie told him quickly.

Outside in the Range Rover, Jones found himself bristling at the unpleasant edge to the speaker's voice, not to mention his obvious attempt to cop a feel, which Allie had fortunately been sharp-witted enough to shut down.

"Sounds to me like Leo can afford to buy the first round," she said, sounding more cheerful. "Is your friend here who can get you the hard seltzer?"

"Um, I'll have to go and see. Let's grab this table first."

Jones looked down as his timer and saw that it had been eight minutes. He then shut it off, deciding it was close enough to head for the line to get inside before Jared or Leo tried anything else.

Before leaving the vehicle, he popped one of the earpieces into his pocket so he could hear what was going on around him while also following Allie's conversation with Jared—since Leo had apparently gone in search of drinks as she'd requested. For the moment, as least, their chatter sounded friendly enough, with Allie easily fielding Jared's questions about where she'd moved to Chicago from and what she was studying before coaxing him to talk about himself.

Jones knew there was no way he could pass for one of the eighteen-to-very-early-twenties set who usually frequented Bowman's, and sure enough, when he reached the head of the line, the bouncer, a beefy, tatted up white guy with a shaved head and a reddish chinstrap beard, looked at him a little oddly when he showed his ID.

It took Jones a moment to realize it was because he knew the man, though he'd had hair back when he'd worked for Jones at a bar he'd managed in downtown Denver. Both hair and a problem with painkillers that had eventually forced Jones to let him go—though he'd found the bouncer help with a rehab program that he'd hoped would serve to get him straight again.

"Hey, Billy, how's it going?" he asked, hoping the man didn't hold any grudges over his termination. But Billy's brown eyes lit up as recognition took hold.

"Jones, man, it's good to see you." The larger man's hand engulfed his as they shook, both of them grinning. "I'm doing great now, thanks to you."

"You're the one who did the hard work. Makes me proud to hear it," Jones said.

Waving off the praise, Billy said, "I heard you had your own high-class place over in West Loop. So what're you doing, slummin' over here?"

"Just taking a little walk down memory lane," Jones told him. "I used to hang out here with friends back in the bad old days."

"Well, I can promise you," Billy said after glancing around as if to make sure no manager was within earshot and lowering his voice, "it's nothing like you're used to. You might want to try Morgan's down the road. It's all twenty-one-and-up there, and the drinks won't be watered down…unless maybe you're cruisin' for some sweet young college girl?"

"Actually," Jones told him, sensing time running short as those in line behind him murmured restlessly with the delay, "I'm kind of looking out for the kid sister of a good friend, trying to make sure she keeps herself out of trouble."

Billy clapped him on the shoulder with one enormous hand. "Sounds exactly like something you would do. You let me know if there's anything you need."

Thanking him, Jones headed in, glad to have a potential ally on-site on the off chance that things went sideways. He headed inside, where he casually made his way through the crowd standing in the aisle skirting the dance floor to try to catch a glimpse of where Allie and Jared were seated.

As he passed the bar, a slightly shorter but muscular male bumped against his shoulder, knocking Jones off-stride and sloshing something cold and wet against his arm.

"Watch where you're going, dude," erupted the younger guy, who was juggling a trio of drinks. "You made me spill it."

When Jones turned, he immediately took in the scowl, and brown eyes, partly hidden by shaggy, dark bangs, smoldering with anger. The chain-wrapped neck and camouflage army-surplus shirt confirmed Jones's shocked brain's initial assessment.

Heat rushed to his face with the realization that he was face-to-face with Leo Styler, one of the men responsible for his father's murder. *Don't blow this now*, Jones warned himself, even as his jaws clenched and his heart pounded so hard that every other sound was drowned out.

"You bastard," he said, the words rumbling low as a wolf's growl—words that had nothing to do with his wet sleeve or Leo's ridiculous accusation.

"*What* did you say?" Leo started.

But Allie was speaking at the same time, her voice coming into Jones's ear over the wire even as he heard her speaking, only feet away. "Oooh, Leo, there you are!" she said, coming up to lay her hand on the punk's shoulder, distracting him from Jones's glare. "You're my hero, scoring those drinks. I was about to die of thirst!"

Handing one of the cups over to her, Leo paused to shoot an ugly glare in Jones's direction before cocking his head toward Allie as if to boast that such a beautiful woman was here tonight with him. But it was Allie's warning glance that had Jones backing off, remembering his promise to her as she deftly steered Leo back in the direction of the table Jared was still saving.

Jones took several deep breaths, waiting for the roaring in his ears to diminish before he headed to the bar. Though he had a direct line of sight to Allie herself, she was too immersed in her role as the friendly and flirtatious Lexi—or too professional—to do so much as look his way.

The bartender wandered over, a bubbly-looking young brunette with a winning smile. "Can I get'cha anything? You look like a man who could sorely use a drink."

"I'll have a club soda with lime," Jones said, unwilling to trust his composure—nor his responsibility to look out for Allie's safety—with so much as a single drop of alcohol.

Standing behind his table outside the door, Billy Morgan frowned at the line of hopeful kids waiting to get in to Bowman's, their faces looking younger to him every night. More than likely, some of them *were* younger than the mandatory eighteen, for every night, he came across at least a handful of bad fake IDs—the kind made on home computer printers by high schoolers desperate for a glimpse of what they thought of as The Promised Land.

Some were caught because of sloppy work, others because they couldn't quit sweating, shaking and avoiding his eyes when he spoke to them. Still others blew it because, instead of trying to pass for eighteen or nineteen and then sneak drinks inside from some sympathetic fellow partier—which wasn't exactly rocket science—

the baby-faced kiddies overshot plausibility by attempting to pass for twenty-one or older.

But as good as Billy had gotten as separating the wheat from the chaff and keeping the peace in this place as much as it was possible in an atmosphere so charged with alcohol, hormones and bad judgment, he himself was feeling too old for the scene—and restless—at the age of thirty-two. Maybe it had been seeing Jones, who though years younger, had gone out and made something of his life and was here playing the white knight for some girl. But then, Colton, to Billy's knowledge, hadn't wasted years of his life fighting to get the monkey of an opiate addiction off his back following a motorcycle wreck on the icy roads outside of Denver.

He winced, remembering what a crap employee he'd been when he'd been at his worst, showing up late for shifts, failing to bother with calling in when he was under the weather, and even, on one occasion that shamed him to this day to think of, looking the other way to a group of underage drinkers after a girl had slipped him a bottle of her mother's prescription oxy.

But as furious as Jones had been after he'd found out and ejected the group, he had still shown compassion, helping to put Billy on a path to getting straight… for as long as sobriety had stuck. Though he had backslid and cleaned up again twice in the years since, he wondered if it was possible that he might do better in a cleaner setting—or if Jones might find it in his heart to hire him if he dropped by his craft brewery and put in an application?

Billy knew he didn't really deserve the second chance, that he hadn't done anything in particular to prove he could live up to that kind of trust. Still, he filed away the idea to think on later, the sight of his one-time friend enough to make him ache for one more chance to pull his life together.

After drawing an X on the hands of a group of nine-teen- and twenty-year-olds, he blinked in surprised to see an honest to goodness relic scowling up at him. Blond and barrel-chested, with a just bit of a paunch going, the man was an easy forty-eight or fifty, maybe even older, with a short, broad neck and tough, muscu-lar build that put Billy to mind of a bulldog on steroids.

Between the pugnacious set of his jaw and the steely blue eyes, Billy reflexively asked him, "What can I do for you, Officer?"

The bulldog choked back a laugh, handing over a Michigan driver's license that was either a quality fake or the real thing. *"Officer,"* he scoffed. "That's rich. But I don't imagine they pay you extra for your brains here."

"No, sir, they don't," said Billy, his creep-o-meter pinging into the red zone, despite the fact that the man was well-dressed, in a button-down blue shirt and a pair of chino slacks with a nice leather belt and good shoes. "But they do pay me to keep the kids who come here safe, so just so you know—" he leaned in, lowering his voice to a conspiratorial whisper "—we've got zero tol-erance for old panty-sniffers creeping on the girls here, so if you're one of those guys here to—"

"Spare me the lecture," the blond guy said, his face darkening with anger. "I'm just here tryin' to keep an eye out for my daughter. She hasn't been makin' the best choices lately. Who knows? She might even imag-ine that sleeping with a dirtbag like you would be a fit-ting way to infuriate her mother."

"Wait—what?" Billy asked, blinking in confusion. "You wouldn't—you wouldn't happen to know a Jones Colton, would you? Because he just came through the line a few minutes ago and gave me damned near the same story."

Surprise gave way to a look of unbridled delight. "Jones is here, too? I can't believe it," the bulldog said. "Did you happen to see which way he went?"

"Um, I think so," Billy said, before walking him to the doorway and pointing vaguely to the left.

But afterward, he was left with the troubling suspicion that he had, without meaning to or understanding, just done something very wrong. Something that was in no way going to earn him points with the man he hoped might once more turn around his life.

Chapter 15

At first, Allie was upset with Jones for nearly spoiling everything with what looked like an eruption-in-progress, in spite of all his earlier assurances. But by the time she'd gotten Leo back to their seats with their drinks, she had to admit—at least to herself—that had she been in Jones's shoes, she would've lost it completely had her father's killer literally blundered into her inside a crowded bar.

Still angry about the loss of most of his beer, Leo said, "I should've popped that jerk in the mouth. *Would've*, too, after what he called me. Damn lucky thing for him you showed up when you did."

"I'm sure he's shaking in his shoes," Jared taunted. "Dude, I saw the look on that guy's face. He was about to hand you your ass and make you thank him for the beating."

Leo made a scoffing sound. "I'd stomp a mud hole

in him for sure. You think I can't? I'll go and prove it right here, right now."

He touched the thick chain on his neck—a chain Allie could all too easily imagine him whipping across Jones's handsome face—or possibly Jared's. Intent on soothing Leo, she grabbed his elbow when he started to get up. "Hey, c'mon. Why not relax and chill for a few minutes? No need to get us all thrown out of here when we're just getting started, right?"

Jerking his arm free roughly, Leo downed the dregs of his beer before angrily smacking down the empty cup. "Sure, I'll chill. As soon as I go and get myself another drink to take the edge off."

"Sure thing." Allie pretended to sip at her seltzer. As desperate as she was to swallow back her fear that there wasn't enough beer in Chicago to cool Leo's outsize temper, she wasn't willing to actually ingest any drink he'd handled outside of her sight.

"I'll grab you another, too, so you be sure to drink up," he said gruffly. "I hate to see good booze go to waste."

"Thanks," she said.

As he started off in the direction of the bar, Jared called, "Don't forget me, too, will you?"

"You're the one who's always bragging about your fat wallet and connections, so get your own damn drinks," Leo said before stomping off.

As fresh alarm pulsed through Allie, she prayed that Jones had had the good sense to take himself to a seat somewhere well clear of Leo's path, though it occurred to her he might not be headed to the bar since he had claimed a friend was getting his drinks for him. But she didn't dare to turn around to suss out the situation, not with Jared regarding her so intently.

And appreciatively, she noticed, so she didn't waste a moment, returning his frank look with one of her own that ranged from his deck shoes and khaki pants to the kelly green designer polo shirt with the oversize horse embroidered on the left chest. With his similarly preppy blond haircut and his straight, white smile, he had a wholesome appeal—one that ended the moment her gaze rose to meet those soulless blue eyes.

But she had a job to do this evening, and her revulsion for this young killer didn't factor into it at all.

"Wow," she said breathlessly, nodding in the direction Leo had taken. "Is he always so…*intense*? Because, I might have a thing for bad boys, but I don't want to end up on the receiving end of…you know." She held up one palm and with the other, mimed a face-slapping motion while giving him a worried look.

"I could be an ideal wingman, tell you my boy Leo's one big teddy bear," Jared said, "but the truth is, his racket's strung a little tight for polite company."

She lowered her lids for a look she hoped might pass for sultry, while simultaneously slipping the hand holding her drink beneath the level of the table to pour some of it out onto the floor. "I'm not so sure I qualify as *po lite* company…but I do like to keep my teeth all in the same neat row as the orthodontist my daddy paid for intended, if you catch my drift."

Jared raised his cup in salute. "Smart as well as pretty, then. *Way* too smart and pretty to be hanging with the likes of Leo."

Hearing a note of suspicion, she raised her now half-empty cup and faked another sip of her drink to at least pretend to keep up with his hearty gulps before squirming in her seat. "You don't think—he isn't imagining I came looking to hook up with him or something, is he?

Because I'm just out to meet some fun new people, and because I was told there'd be a *par-tay*."

"Yep." Jared's smile widened. "You're sounding smarter by the second. And, yeah, there will be little get-together, at my place a bit later, since my parents are away."

"Please don't tell me you're out to lure me to your lair *alone*, you bad boy," she scolded, keeping her tone strictly playful.

"Would I do that?" he asked, his smile practically crocodilian. Or maybe she was only imagining the malice in it, and he was simply attempting to do his best impression of a bad boy to attract her. Not that it required much of him in the way of acting, since where bad boys were concerned, he and Leo were the worst.

At the thought of what the two of them had done to Jones and his family, along with the families of the two others killed, made her slightly dizzy. Since she hadn't actually drunk any of the hard seltzer, she chalked it up to the exhausting and emotional day she'd had already.

"Listen," said Jared, "if you're worried, your friend Kyrie'll be there, too. Leo said you knew her."

"Um, not really all that well. We have a class together." Allie raised her voice to be heard over the swelling music and blinked in respond to the flashing lights from the dance floor, which were making it more difficult to gauge his expression.

"You sure about that, 'cause Leo made it sound like you two were tight?"

"He must've misunderstood, that's all. Now, if you'll excuse me for a minute," she said, her face feeling warm and oddly flushed as she rose from the table. "Do you know, are the restrooms over this way?"

"Over there." He pointed in the opposite direction.

"You want anything else? Maybe a soda or something?" Jared asked her. "I can see you aren't really into your drink, are you?"

"Oh, no, it's great," she lied, making a mental note, to stop at the bar on the way back to grab herself water or a clear soda, something nonalcoholic she could sip while her head cleared—even though she was certain Leo would be less than pleased about her letting his offerings go to waste.

"Sure thing, but, Allic…if you were thinking of cutting out and—"

"Whatever gave you that idea? I just have to go use the—"

"I'll have some of the primo stuff over at my party, and I'm not talking any penny-ante beers and seltzers."

She faked an enthusiastic smile. "Honestly, you don't have to *bribe* me, Jared. I'm having fun enough just talking to you…though maybe I wouldn't turn down a little…" She brought a tiny, imaginary cigarette to her lips—miming an action she had no intention of taking part in—eliciting a second predatory smile on his part.

On her way to the restroom, she deftly avoided being seen by Leo, who was headed back to their table with a couple of more drinks. Judging from his relaxed posture and relatively benign expression, she decided that he couldn't have crossed paths again with Jones—and thanked her lucky stars for that small favor. But her vision was a little blurry, which annoyed her greatly. She couldn't afford to allow fatigue to have its way with her—or choose tonight to come down with some bug.

After briefly switching off her microphone to use the restroom, she washed up. Once she was finished, she splashed some cold water on her face and told herself she was fine, just a little strung out from all the stress she had been under, but she could power through this. She only needed to keep leading Leo—or perhaps Jared, with his overconfidence, might make the better target—to the subjects she needed to discuss.

Remembering to turn her microphone back on, she headed out the door—and nearly ran straight into Jones, who had evidently been waiting for her, his blue eyes blazing with an urgency she hadn't seen before.

"We have to get out of here, Allie. Right now," he said.

"What's wrong?" she asked, reflexively looking around the narrow corridor that led off to both sets of restrooms. "You haven't seen one of those creepy guys flashing my photo around, have you?"

She couldn't imagine worse timing than having to deal with another of the sex trafficker's recruits here— or worse yet, one of the organization's far more frightening assassins. In either case, she had no way of guessing what such an enemy might look like. Though the traffickers' kingpin and much of its key leadership had been arrested and faced long prison sentences, the large crime family from which they'd sprung extended across several national borders and had in the past included some unusual affiliations. So her would-be killer might be anyone: young or old, of any ethnicity or gender.

But Jones was shaking his head. "It's not that. It's those two bears you've been baiting—they're just plain evil. Can't you feel it?"

"Of course I can. That's why I'm working my tail off to stop them, if you'd quit interfering." Her voice came out louder and sharper than she meant for it to, her face heating once more as anger and impatience roared to life. "This is ridiculous, Jones. You knew coming in what I'd be doing, and now you're risking everything by delaying me. If either of them happens to walk back here to use the facilities and see us—"

As if to underscore the point, a lanky younger guy with a shock of spiky black hair left the men's room and squeezed past them.

Once he was gone, Jones shook his head. "No, Allie. You don't get it. Risking *everything* would be letting you go out there and go off with them. I heard Jared inviting you to his house."

"To a party there tonight, yes."

"You go there and you'll *be* the party," he insisted. "I can feel it in my bones. The evil oozing through their every word and action—and didn't you catch on the way that Jared was testing you, the way he offered to brush off your breasts the moment you met him— "

"As if I was about to fall for that trick," she said, "but there really was white powder down my front…"

"And what about the way he brought up that girl's name?"

"Kyrie, you mean?" She shook her head, which made her vision wobble, bringing with it a surge of nausea that only made her mood worse. "You're just suspicious because of what you know, or think you know, about them, what we both suspect, based on their on-line postings—"

"Look me in the eyes and tell me you have a single shred of doubt about it now. They're stone-cold killers."

She blew out a breath before admitting, "I can't prove it yet, but I can't deny my feelings, either. I agree with you." The needle on her instincts had been deep-diving into the red-zone since their arrival.

"Which means that you absolutely can't leave here with those two, not under any circumstances."

"But you know this is our one chance, our *only* shot

with these two," she whispered furiously as a pair of women entered, passing them to head into the ladies' room. "I can nail them, Jones. Tonight. I *know* it." She was feeling too out of sorts to stand here and argue with this stubborn man about it. Why couldn't he just let her finish her job so she could wrap this up and then find someplace dark and quiet to lie down?

"I've heard enough. *I* know for sure now, and you've done what you were paid to do—and then some. As the person paying your fee, I'm telling you it's time now to step back and allow the FBI to do their jobs."

"How are you going to feel tomorrow, knowing that we were right there, on the cusp and blew it—all because you lost your nerve because we've slept together?"

"I don't regret it for a moment. Do you?"

"The sex? Of course not—except for the part where you think it gives you a license to tell me how to do my job."

"That's all it was to you? Sex?"

"Jones," she said sharply, her head once more spinning, "this is *not* the time for this discussion. It's the time for getting the justice that we've both already risked a lot for. And that's exactly what I'm *going* to do, both for you and for your family. Out there, right now—" she thumbed a gesture to the door to the bar area "—before they get suspicious something's up and walk out."

"But you won't leave this bar with them?"

"I won't leave here without you, I promise."

Though he still looked troubled, he nodded, saying, "Another half hour, tops, if things sound as if they're going well. But before you go—" he caught her wrist as she began to turn away "—are you feeling okay? You look a little—"

"I'm *fine*, just impatient not to have this whole thing blown because you've gotten cold feet," she said, nearly tripping in her haste to push through the frosted door leading back into the bar before he could get another word out. "I'll catch you later…"

As Jones watched her stumble out the door, the anxiety he'd been feeling since his encounter with Leo shifted into overdrive. Though Allie had seemed off during their conversation, he'd at first chalked up her unwillingness to listen and her irritation with his interference to stubbornness or perhaps the excitement of the chase. But there had been a manic gleam in her eyes, a frenetic quality to her speech—and that moment of clumsiness tipped off the longtime bar manager in him to the signs of inebriation…

Except there was no way he could believe that she could have or would have consumed enough alcohol to become intoxicated in the short time they'd been here. Aside from that, she was far too much of a professional to risk getting drunk when she needed to trick Jared and Leo into making incriminating statements, so he couldn't believe that she'd willingly ingest more than a sip, if she'd drunk anything at all, from the drink that Leo had brought her.

That Leo had brought her, after getting it from some-place out of her sight… Jones groaned at the thought.

During his time as a bar manager and owner, one of the things he'd been adamant about training his employees to watch out for was any sign that a customer's drink may had been tampered with. Sudden, apparent intoxication out of keeping with the amount of alcohol consumed could be a prime sign that a fellow drinker—usually a male sexual predator but occasionally a thief of either gender looking for an opportunity to make off with an expensive watch or wallet—had slipped in some liquid or powder. There were any number of drugs, from roofies to Special-K to tranquilizers and antianxiety prescriptions that could reduce a victim's resistance and alter his or her level of consciousness—sometimes extremely quickly, if the dose was far beyond what would normally be considered safe.

Coupled with Jared's possibly testing Allie with his comment about a "friend" she'd claimed named Kyrie, it was enough to convince Jones that in the wake of their FBI scare this afternoon, the two young men were suspicious of "Sexy Lexi's" sudden appearance and interest. Suspicious enough to mean her serious harm.

The conversation he heard from Allie's microphone only served to confirm his fears.

"Hey, Lexi, you okay there? Here, let me help you up," said a voice he recognized as Leo's.

"Here, have another drink," said Jared. "C'mon now, drink up. There's a good girl."

"No, I don't *wanna…*" Allie said, slurring her words.

It was all Jones needed to hear. Heart pounding out an urgent rhythm, he started through the frosted-glass door—only to be forcefully shoved back inside the corridor by a tough-looking older blond guy with a thick, muscular build and a hard expression.

"We need to talk, Colton," the man said, bulldozing him so fast and hard that Jones had no choice but to take several steps back to avoid being bowled over.

As two young women left the ladies' room, a petite brunette screamed, clearly startled, while her taller, red-haired friend shouted angrily, "Watch out, losers! Coming through!"

Jones reflexively sidestepped to avoid crashing into

the pair, banging into a picture frame hanging on the wall—a collision that sent the single earbud he was wearing popping loose and falling to the floor.

Carried forward by his own momentum, the older man continued forward, contorting his body to avoid the females. Somehow, both women narrowly avoided contact, shrieking as they darted between the men to flee through the frosted-glass door, with the redhead threatening, "I'm reporting you jerks right now!"

Seeing his chance, Jones decided to forget the fallen earbud in favor of getting straight to Allie and moved to follow them out.

"Freeze, right there!" shouted the blond man, who was now standing directly behind him.

The firm authority in his voice had Jones gritting his teeth, the skin between his shoulder blades crawling as his steps slowed.

"I said freeze or I *will* pull this trigger!" Sounding exactly like a cop's, the bellowed order echoed in the narrow space.

"I do *not* have time for this now," Jones growled, turning slowly, "so what the hell do you want?" The man's shooting stance as he faced him, feet apart and knees slighted bent and sighting down the barrel over his outstretched arms, seemed to confirm that he had law enforcement training and dredged up the only name that made sense.

"It's Oz, isn't it?" Jones asked, remembering the name of the disgraced detective that had given Allie so much trouble. "Oz Sullivan, from Phoenix?"

At the ripple of surprise that crossed the man's expression, Jones pushed his luck, adding, "She told me how you couldn't hack it, being shown up by someone better at your job than you were. And a woman half your age to boot."

"She's damned well *not* better," Sullivan responded. "She stood on the shoulders of the work I'd been pouring my sweat and blood into—and any lingering goodwill left in my marriage—for two freaking years and then swooped in to steal my glory after giving that bitch of a chief the excuse she'd been looking for to finally run me off."

"To be fair, it sounded like a damned *good* excuse to me. Destroying evidence, threatening to beat a woman—I don't know any boss who'd put up with that."

"They were all conspiring against me—my wife, that incompetent slut they gave the chief's job just to be politically correct, and then of *course* she brings in a girl consultant, just to show anyone with a set of balls that their hard work was worth nothing."

"It was you who did it, wasn't it?" Jones demanded, ignoring the gun to step forward. "You outed her to the very criminals you spent most of your life hunting. Do you know what they threatened to do to her, if they get hold of her?"

"Of course I do. I wrote the damned letter myself."

That was when it clicked, belatedly, that Sullivan hadn't doxed Allie to the murderous sex traffickers at all. He wouldn't give them the pleasure, not when this vendetta was so personal to him. So very personal that he'd evidently tired of waiting for one of the thugs he'd recruited to get the job done and come after them himself.

"So where is she?" Oz demanded. "I knew you'd been in this area, so I was cruising and got lucky, saw you get out of your car and come in—"

"After I'd dropped off Allie at the airport," Jones

said, improvising. He just wanted to get rid of this guy so he could rescue Allie before it was too late. "If you hurry, you might just catch her before her flight leaves for London."

"London?"

Jones shrugged, as if he weren't looking down the barrel of what appeared to be a 9 mm semiautomatic. "Yeah. She couldn't very well stay here—your recruits' attempts on our lives saw to that. And she told me she had an offer to present this paper she'd written to some crime symposium. Apparently, it's quite an honor." Twisting the knife, he added, "I think it was about how she broke that big sex trafficker case wide open for your department—"

"Are you freaking *kidding* me?" Oz erupted, going red in the face. "Figures, she would try and steal my credit—and brag about it to boot."

"It leaves from Terminal 5 at O'Hare," Jones said, thrilled to think he had bought the wild story. "Do you need directions or—"

"Hell, no, I don't need directions." Oz gestured past him, toward the frost-glass door. "*You'll* be driving us there."

"Forget it. I can't—"

Pointing the gun toward Jones's face, Oz roared, "Do I look like I'm *asking*?"

A swell of music alerted Jones as the door behind him opened and a male voice shouted, "None of that! Hey!"

Recognizing the speaker as his former employee, Billy, Jones tried to warn him, yelling, "Gun!" At the same moment he spun around, instinctively attempting to flatten himself against the wall.

It turned out to be a lifesaving instinct, as gunfire

filled the corridor—two shots, three—Jones couldn't be sure how many were fired, only that it was Billy's shout of pain or alarm that had Jones tackling the former cop, taking them both to the floor with another crack of gunfire.

Desperate to take out the threat before the older man managed to blow his or Billy's head off, Jones launched a flurry of punches, but it was the bald bouncer who ended the threat—by stepping on Oz's wrist and snatching the gun out of his hand.

Turning it on the disgraced former cop, Billy ordered, "Quit fighting, you, or maybe these bloody fingers will slip on this damned trigger. And I can tell you, it wouldn't break my heart paying you back in kind."

It was only then Jones saw the blood running down Billy's left arm and dripping off his elbow.

"I'll call 911 and tell them to send police and paramedics," Jones offered, as a panting, cursing Oz slowing raised his own hands.

"Search him first," Billy said, panting. "We don't need any unpleasant surprises."

"Get up," Jones ordered Oz as he himself rose. "Put your hands against the wall and spread your feet wide."

When Oz was slow to comply, Jones kicked his leg to get him moving.

"You smug son of a—" As he reached for something tucked in the rear of his waistband, his head jerked at the same moment a single *crack* exploded. His chest blooming bloodred, he slumped backward, his sightless eyes wide open.

"Can't say I didn't warn you, dumbass," Billy muttered, the gun in his hand smoking slightly. And shaking as well as he looked at Jones. "Please tell me that was another weapon he was going for behind him."

Glancing at the bloody mess, Jones hesitated. "I'm not sure I want to touch—"

"Please, Jones," Billy repeated, his brown eyes not only pained but desperate.

Realizing that he owed him that much—and probably his life—Jones nodded. After pulling loose a handkerchief he saw sticking out of the dead former detective's front pocket, he shook it out and wrapped the cloth around his hand before doing as Billy had asked.

"I'm not about to pull it out," he said, "That's for the police to do. But I feel something inside his waistband. I'm almost positive it's the handle of a good-sized knife. He was about to throw on you—I'll swear to it."

Billy closed his eyes, a look of relief passing over his face as he leaned against the wall. "You better call that ambulance now. I'm not—not feeling so great..."

Once more, the frosted-glass door opened, and female screams erupted as Billy slumped to the floor. "Call 911!" Jones ordered the young women, who looked to be no older than their late teens. "These two men have shot each other. I'll go grab the manager!"

As he stepped past them, Jones mentally apologized to his former employee, vowing, *I'll explain everything to the police later and make this up to you. I swear it!* But his first priority was to make certain Allie was safe and well clear of Jared and Leo.

Abandoning the fallen earbud, he pulled the other, from his pocket and stuck it into his right ear to see if he could pick up any of Allie's conversation. Without wasting time to listen, he then raced across the bar, his passage drawing cries of alarm—and not a few curses when he cut off people trying to walk or brushed too close to someone. Between these protests and the music playing, he heard nothing in his earpiece, but he did catch snatches of conversation as the fresh news spread like a wildfire throughout the club.

"Old guy with a gun over by the men's room…"

"Some dude got shot!"

"There's a dead body! Bouncer's shot, too."

The swell of excitement growing, people began moving, some of them—predictably—pushing in the direction of the restrooms, their cell phones at the ready to record any potential excitement. Others, more alarmed than curious, made a beeline for the exit, blocking his path.

But at the moment, it didn't matter. Jones was frozen in place, staring at the empty table where Allie, Leo Styler and Jared Garner had been sitting. Though he cupped his hand over his right ear, he still heard nothing from the earbud, as if her wire had gone dead.

Heart thundering in his chest, Jones ran to the spot before drawing gasps and stares by clambering up, one foot on the seat and the other on the table to scan the crowd.

"Allie!" he bellowed, his voice barely making a dent against the noise until, abruptly, someone cut off the music.

"Allie!" Jones yelled again, desperate to catch a glimpse of her or one of the two young killers among the sea of heads.

Over a loudspeaker, a male voice spoke in deliberately friendly, conversational tones. "Sorry to interrupt your evening, folks. Everything is safe now, but we're having an issue with the restroom facilities. Unfortunately, that means we have to ask all of you to clear out now, in a quiet and orderly manner—"

Though Jones thought the club manager was handling the situation about as well as possible under the circumstances, shouts quickly drowned him out. "We want a refund!"

"How about one for the road?" But as soon as someone yelled, "Does someone have a gun?" people started charging for the exit.

"Let's take it easy, everyone," the manager's voice came over the speaker. "There's absolutely no need for panic—and no unsecured weapon."

But by now, no one was listening, and in his haste, someone knocked the chair Jones had been standing on out from underneath him. Waving his arms for balance, he managed to land on his feet but crashed down anyway when a second male barged into him.

Slamming down onto his side, he hurried to push up off the floor before he could be trampled. But as he was rising, a rectangular shape lying only a couple of feet away caught his eye. Reaching out, he grabbed it— and was dismayed to recognize Allie's purse, her cell phone still inside it.

As he came to his feet with it, the black maw of panic threatened to engulf him. Allie had told him her wire would only work if she were within a short range of her phone...

Which meant he wasn't hearing her because Jared or Leo—or most likely both of them—had taken her from the building. And with neither her phone's GPS nor the working wire, he had no way to either track her location or any idea of what the pair of murderous sociopaths might be doing to the drugged and most likely helpless woman.

Chapter 16

Ten minutes earlier...

"What the hell was it you put in her drink? Horse tranquilizers?" Jared demanded.

Or at least Allie thought that it was Jared speaking after she'd missed her chair and found herself suddenly, embarrassingly, sitting on the floor, the club's lights all blurring as they swirled around her.

"It wasn't the drink at all," said Leo. "I dumped a vial of dance fever on her when I hugged her as soon as she walked in."

"Fentanyl?" Jared exclaimed. "Dude! Why didn't you warn me? I could've absorbed it through my own skin and OD'd, too, if I'd accidentally touched that!"

"Would've served you right, for trying to grope my date, man, offering to brush her chest off like that."

"Forget that," Jared said. "I thought we wanted *answers*, not to knock her out cold right here."

"Am I going to die?" Allie tried to ask, but her tongue was thick, causing the words to loosen and collapse in the same heap that her legs had.

"Never mind that right now," Leo said. "Help me get her back up before anybody notices."

A moment later, she felt herself hoisted back into her seat while someone—Leo, she thought, tried to coax her into drinking something else, but she refused to swallow, allowing the liquid to spill down her neck and front when he tipped the glass back.

"Don't give her anything more. Damn," said Jared. "She needs to be able to walk out of here on her own power."

"This one's just plain water," Leo answered in a low voice. "We want her compliant, not unconscious. I may've gotten a little heavy-handed on that dose."

"Sure as hell looks like it," Jared said before telling Allie, "C'mon, sweetheart. Let's get some fresh air and clear your head. Give me a hand here, will you, Leo? Let's take her for a little walk, and she'll snap out of it—enough, at least."

"C'mon, Lexi. Let me help you up," Leo said, his look of concern at odds with what she'd heard him say.

But the drug he'd given her had left her mind as clumsy and sluggish as her body, so that she was already out of her seat and being walked between the two of them toward the exit by the time she realized that her phone wasn't in her pocket, and that wasn't the only thing that she was missing.

"My purse!" she said, her slurred voice sounding like a stranger's and the edges of her vision darkening.

"Don't worry. I've got your stuff," Jared said, though she didn't see it on him.

"B-but my—" *Phone*, she meant to tell them. *And anyway, I can't go anywhere with you. I promised.* Jones's face flashed through her mind, the worry and the warning in it. And something more as well: the concern of a man who truly cared for her...

Just as deeply as she'd come to care for him, she realized as pure panic streaked through her and she fought to pull away. "No!"

But in her weakened state, she was no match for the men holding her arms, who had picked up their pace so that it was all she could do to keep up without being dragged behind.

"Stop!" she tried again, fighting to break away—or at least to make her voice heard. "Jo—"

Somehow getting an arm free, she flung it outward, grabbing the sleeve of passing T-shirt. When the young man they'd been passing—a wiry, freckled guy with shoulder-length reddish hair—looked her way with startled blue eyes, she begged, "Don't let them take me—help me."

"Ignore my girlfriend," Jared lied smoothly. "She's had a few too many and doesn't want to leave."

"She's underaged, so we're getting her outta here to buy her some coffee before she ends up getting us all busted and her old man all over us," Leo added. "You know how it is."

The freckled kid laughed. "Good luck with that, my dudes." Looking to Allie, he added, "Now you behave yourself, sweet thing."

If Allie could have screamed or raged, she would have, but in the wake of her burst of energy, a wave of fatigue overwhelmed her and she found herself collapsing. But that no longer mattered, as Leo and Jared were supporting her full weight now and already had her out the door.

"Help me get her to my car," Jared told Leo, "before she passes out completely. We've gotta find out who put her up to contacting you."

As they continued walking with her, Allie's head drooped, her eyes closing. Unable to respond in any way, she zeroed in on what they were saying, willing herself to remember every word so she would be able to pass on the details of their conversation…assuming she survived this.

"I think maybe we got this wrong," Leo said, sounding suddenly uncertain. "Who's to say she isn't just into me? Why would you assume that's so freaking impossible?"

"I *told* you, Kyric's never heard of her, and there's no way the answer to your dirtiest dreams just happens to contact you the day before the Feds start asking questions."

"She seemed really cool, though," Leo told him. "Like the kind of girl you'd really want to hang with, not just—"

"You're dreaming, man, and anyway, *you're* the one who doped her up, so there's no point in crying over spilled milk now."

"Yeah, well, maybe I just didn't want her taking off after an hour to work on some damned paper," Leo told him, sounding hopeful. "Just *look* at her, man. She's definitely our age, and a straight-up babe, not some FBI suit."

She heard the chirp of a car unlocking, and Jared said, "Here. Hold her up, and then we'll get her into the back seat."

Panic surging through her at the thought of being forced half-conscious into the vehicle—and what the two murderers might do to her while she lay helpless—Allie struggled fiercely, crying out and clawing like a wildcat caught in a snare.

"Damn it, bitch, quit your scratching!" Leo backhanded her hard across the face before Jared helped him shove her into the car's rear seat, where she landed on her back beneath the dome light, her nose throbbing from where she'd been struck.

Choking and sputtering she wiped at it, and then saw her hand coated in crimson—so much blood before her eyes that everything went dark.

Jones's first order of business was getting out of Bowman's without being trampled, since it was far too noisy and chaotic inside to call anyone for help. And help is what he needed, fast, if he was going to rescue Allie. He only prayed that he could reach Special Agent Howard—or perhaps Detective Parker—quickly enough and that they would put their resources into motion immediately rather than wasting time berating Jones over the risks that Allie had been so determined to take.

Risks he doubted she would have insisted on if what should have been a simple business relationship hadn't ignited into an affair that had blazed hot enough to burn away their better judgment. But as he threaded his way through the crowd, Jones knew that wishing they had made different choices wasn't going to change things. The only thing that mattered now was getting help to her—and fast.

As he spilled outside into the night air, he found himself still surrounded by a noisy and confused throng.

Heedless of the other bouncer, who was trying in vain to disperse the crowd, some of the club-goers were running about shouting the names of friends from whom they had gotten separated in the confusion. Others stood in clusters, excitedly comparing what they'd seen or heard inside or attempting to talk or text on their cell phones.

Scanning the chaos, Jones prayed that he would catch a glimpse of Allie somewhere in the mix. Realizing it was useless—and still far too noisy to make a call here—he jogged clear of the mass, keeping his eyes peeled as he traveled the short distance to the Range Rover.

Once inside the relatively quiet interior, he pulled out the card Special Agent Howard had given him, though he feared he would reach the man's voice mail, calling at this time of night. Instead, he reached the FBI field office, where he briefly explained the situation to another special agent, emphasizing that a woman's life was at stake. A couple of minutes into the effort, the man—whose name Jones, in his mounting panic, hadn't caught—interrupted.

"I need you to hold on—do *not* hang up on me— while I reach out to Special Agent Howard. He's working in the field at the moment, but I know he's going to want to hear this," he said, his voice brisk and serious. "Then I'm going to patch your call through to him directly. Is that understood?"

"I hear you. I'm holding," Jones said, his relief warring with the worry that Howard might be too busy on some other operation to help with this immediately. As his wait turned into several minutes, doubts assailed Jones. Instead of wasting time with the FBI and all its red tape, he should've tried Joe Parker—or better yet called Micha, since the former Special Forces soldier would be sure to show up to help first and ask questions later.

But even if he had Micha right here, Jones realized that Allie had never shared Jared Garner's home address with him, only with the special agent when she'd passed along her background research on the two suspects. And without that crucial piece of information, Jones wouldn't have the slightest idea of where to look for Allie.

What the hell do I do?

Just as panic threatened to completely overwhelm him, a new voice came on the line, sounding urgent but in control. "This is Brad Howard. I'm maybe two minutes away from Bowman's, so tell me, where are you exactly?"

"I'm parked on the street half a block north of the front door, inside a white Range Rover SUV with paper plates."

"Be right there to pick you up," he said, the connection going dead an instant later.

While Jones waited with what felt like a swarm of angry hornets buzzing in his stomach, an ambulance pulled up, a pair of Chicago PD cruisers not far behind. He thought of Billy inside, injured and alone as he faced a slew of questions regarding the man he had been forced to kill. But as bad as Jones felt about it, he'd made the only choice he could live with. He only prayed that Howard would hurry up and get here and they could get to Allie in time to make the difference between life and death.

It was the fall that woke her, when Allie thumped against the back of the front seats and rolled down onto the rear floorboards as the driver took a turn too sharply. Something underneath her crinkled—a fast-food bag, she thought, part of the heap of refuse indicating it had been some time since anyone had cleaned out the back seat of the car.

"Should've belted her in," one of the pair in the front said. Though the voices sounded slightly muffled, she thought it was Leo speaking.

"So she gets a couple of bumps and bruises. Big freaking deal."

"She's already bleeding all over my freaking car, getting her DNA all over the place."

Allie barely managed to keep from groaning aloud as she remembered about the blood, which accounted for her stuffed and painful nose—and the fact that she had once more blacked out—but right now, a little red stuff was the least of her worries. Since she had no idea whether Jones had seen her taken from the club or had been able to follow, her life depended upon clearing her head and coming up with some way to buy time— or better yet, to talk or fight her way out of this mess.

"Don't cry to me about it." Jared sounded even more condescending than he had inside the club. "You're the one who had to go and hit her so hard."

"What else was I supposed to do, with her coming unglued like that? And those damn scratches. If the cops decide to make us take our shirts off and take photos, they'll know for sure that we—"

"You need to chill," Jared said smugly. "After those lawyers our parents sent in finished shredding the Feds this afternoon, they won't dare lay a hand on us until they have a solid case. And we'll be out of the country at my nana's long before then, as soon as our parents can arrange our tickets—"

"That's the Feds. If she goes to the local cops…"

"Maybe she won't be going anywhere," Jared said, his chilling tone slicing through Allie's stupor to leave her shaking.

I have to get out of this car now—jump out when we slow down, maybe. Yet she couldn't seem to make her arms and legs work, couldn't even push herself onto her hands and knees to climb back up onto the seat.

"I don't know about this," Leo said. "Blasting randos is one thing. Like you've said yourself, we'll never be connected to them. But I've been seen more than once with this girl—and you, too, tonight."

Allie was beginning to realize that her earlier suspicion that Leo was a mindless killing machine, completely reliant on Jared for guidance had been wrong. Violent and impulsive as he might be by nature, he sounded as if he at least had a decent self-preservation instinct. But could it be enough to save her?

"We'll scrub the car, after," Jared told him. "Burn it if we have to."

"We won't have to if we dump her somewhere, alive," Leo told him. "We can say she headed back to her car after we left Bowman's, and someone must've grabbed her. She probably won't remember crap, as out of it as she is."

"You really willing to take that chance?"

"Better that than going away for her murder when we don't even have any proof she's what you think. For all you know, that airhead Kyrie just happened to forget her name when you mentioned her earlier."

"Well, let's find out, why don't we? We're almost to my house, and Kyrie should be here in just a little while. Just help me get your little friend down to the basement."

"I'm not—"

"You're in this now, so do your part." The threat edging Jared's voice was icy cold.

As the car slowed, Allie's heart swelled with dread, and she felt around the debris, desperate to find her purse with the stun gun she'd packed inside, if Jared had really picked it up on the way out as he had claimed. Instead, her hand curled around something hard and cylindrical. With her vision blurred and the light nearly nonexistent, she couldn't quite make it out, but her sense of touch told her she'd grabbed a T-headed plastic-and-metal windshield ice scraper. Though it wasn't much of a weapon against two larger, stronger and unimpaired males, it might at least buy her precious seconds—and make them pay in the form of wounds they'd have a hard time explaining later.

Once they've murdered you... Shivering, she shook her head, determined to fight to her last breath—and the chance to beg Jones for forgiveness for risking any opportunity to explore the powerful feelings that had blazed to life between them. What she would give now for a single chance to do things over...

The car glided to a stop, and Allie braced herself, her heart beating like the wings of a hummingbird and her fist clenching the ice scraper when she heard both front doors open.

When Jared opened the rear door closest to her head and leaned in, she held her breath and took a wild swing, aiming for his face.

"Whoa!" he shouted, jerking back and out of range before darting in to grab her wrist with crushing force, forcing her to drop her last means of defense. "Damn you! Out of there!"

Crying out in pain, she found herself jerked roughly

from the car, where she came down on her knees on the hard concrete of a security-lit driveway of a large two-story house. As Jared hauled her to her feet by her wrist, she yanked free. She tried to run, but Leo grabbed her around the waist and slung her hard against the side of the car, where she stood panting, her shirt torn partly open.

"What the hell is this?" he asked, reaching to run his fingers along the strap of her bra.

Revulsion climbed the back of her throat, but Allie realized he wasn't trying to molest her. Instead, he'd found the wire—the microphone she had earlier sewn to her bra.

When she didn't respond, he shook her hard. "I asked you to tell me what the hell is this? What've you done?"

Rattled as she was, Allie did her best to run a bluff, laughing wildly. "I've led my coworkers straight to you idiots—and they're not going to be a bit happy that you've roughed up a fellow cop."

After looking around nervously, Jared said, "Nice try, but something's gone wrong with your grand plan. There's nobody else here. No witnesses at all…"

"They already know you two are killers," she said, "and now, thanks to the digital recording I'm broadcasting, they've heard you confess to 'blasting randos'—and we'll have enough to prosecute you both for kidnapping, as well."

Leo started pacing wildly, cursing to himself and running his hands through his hair before telling Jared, "We should just get grab our go bags and take off. Right now, while we still can."

"Stand still and settle down. This is what she wants, for us to freak out and give her a chance to get away,"

Jared told him, moving his hand to her neck to keep her pinned against the car.

With his free hand, he grabbed the microphone roughly and tore it free before examining it closely and glaring into Allie's face. "Sorry to be the bearer of bad news, 'Lexi,' but the transmitter for this thing was in your purse, wasn't it? Your phone, most likely, and we didn't bother bringing either one when we left the club, which means that no one heard what we said— nobody except you."

"So what now?" Leo asked.

"We've got to get rid of her," Jared told him. "My parents have a big chest freezer in the basement. That'll do for now."

Chapter 17

The air filled with the thrumming rush of a rotor a split second before the FBI's helicopter lit the driveway with its lights and dust spun up into a vortex. In the confusion, Jones—who'd been ordered to wait inside Special Agent Howard's sedan while he and his partner rushed in—couldn't stop himself from opening the car's door and standing outside along the curb.

Shielding his eyes with his forearm against the flying grit, he strained his ears, struggling to decipher the shouts puncturing the helicopter noise. His heart leaped as he caught another sound. Was that *Allie*, screaming in either pain or terror?

As Special Agent Howard flipped over one of the sputtering, cursing suspects—Jones recognized Jared's blond head—and cuffed him on the driveway, his partner took off chasing the second, who vaulted a fence into a neighbor's tree-shaded backyard. With the helicopter repositioning in an attempt to keep a spotlight on the fleeing suspect, Jones ran to the side of a red Camaro, where he found Allie crouched down and shaking, her arms raised to protect her face.

"Allie, it's me, Jones. You're safe now. I've got you," he said, taking her by the arms and helping her to her feet.

"Wh-what—how?" she asked, tears slicing through the blood that had spread across her lower face. "They were going to put me down in the basement, in the freezer. Th-they meant to kill me because I h heard them—"

Wanting to murder both of the sociopaths who'd terrorized her, he wrapped his arms around her. "No one's touching you again. Do you understand me? You're mine, Allie—*mine*, and anyone who wants to hurt you is going to have to damned well go through me."

He felt her head shaking as she pushed him away, her eyes glazed with terror—or whatever it was she'd been drugged with. "They'll be back. I know they will."

Desperate to make her understand, he explained, "Special Agent Howard and his partner were watching Leo and Jared. They'd lost them just before they entered Bowman's, but they were in the area when I called. They're *on* this, Allie, and there's an ambulance on the way, too. We're going to get you taken care of."

Chicago PD cruisers arrived first, additional support called in to assist in the ground search for Leo Styler, who had somehow managed to evade capture so far. After securing Jared Garner in his vehicle, Brad Howard walked over and frowned at Jones, who was still holding Allie tight against him.

"I thought we understood you were to stay inside the vehicle."

"Arrest me if you have to, but I couldn't do it—especially not after I heard her."

The special agent nodded, his blue eyes sympathetic. "I get it. I heard her, too." Voice gentling, he produced a clean handkerchief from his jacket and handed it to Allie. "I can have a female agent meet you at the hospital to go over what happened to you tonight, and there are forensic nurses who are specially trained to—"

"Th-that won't be necessary," Allie told him, blinking away tears and wiping gingerly at her face. "They didn't—other than a little manhandling, a smack to the face was the worst of it."

Thank God, Jones thought, knowing if they'd done more, he'd end up in jail tonight himself for certain. "We'll definitely want that nose of yours X-rayed," he told Allie, "and figure out what they spiked your drink with, because you were clearly drugged."

"I heard them talking about it," she said, disentangling herself from his embrace and standing more or less steadily beside the car. "It was fentanyl. Leo intentionally spilled some on me, and I brushed it off with my hand. I think the adrenaline's burned off the worst of it, though."

"They drugged you with fentanyl?" Jones asked, alarm spiking through him at her mention of the dangerous opiate that had been in the news recently, the cause of many tragic overdoses. Though she looked far more alert now, it hit home once more how close she'd come to death.

"Let's get you to the medics the second they arrive them. They'll have an antidote on board the ambulance to give you," Howard told her. "And we'll need your blood samples from the hospital as well as soon as possible to aid in the prosecution of Garner here on the abduction charges."

"If you'd been a little slower, you could've had 'em

both on murder," Allie told him before recounting what she'd said to Jones about the teens' plans to put her in the basement freezer. "I suppose I'll always wonder if they meant to kill me first or just tie me up and let me freeze to death in there."

Jones closed his eyes and groaned, wishing she hadn't put the horrifying images in his head. He already knew all too well what it was like living with the aftermath of the two young killers' senseless carnage. If they had taken her from him, too...

Apparently sensing his distress, she laid a hand on his arm. "I'm sorry I ever put myself in this position."

"You should be," he said, lashing out abruptly, and, he knew, irrationally angry, but he was sick at the thought of standing by her casket the way he'd stood beside his father's and his uncle's. "I asked you, practically begged you not to risk this and yet you still charged straight ahead and did it anyway. Don't you understand, if anything had happened to you, there's no way I could have ever lived with myself?"

"What on earth's happened to us, Jones," she asked, eyes gleaming, "to the idea that we were the kind of people who—who could love with no strings attached?"

"Ah, looks like the EMTs are here." Looking deeply uncomfortable to witness such a personal moment, Special Agent Howard gestured toward the approach of yet another set of flashing emergency lights on a street that had by now grown crowded with vehicles, law enforcement personnel and neighbors who'd emerged from their homes to watch the unfolding situation. "Let me go and help direct them over and check in with my partner."

Ignoring his departure, Jones said, "Let's say we spend some quality time exploring the answer to that question, Allie, as soon as we know you're okay, because I don't want to—I don't think I can bear to let you go again."

"But the sex traffickers—they'll keep sending—"

"It was never the sex traffickers," he told her. "It was Oz Sullivan himself. He finally came out of the woodwork and pulled a gun on me back near the restrooms at Bowman's. He admitted mailing you that threat himself, and if the bouncer hadn't showed up—"

"Oz himself? Oh, no, Jones! What happened?"

"Jackass went for a knife after Billy'd grabbed his gun and ended up shot."

Eyes widening, she asked, "Is he—"

"You won't have to worry about him anymore. Sullivan is dead, and as soon as word gets around that he won't be paying off his markers, I figure you and I will be safe, as well."

She blinked slowly. "So this means…"

Cupping her face with his hands, he used his thumb to gently brush a tear from beneath her eye. "It *could* mean everything for us, if we'll only grab hold of this chance and take it. Please, Allie, say you'll do it—that you'll take a chance on me."

Smiling through her tears, she wrapped her arms around his neck, pulling him in closer.

"That's the best offer I've had in ages," she said before he ducked his head a little lower, eager to taste all the possibility and the promise that their future offered.

"There's no need to be so nervous," Jones told her as he opened the door of his BMW on a beautiful afternoon two days later. He offered her a hand up, since she remained stiff and sore following her ordeal with her abductors. "I promise you my aunt Farrah and my grandmother won't eat you alive. Neither will my mother or any or the others."

But ever since they'd driven into this elegant, tree-lined Oak Park neighborhood, Allie had been staring, her mouth too dry to swallow as she took in mansion after mansion, each more impressive than the last. Now that they'd passed the gates and entered the Colton family compound, she kept right on staring past him at the elegant, brick two-story home that all but screamed prosperity, security—all the things her own humble upbringing had lacked.

Had her choice to wear a coral-colored jacket, a crisp, white top and nice jeans been too casual? Or by dressing up her outfit with a pair of silver earrings and a simple necklace, would she give the impression that she was trying too hard to look like something she was not?

"So this is where January and Tatum grew up?" she asked, accepting his hand—because she'd realized that he needed to dote on her right now far more than she needed his assistance, and because she'd found, to her amazement, that it felt good to lean on someone else's strength for once.

"With their sister, Simone, yes. I see her car is here, so you'll finally get to meet her, too," Jones said, leading Allie past a number of parked vehicles in the large, semicircular brick driveway.

So many parked vehicles that Allie felt her apprehension ramp up even higher at the thought of the many people gathered, waiting to meet her inside.

"The psychology professor, right?" Allie asked. "She's the single one?"

"That's correct. The others, including my two siblings, will each have their partners with them. But you've met most of them already."

Face heating, she stopped walking abruptly, shaking her head. "I'm really sorry, Jones, but I can't do this. I can't walk into some giant family reunion, where everyone will be staring at my two black eyes and broken nose—"

Stopping to turn to her, Jones pleaded, "First of all, you're nothing short of gorgeous on your worst day, and the nose isn't bad at all. The makeup covers most of it."

"Then why do you wince practically every time you look at me?"

"Because I keep remembering how they drugged you and all that blood on your face, but we got lucky, remember? More than lucky."

She nodded, grateful that the hairline fracture to her nose had required neither surgery nor a splint and should heal on its own within a few weeks. She'd suffered no lingering effects from the fentanyl she'd been given, either, since she'd absorbed only a fraction of Leo's full dose through her skin, and already, Jones's tender loving had gone a long way to ease the jumpiness that she'd been feeling for weeks.

But all the loving in the world couldn't change the way she'd always felt about being the center of attention, so once again, she shook her head. "It's not only my appearance, Jones. It's the idea that we lied to them, well, all of them except for Carly, about why I came here in the first place."

"That's on me," he said, "and I'll take full responsibility. Besides, they're going to be as grateful as I am when they find out what you've risked to get our family answers—and put Jared Garner behind bars."

"But *only* him," she said bitterly, beyond disappointed that Leo Styler had somehow managed to elude capture. Because of his anger issues and poor social skills with women, she had definitely underestimated his intelligence, but the way he had so far avoided returning to his own home or any known haunts had her reconsidering. Might he have been the real brains behind the duo this entire time? "And so far, Jared's only being held on charges of kidnapping me, even though I swear I overheard them talking about shooting people."

"You understood what Special Agent Howard told us, though?" Jones asked, referring to the meeting they'd had yesterday, when Allie had given her formal statement at the FBI field office. "Any vague reference you may have heard while doped up and half-conscious isn't nearly enough evidence to file charges, not when there's no recording of a real confession and no hard evidence. We're going to have to take Howard at his word when he says he means to do this the right way and bring those two to justice."

"I only wish I could have finished this for you and your family."

"Don't you see how much further you've gotten us than we've been before? Without you, Brad Howard wouldn't have a clue to go on, Jared Garner would still be running the streets, killing at will…and I'd still be floundering in the same useless guilt and grief that have been eating me alive all these months."

She looked up into his handsome face. "Then this has— I've somehow made things better for you?"

"I won't kid myself into thinking that my grieving is all over, but because of you I've found there's room in my life, and my heart, for so much more. And I'll always love you for it, Allie… Just the way my family's going to love you, too, once they're lucky enough to get to know you. But if that can't be today—"

"I love you, too," she said, her heart thumping with

the enormity of what she felt for this generous, thoughtful man. "But I'm still scared to go insi—"

"Hi, there, you two. Are we interrupting anything?"

Turning in surprise, Allie spotted January coming toward her, with Carly on her heels, both of them smiling warmly and dressed even more casually than she was, their blond hair bright in the spring sunshine.

"I'm so excited you could be here," January said, swooping in with an embrace that felt completely genuine. "I understand you've really been through the wringer lately, Miss Secret Sleuth."

"Careful of her nose now," Carly warned, her blue eyes sympathetic. "It may not look bad, but I'm betting it hurts like anything if you bump it."

Extracting herself from January, Allie gave Carly a hug as well before raising an eyebrow in Jones's direction. "I see that someone's been spilling secrets."

Jones shrugged. "Not everything, but I may've confided to my sister and my cousin that you were injured investigating our fathers' murders, after you assured me it was safe to talk."

Carly blushed. "And I *may* have spoken to a couple of people in the family, as well."

"Me, too, I'm afraid," January admitted before smiling at Allie. "If you're going to hang around this bunch, you'll have to understand the Colton grapevine is a very real thing. We did all grow up practically in the same household."

She nodded in the direction of a neighboring mansion, which Jones had pointed out as they'd driven in. Looking at it, Allie could only wonder how it must have been, not only sharing two sets of parents who were each twins, but also a combined backyard with a common pool, pool house and swimming pool, and tennis courts. Though most kids would probably find such a setup a paradise, for people like herself or Jones, who were meant to have their own space and march to their own drummers, all the togetherness must have been pretty overwhelming at times.

Carly looked at Jones. "Sorry, brother, if we stole your thunder."

"Please don't be," Allie told them. "You have no idea how much I've been sweating the idea of admitting that I've been an imposter."

"Forget that." January shook her head, her green eyes brimming with sincerity. "Everyone thinks you're incredibly brave and smart and absolutely amazing for going toe to toe with dangerous criminals. I don't know how you found the courage."

"Me, neither," Allie admitted, "since I'm practically having a nervous breakdown over the thought of going inside this gorgeous home and facing the mothers and grandmother and everybody else."

"I sort of thought that might be the case when I spotted you hesitating out here," January said. "That's why Carly and I decided to give you a personal escort. Please come in. I promise you, it'll be a very warm reception."

Allie glanced from the one to the other to Jones, seeing the hopeful looks in all three faces, and nodded. "Let's go then—and thank you. I can't tell you what it means that you all get who I am and are still more than willing to very literally meet me halfway."

"Isn't that what friends do for each other?" Carly asked her. "I know it's what I hope you'll do for me once you get to know me well enough that all my issues come spilling out—"

"And mine," January laughed.

"And you already know I've got a whole footlocker of them stashed down in my man cave," Jones joked.

"He's not kidding," Carly said.

"Oh, don't let them fool you. His deepest, darkest secret's what an absolute sweetheart he is—well, that and his crazy hops obsession." January winked at Jones just as they reached the door.

"I've got that much figured out already," Allie told them.

The three Coltons led her inside, welcoming her into a large living area, where everyone had gathered, and introducing her to family members she hadn't met before, including January and Tatum's sister, Simone, and Jones's grandmother, a slender woman with short, silver hair who had come to live in a mother-in-law suite after a stroke the year before had left her a bit unsteady.

Recalling what Jones had told her about his aunt and mother both being interior decorators, Allie had expected the space to be tastefully elegant, but she wasn't prepared by how warm and inviting it felt for a room of its size, with its earthen tones and Tuscan-style furnishings and fabrics.

"You home is so inviting," Allie told Jones's aunt Farrah, once he'd introduced them. Standing near one of the sofas beside a large fireplace, she was an attractive middle-aged woman with lustrous, dark curls and warm, green eyes gleaming with emotion. "Thank you so much for inviting me."

"Thank you, and we're so glad you've come," she said a moment before her twin, Jones's mother, Fallon, came up behind her.

A bit slimmer than her sister, she wore her dark curls longer and her clothing a bit more tailored, but the welcome in her gaze was equally sincere. "We're all in your debt," she said, before taking her son's hand and giving it a squeeze. "I understand you've brought us closer to the answers we've all been praying for."

At this point, Allie realized that the conversations all around the room had fallen silent. She saw faces tilted toward her. Some she recognized from the evening of the beer tasting, such as Cruz and Tatum, Sean and Micha, and Heath and his fiancée, Kylie. Others she had just met, but all, she realized were waiting for information that she and Jones still were not at liberty to share freely, not without risking any eventual case that might be prosecuted. But the two of them had agreed, the family had to be told something.

And now, while everyone was listening, seemed as good a time as any if she could only find the right words.

Jones laid a hand atop her shoulder, before sparing her the task by saying, "I'm afraid the FBI has asked us not to share any of the details at this time, but I do want you to know that thanks to Allie's work, they believe they're now close to making arrests...and finally bringing the murderers to justice."

A wave of emotion swept the gathering. Allie heard it in the gasps and more than one "Thank God" and saw it in the eyes that closed and arms that reached out as couples, siblings, cousins and generations embraced one another. Jones went to his mother, comforting her as she broke down. Allie's eyes misted over as well as she imagined what it might have been like for her own mother to receive the official answers she'd been denied regarding her husband's death.

But a moment later, Jones's cousin Simone, with her stylish brown bob and her blazing blue eyes, caught Allie's attention. With her arms crossed over her slim frame, the psychology professor turned away and stalked into the kitchen, away from any comfort her family might offer.

Remembering her own burning anger following her father's death, Allie slipped out of the room to follow.

"I know we've only just met," she said, stepping up behind Simone, "and that probably the very last thing in the world you want right now is someone acting like they know how you're feeling. But I know what it is to lose a father the way you did—and to want to personally be the one to deal out justice. I'm here to tell you it's not what it's cracked up to be. This will be so much better in the long run, so let the FBI do their jobs."

"I—I loved my uncle Ernie," Simone told her, her breath hitching and tears shining in her eyes, "but my f-father was everything to me. I should've been the one—the one to find these people." Pounding her fist against her chest, she repeated, "You have no idea how much I *needed* to be the one to finish this for him."

"Simone, please," said Jones, who had stepped into the kitchen doorway and evidently overheard their conversation. "Let's talk this through. I know you're hurting, and I want to help—"

"You can't help. You have no idea," she said. "I have to go. I'm sorry. I can't—I just can't be here for the rest of you right now."

"Simone," Jones tried once more, reaching after her, but it was too late. She had turned already and fled through the back door.

"Should you go after her?" Allie asked.

Jones shook his head, the look on his face both sad and wistful. "I hate like hell to see her hurting like this, but I don't think I'm the right person to help her right now. She really did have the relationship with her dad that I wish I'd had with mine. She's going to have to find her own path through her grief, just the way we both have."

"You're probably right about that. I know I wouldn't have listened to anyone else after my dad's murder, and I'm sure you weren't in a place to, earlier, yourself."

"I wasn't," he agreed, as Allie wrapped her arms around his waist and leaned her head against his chest. "I only hope she understands that whenever she's ready to open up, we'll all be waiting to welcome her home with open arms."

Smiling up at him, Allie said, "Even the family's lone wolf?"

"Wherever I might be, I'll come running..." Leaning down, he brushed his lips across hers, adding, "Preferably with my brave and beautiful lady by my side."

"I like the sound of that. Your lady," she told him before raising herself up onto her toes and sealing the bargain with a long and lingering kiss.

* * * * *

Don't miss the next story in our
Colton 911: Chicago miniseries
Colton 911: Guardian in the Storm *by Carla Cassidy,*
available next month from
Harlequin Romantic Suspense!

WE HOPE YOU ENJOYED THIS BOOK FROM

◈ HARLEQUIN

ROMANTIC SUSPENSE

Danger. Passion. Drama.

These heart-racing page-turners will keep you guessing to the very end. Experience the thrill of unexpected plot twists and irresistible chemistry.

4 NEW BOOKS AVAILABLE EVERY MONTH!

HARLEQUIN

*Uplifting or passionate,
heartfelt or thrilling—
Harlequin has your
happily-ever-after.*

With a wide range of romance series that each
offer new books every month, you are sure to
find the satisfying escape you deserve.

**Look for all Harlequin series
new releases on the
last Tuesday of each month
in stores and online!**

Harlequin.com

#2139 COLTON 911: GUARDIAN IN THE STORM
Colton 911: Chicago • by Carla Cassidy

FBI agent Brad Howard is trying to solve a double homicide—possibly involving a serial killer. He never expected Simone Colton, daughter of one of the victims, to get involved and put herself in jeopardy to solve the case.

#2140 COLTON'S COVERT WITNESS
The Coltons of Grave Gulch • by Addison Fox

Troy Colton is a by-the-book detective protecting a gaslighted attorney beginning to fear for her life. Can he keep Evangeline Whittaker—and his heart—safe before her fears become reality?

#2141 CLOSE QUARTERS WITH THE BODYGUARD
Bachelor Bodyguards • by Lisa Childs

Bodyguard Landon Myers doesn't trust Jocelyn Gerber, the prosecutor he's been assigned to protect, but he's attracted to the black-haired beauty. Jocelyn finds herself drawn to the bodyguard who keeps saving her life, but who will save her heart if she falls for him?

#2142 FALLING FOR HIS SUSPECT
Where Secrets are Safe • by Tara Taylor Quinn

Detective Greg Johnson expects to interview Jasmine Taylor for five minutes. But he's quickly drawn to the enigmatic woman, and the case surrounding her brother becomes even murkier. With multiple lives—including that of Jasmine's niece—in the balance, can they navigate the complicated truths ahead of them?

HRSCNM0621

*Detective Greg Johnson expects to interview
Jasmine Taylor for five minutes. But he's quickly drawn
to the enigmatic woman, and the case surrounding her
brother becomes even murkier. With multiple lives—
including that of Jasmine's niece—in the balance, can
they navigate the complicated truths ahead of them?*

Read on for a sneak preview of
Falling for His Suspect,
*USA TODAY bestselling author Tara Taylor Quinn's
next thrilling romantic suspense in the
Where Secrets are Safe miniseries!*

Greg had been heading to his home gym when his phone
rang. Seeing his newly entered speed dial contact come up,
he picked it up. She'd seen his missed call.

Was calling back.

A good sign.

"Can you come over?" The words, alarming in
themselves, didn't grab him as much as the weak thread in
her voice.

"Of course," he said, heading from the bedroom turned
gym toward the master suite, where he'd traded his jeans for
basketball shorts. "What's up?"

"I...need you to come. I don't know if I should call the
police or not, but...can you hurry?"

Fumbling to get into a flannel shirt over his workout T-shirt, Greg was on full alert. "Are you hurt? Is Bella?" Had Josh been there?

"No, Bella's fine. Still asleep. And I'm…fine. Just…"

He'd button up in the car. Was working his way one-handed into his jeans.

"Is someone there?"

"Not anymore."

Her brother had shown her his true colors. And she'd called him. "You need to call the police, Jasmine." They couldn't quibble on that one. "He could come back."

"He?" For the first time since he'd picked up, he heard the fire of her strength in her voice. "Who?"

"Who was there?" She'd said *not anymore* when he'd asked if someone was there.

"Heidi."

Not at all the answer he'd been expecting.

Grabbing his keys and the gun he didn't always carry, he headed for the garage door and listened as she gave him a two-sentence brief of the meeting.

"Hang up and call the police and call me right back," he told her, pushing the button to open the garage door and starting his SUV at the same time.

He was almost half an hour away. The Santa Raquel police were five minutes away. Max.

Heidi could still be in the area.

Don't miss
Falling for His Suspect *by Tara Taylor Quinn,*
available July 2021 wherever
Harlequin Romantic Suspense
books and ebooks are sold.

Harlequin.com

IF YOU ENJOYED THIS BOOK
WE THINK YOU WILL ALSO LOVE

INTRIGUE

Seek thrills. Solve crimes. Justice served.

Dive into action-packed stories that will keep you
on the edge of your seat. Solve the crime
and deliver justice at all costs.

6 NEW BOOKS AVAILABLE EVERY MONTH!